FORGIVING
PARIS

Other Life-Changing Fiction™
by Karen Kingsbury

Lost Love Military Series
Even Now
Ever After

Forever Faithful Series
Waiting for Morning
A Moment of Weakness
Halfway to Forever

Women of Faith Fiction Series
A Time to Dance
A Time to Embrace

Cody Gunner Series
A Thousand Tomorrows
Just Beyond the Clouds
This Side of Heaven

Red Glove Series
Gideon's Gift
Maggie's Miracle
Sarah's Song
Hannah's Hope

**Life-Changing Bible Story
    Collections**
The Family of Jesus
The Friends of Jesus

**Children's Chapter Books
    Ages 8-12**
*Best Family Ever (Baxter
    Family Children)*
*Finding Home (Baxter Family
    Children)*
*Never Grow Up (Baxter
    Family Children)*

Children's Picture Books
Let Me Hold You Longer
Let's Go on a Mommy Date
We Believe in Christmas
Let's Have a Daddy Day
*The Princess and the Three
    Knights*
The Brave Young Knight
Far Flutterby
*Go Ahead and Dream (with
    Quarterback Alex Smith)*
Whatever You Grow Up to Be
Always Daddy's Princess

Miracle Story Collections
*A Treasury of Christmas
    Miracles*
*A Treasury of Miracles for
    Women*
*A Treasury of Miracles for
    Teens*
*A Treasury of Miracles for
    Friends*
*A Treasury of Adoption
    Miracles*
Miracles: A Devotional

Gift Books
*Forever Young: Ten Gifts of
    Faith for the Graduate*
Forever My Little Boy
Forever My Little Girl

e-Short Stories
The Beginning
I Can Only Imagine
*Elizabeth Baxter's 10 Secrets to
    a Happy Marriage*
Once upon a Campus

www.KarenKingsbury.com

KAREN KINGSBURY

FORGIVING PARIS

A Novel

ATRIA BOOKS

New York   London   Toronto   Sydney   New Delhi

ATRIA
BOOKS

An Imprint of Simon & Schuster, Inc.
1230 Avenue of the Americas
New York, NY 10020

Published in association with the literary agency Alive Communications, Inc.,
7680 Goddard Street, Suite 200, Colorado Springs, Colorado, 80920,
www.alivecommunications.com.

First Atria Books hardcover edition October 2021

ATRIA BOOKS and colophon are trademarks of Simon & Schuster, Inc.

For information about special discounts for bulk purchases,
please contact Simon & Schuster Special Sales at
1-866-506-1949 or business@simonandschuster.com.

The Simon & Schuster Speakers Bureau can bring authors to your
live event. For more information or to book an event, contact
the Simon & Schuster Speakers Bureau at 1-866-248-3049
or visit our website at www.simonspeakers.com.

Manufactured in the United States of America

1 3 5 7 9 10 8 6 4 2

Library of Congress Cataloging-in-Publication Data has been applied for.

ISBN: 978-1-9821-0441-2
ISBN: 978-1-9821-0443-6 (ebook)

Dedicated to Donald, the love of my life, my husband of 33 years, and to our beautiful children and grandchildren. The journey of life is breathtaking surrounded by each of you, and each minute together is time borrowed from eternity. I love you with every breath, every heartbeat. And to God, Almighty, who has—for now—blessed me with these.

1998

1

The incessant pounding rattled the living room window and shook the walls in the small Parisian flat where Marie Michel was trying to sleep. She folded the pillow over her head and squeezed her eyes shut. She was a terrible mother. How could she have raised a daughter who ran with drug dealers? An addict who had stolen from Marie . . . from her own mother.

"Change the locks," the police officer had told her last time it happened. "You're not helping by giving her a way to keep using."

More pounding.

Marie's heartbeat skipped and jumped and raced inside her chest. It was after midnight. What was her daughter thinking? Why wouldn't she get help? Marie threw the pillow on the floor and swung herself out of bed.

As she did, the pounding stopped. Marie held her breath. Ten seconds. . . . Fifteen. Still nothing. Silence. Marie exhaled. Alice must've moved on, scurried off through the dark of night to find the place where she slept—under some bridge or in a shelter in the most dank and undesirable part of Paris. Wherever the drugs were easy.

Marie lay back down and stared at the ceiling. *Baby girl, I'm sorry . . . I never wanted it to come to this.* A chill ran down her arms and she pulled the blanket over her thin body. She hadn't paid her gas bill again and this was the coldest night in May.

Life was eroding like the beach at high tide.

If her own mother were still alive, Marie knew what the woman would say. *Pray, Marie. Pray. God has all the wisdom in the world. Talk to Him . . . ask Him. He loves you, Marie.*

But what would it matter, praying to God now? Alice had been gone long before tonight. Marie's precious baby girl was eighteen and a child of the streets, running with derelicts and drug dealers. Marie wasn't even sure when she'd lost Alice. Three years ago, maybe. Sometime between shifts, when Marie was out working two jobs to keep food on the table. They would've been better off starving.

Then she might still have Alice.

Marie leaned over and clicked on the lamp by her bedside. A yellow haze filled the cramped room. Marie let her eyes adjust. She stood and pushed herself to the dresser by the window. Every step stirred the ache in her bones, the ache that always came with twelve hours of cleaning hospital floors.

Don't look at it, she told herself. *You need to sleep. Morning comes quickly.*

But her hands had a mind of their own.

They pulled open the second drawer and there, sitting atop a heap of worn T-shirts, was the photo album. The one Marie had put together for Alice's sixteenth birthday. An attempt to win her back and pull her from the seedy world she'd fallen into.

The effort failed, but the photo book remained. Proof that their time together hadn't been all bad. Marie picked it up and ran her thumb over the cheap cloth cover. At the center was a photo of Marie and Alice, cheek to cheek. In the picture, her precious girl was maybe ten or eleven. Before the streets had gotten her.

Marie stared at the image. "What happened to you, baby girl? Why aren't you here? Down the hall?" Her voice fell. "Your mama still loves you, Alice." A rush of tears came and Marie shut her eyes again. "I'll always love you, Alice."

Sleep wasn't going to come anyway. Marie took the album to the edge of her bed and settled in.

The first few pages were full of baby Alice, as if she'd come into the world like any other child. Alice on her blanket and in her crib, crying in her first bath and laughing at her favorite toy bunny. And Marie, a much younger version of herself holding baby Alice and walking her along the streets of Paris in the pram Alice's grandmother had given her.

But there were other moments the pages didn't show. Her mother's warning in the beginning, when Marie came home pregnant after her first year of college.

"You'll keep the baby, of course." M'man had pulled her into a hug. "I will help you." Then she had stepped back and looked deep into Marie's eyes. "But mark my words, Marie. Being a single mother will be the hardest job you've ever had. I should know."

Marie's father had left when she was six. That was the year her mother refused to go along with her father's affairs. "It's a Parisian thing," Marie could still hear him saying. "French men need more than one woman."

Finally, her mother had sent him on his way. "You can have all the women you want," she had told him. "Just not this one."

Whenever Marie had asked about her father, her mama would stand a little straighter and her eyes would cool. "We don't need him, Marie. We have each other . . . that's enough."

And it was. For Marie's mother.

But no one ever asked Marie if having only a mother was enough for *her*. She remembered her first day of third grade and her classmates talking about their fathers. *My papa works in sanitation. Mine works at the hospital. . . . My papa is taking me to Normandy. . . . My papa is taking me to the Seine.*

She could hear their voices, feel herself shrinking toward the back of the classroom. "What about you, Marie?" her best friend had asked. "What does your daddy do?"

"He's a soldier." The answer was out before Marie could stop herself. And that's what she told herself every day after that. Right up until high school, when her mother told her it wasn't nice to lie.

"Your father wasn't a good man." Her mama had put her hand on Marie's shoulder. "Stop calling him a soldier."

And so, Marie was left with the truth. Her daddy had done just one thing in his role as a father—he had gotten her mother pregnant. After that he had disappeared.

Even now Marie missed the imaginary soldier father she had created. But as she worked her way through high school, and as she met friends like her with single mothers, Marie promised herself one thing—she wouldn't repeat her mother's mistakes. Not ever. When she fell in love it would be for life and the children she bore would know what it meant to have a father.

In her last year of lycée, Marie attended a dance at the community center and met a real-life soldier. Philippe promised to marry her and show her the world. Three months later Marie was pregnant, and Philippe had shipped out. Never to be seen again.

Marie stared at a photo of her younger self holding baby Alice. That was the main thing missing from the photographs: Alice's father.

Tears stung her eyes. Years had passed since she'd cried about her own story, the way she'd repeated her mother's mistakes and become a single mom to Alice.

The next page of the book showed her and Alice at a Paris playground, side by side grinning from the swings. Despite her watery eyes, a slight smile tugged at Marie's lips. Before Alice started using heroin, Marie had felt proud of the work she'd done as a single mom. She didn't believe in God back then, not really. But often she felt like she had some sort of invisible help. Maybe because of the things her own mother would constantly tell her.

"You're never alone, Marie. Alice isn't alone, either. Your Heavenly Father is only a whisper away," she would say. "Who could ask for more than that?"

Her mother had felt that way right up until her death last year from cancer. Peace had filled her face even as she took her last breath, off to meet the One who had carried her all her life. But Marie had none of that assurance.

She turned the next page and the next. More pictures of her and Alice, making a life for themselves. *I didn't see it coming, baby girl. How could I have seen it coming?*

The change in Alice happened midway through her first year of secondary school. That's when students were allowed to have cell phones in school. Overnight it seemed Alice was different. She ran with a wilder crowd and lied about where she'd been. Months later Marie was rummaging through Alice's room, looking for signs of trouble, when she found tiny bits of balloons and other plastic pieces, along with miniature fragments of tinfoil and short sections of string.

Her heart in her throat, Marie moved to her bedroom telephone. A quick call to a drug counseling office and she had the truth. Alice was doing heroin. The man who spoke with her said addiction could happen the first time a person tried the drug. Before long, heroin was all a person knew, and buying and using became a full-time obsession.

Cold chills had run down Marie's arms. She confronted Alice that day and after a spate of lies, her daughter left in the dark of night and didn't come home for a week. When she did, her clothes hung on her shrinking body and her eyes were sullen, framed by dark circles. Alice tried to run past Marie toward her bedroom down the hall. But Marie grabbed her daughter's arm. "Where are you going?" *Stay calm*, she had told herself. *Alice won't talk to you if you're hysterical.*

"To my room." Alice glared at her. "Leave me alone."

"No." Marie's grip tightened. "We need to talk."

"There's nothing to talk about." Alice jerked her arm free and that's when Marie saw the marks. Needle tracks up and down the inside of her daughter's left arm. Alice must've realized what her mother had seen because she ran to her room and slammed the door.

Marie didn't give up. She followed Alice and tried to open the door, but Alice must've been sitting against it because it barely budged. "Move, Alice! Let me in!"

"No. I said leave me alone!" Alice's voice was muffled.

"I know about the heroin." Marie's voice had grown louder. "I want to help you."

"It's my life." Alice started crying. "I don't want help."

And so it went for five minutes until Marie had no choice but to wait it out. She returned to the kitchen and an hour passed. When it was long after dark, Marie tried again. This time when she pushed her way into her daughter's room there was no resistance. Alice was passed out on her bed, still in her dirty clothes, her stringy hair strewn across her beautiful face.

Marie wasn't sure if she should wake her daughter up and finish the discussion. For several minutes she stood there and watched her sleep. Just staring at her precious Alice. *Baby girl, how did this happen? Why would you do heroin?* She barely noticed the tears falling onto her face. *Didn't I give you what you needed? Wasn't this life enough for you?* In that moment a thought had occurred to Marie. Something else her mother had always told her. Without God, life would only be a series of meaningless efforts and irredeemable failures. *You need Him, Marie. Alice needs Him. This life is empty otherwise.*

Marie had always figured—then and now—that if God were real, she would've had a father. Alice would have one, too. She and Alice wouldn't struggle to pay the bills and keep food on the table, the way her mother had also struggled. Every day of their lives.

If He loved them, where was He when Alice took her first hit of heroin?

Marie ran her finger over the next photo. Alice grinning from the second row at her middle school graduation. She was so beautiful, so full of light and love. Friends surrounded her in the photograph, the way they always had back then. Marie held the book a little higher so she could look deep into her daughter's eyes. The eyes of a child with all of life ahead of her. *I have no answers, Alice.*

Marie sighed and lowered the book again. *None. Why would you throw your life away?*

That night in her daughter's room, despite Marie's best efforts to stay quiet and motionless, Alice opened her eyes. Not like when she was a little girl. Sleepy and slow with a smile that gradually lit up the room. Back then she would hold out both arms and call for her. "Maman. . . hold me."

No, that child was gone forever. Instead, that terrible night Alice's eyes had flown open. Unnaturally wide and panicked. She breathed fast and hard. "Go away!" Her words were a shrill scream. "Go! Now!"

Marie had felt her anger rise. Forget being calm. If this were a fight for Alice's life, Marie was going to start swinging. "You will *not* talk to me like that, young lady. Do you hear me?"

And Alice was on her feet. Her breaths came in jagged gasps and she raked her trembling fingers through her hair. Then she faced Marie and screamed again. "Get away from me!"

"Alice, you're not yourself." Marie was no longer crying. She was too terrified for tears. "You don't want this . . . this life."

"You don't know what I want." She tried to push past, but Marie stood her ground, blocking the doorway. Alice's face grew red. "Move! You don't own me!"

"If I have to get locks for your bedroom door, I'll do it," Marie had shouted. "I will not let you leave this house for a life on the streets. That isn't who you are, Alice. Get back in bed."

A switch had seemed to flip in Alice's heart at that, and suddenly the fight left her. Slowly, like the sick child she was, she returned to her mattress and slipped beneath her blanket. She buried her head in her pillow and turned her back to Marie. Just one word came from her before she fell asleep again.

"Go."

That was the last word Marie heard from Alice for a month. In the morning when Marie went back to her daughter's room, the girl was gone. So were her bedsheets and pillow and most of her clothes.

And life had been like that ever since. For two years. Marie had no idea who Alice had been living with or what she was doing to survive. She didn't want to think about it.

Then a few months ago, Alice began stopping by the flat, acting like she was interested in changing, like she wanted a relationship with Marie again. But each time she left, Marie found money and valuables missing.

Whatever little Marie had, Alice found a way to take it.

The local authorities knew about the situation, but the least of their troubles was a teenager strung out on heroin and stealing money from home. They had promised to bring her back to Marie if they found her, but Alice didn't have a driver's license or ID. So how would police know if it was her or not? Alice was an adult, yes, but she was also Marie's daughter. Stealing from a parent was more domestic disturbance than theft.

Which was why Marie had changed the locks. So

that Alice couldn't come through the front door looking for money and items to steal. So she couldn't use Marie to stay in her wretched addiction. But now that Alice's key didn't work, Marie wondered if maybe this was worse. Hearing Alice pound on the door, listening to her cry out for Marie to let her in, let her have what she wanted.

Marie shuddered. She felt sick. The echoes of her daughter's desperate voice still played in her heart and mind. Would Alice come back tomorrow, pounding on the door and wanting only to find something to steal?

It was late, hours from sunrise. Marie dried her cheeks. Time to put the photo book back where it belonged. Once more she stood and pushed through the ache in her muscles. When the pictures were back in the drawer, out of sight, she returned to her bed. But before she dropped to the sheets, she stopped.

Through it all, through every heartbreaking day knowing Alice was a drug addict living on the streets, Marie had never done the one thing her mother had asked her to do. She had never prayed to Jesus about Alice. Marie didn't believe like her mother believed. Alice didn't, either. What had God ever done for them? And why should she believe He was even real?

But here, now . . . Marie was out of options.

The gravity of the situation pulled her to her knees in a way she was helpless to stop. And there, she buried her face in her hands and did the one thing she swore she'd never do.

"God . . . if You're there . . . help Alice." Her voice was tired, desperate. "Please, I beg You. Help Alice."

Then she struggled to her feet and crawled back into bed. There. She had followed her mother's wishes. Not so much because she believed. Not because she really thought some Almighty Heavenly Father would hear her prayers.

But because she had nowhere else to turn.

2

$\cdots\cdot\cdot\cdot\cdots$

Death was calling for Alice Michel.

In a hissing sort of whisper, it called her name, threatening her, taunting her, clawing at her. And it never stopped. Not ever. Like a living, breathing being of darkness, death wrapped its tentacles around her, dragging her into ever deeper levels of hell.

Until she hardly knew if she were dead or alive. Even her mother had rejected her. Alice didn't blame her.

How could you change the locks, Maman? Alice trudged down the cold, indifferent allée—four blocks from what used to be her home. She clenched her jaw. *I'm not your daughter. I never will be again.* The thought weighed on her and worked its way into the vast cavern where her heart used to be. She wouldn't go home ever. There was no turning back.

Alice shivered and ran her fingers over her right arm, then her left. They felt heavy and cold. Like the arms of a corpse.

There was only one place to go now, back to the underpass alongside the Seine. Cops hated that homeless people shuffled along the river. But the shelters were full and in the homeless camps around Paris, drugs ran the day. Indeed, Alice wasn't sure how long the prison of heroin had held her. Two years, three? Time stopped under the haze of heroin.

She shook harder now. The dull ache in her arms worked its way up through her bony shoulders and along her collarbones. Her legs hurt, too. Streaky pain from her hips to her knees and her knees to her ankles. A few more steps and the headache set in. Alice knew what this was. The feeling was as familiar as her name. *Drug sick*. She was drug sick.

Faster, she told herself. *Move your feet.*

And she did, as fast as she could until the group of tents came into view. Dirty, dilapidated, rain-beaten and sun-bleached. Yes. She was almost home. The only home she knew these days.

Already she could imagine the relief, sense the way her body was about to come to life again. Because someone would have the drug for her. The people of the underpass shared. Last week she'd bought the junk, so today her tent friends would step up. They all swapped needles, so Alice didn't need one of those, either.

She'd take the hit anyway she could get it.

Anything to feel alive again—normal . . . even for a few hours.

Alice carried a bag with her, a crocheted bag with a long strap that once was the colors of the rainbow. Now it was the color of dirt, like everything about her existence.

Push, she told herself. *Get to the tent.* Just . . . a few . . .

more . . . steps. Alice pushed herself until she dropped to the mouth of a crowded tent. Three girls were passed out near the back. Another two—a married couple—were nodding, succumbing to the rescue of their latest dose of heroin.

"I need it." Alice's entire body convulsed now. She pulled her knees to her chin and rocked. "Please, someone. Hit me up."

Needles lay scattered on the torn tent floor. Tonight, sweet, handsome Benji was the most alert of the group. "I got you." He grabbed a needle from a filthy bowl and grabbed Alice's hand. "Hold out your arm, Alice."

It was all she could do to obey. Her muscles were tense, cramping. Benji looked a little high, and he wobbled as he crawled to her with the needle. But the sharp silver point found its mark, somewhere along the tracks of heroin memories that made up her arm.

"There, Alice, baby." The minute the needle was out of Alice's skin, Benji used the syringe to fill the vial again. "My turn."

With every heartbeat, heroin flooded Alice's veins and pumped through her body. And as it did, the aching stopped. Her arms fell to her sides, no longer shaking, and her legs stretched out in front of her. "More, Benji." She closed her eyes. "Give me more."

"No." He leaned back against the tent pole. The drug was working for him, too.

"I need it." Alice leaned closer and put her hand on Benji's arm. "The sick . . . it's worse today."

Benji shook his head. "This is strong stuff, baby. That's enough." Benji used to be a med student with a dream of being a surgeon. The druggies in the camp trusted him.

"It's not that strong." Alice stared at the man. He was twenty-five, maybe thirty. No telling with heroin. Addicts aged a decade overnight. Alice had asked him once, but Benji said he didn't know. "Too many years." That's what he had told her. Too many since he'd checked out of life and given himself to the drug. Everything about his old self was gone. All he had these days was the needle.

By now Alice's headache should've let up. But instead her temples pounded. She stood on her knees and looped her arms around Benji's neck. The two of them had found solace in each other's arms more than once. When they were sober. When they weren't sick or high. She kissed his dry lips and stared into his droopy eyes. "I need it, Benji. Give it to me."

If he were sober, Benji never would've agreed. He knew when a batch of heroin was strong, and he knew when it was maybe laced with fentanyl. *Peppered*, he called it. But tonight, in this moment, Benji was too high to care. He returned the kiss and worked his hands into her hair. "You're beautiful, baby." His words were slurred. "You know that?"

"Give me more." She pressed herself against him. "Please, Benji."

And then, as if he was as intoxicated by her presence as he was by the drug, Benji did as she asked. He leaned back and felt around for the still half-full syringe. She helped him stay steady long enough to find her arm, to find a vein strong enough to take the jab.

"I'll do more, too. We can find the high together." Benji kissed her cheek and aimed the needle. And just like that he was feeling the same euphoria she was feeling. She knew because she could see it on his face.

In a rush the second hit overtook her, warming her and offering a peace she only knew after a hit. Her headache faded and she fell against Benji's chest.

"You okay, baby?" He ran his hand over her matted hair. "You okay?"

Suddenly a sense of panic came over her. Because she couldn't make her mouth work, couldn't find the words. And something else. She couldn't draw a breath. "Ben . . . Ben . . ."

He was up on his knees now, taking her by the shoulders. "I told you . . . not to, Alice!" His voice was loud, frightened. "This stuff is peppered. It's too strong."

Alice could feel herself losing consciousness, her breathing deep and labored. Why couldn't she fill her lungs? What was happening? Then she remembered. This had occurred before when one of the heroin batches was laced. When it was peppered. That time one of the tent people had shot her up with Narcan and she'd lived.

It was her last hope. "Narc . . . Narcan."

"I don't have it, baby. It's all gone." Benji shook her again. "Stay with me, Alice. Stay with me."

Alice was in a whirlpool. A deadly, dark horrific tunnel, and she was falling down . . . down . . . into the thickest, dankest liquid. And she couldn't breathe. She couldn't take another breath.

She remembered how she really loved Benji and how the man had turned to illegal pain meds when he tore his meniscus playing football with a few friends, and how he'd gotten caught stealing from the hospital where he was doing his residency and how they'd fired him. He would never work in the medical field again, Benji had told her. And in a thick fog of shame and addiction, Benji had left home and never looked back.

His family still didn't know where he was.

I love you, Benji. I'm sorry. M'man, if you'd only opened the door. She was out of oxygen, and she felt herself fall to the cold tent-covered ground.

"Baby, stay with me!" Benji shouted at her and shook her again and again. But his words began to fade until eventually her heartbeat stopped. And then there was nothing but eternal darkness and one final thought before death had its way with her. The thought she couldn't bear to admit to Benji or even herself.

Alice was pregnant.

• • •

THE BEEPING SOUNDS must've been some part of hell. That's all Alice could imagine. Because she had died. She had felt her heart stop beating.

But like the wings of a butterfly spreading on the first warm day of spring, Alice finally blinked her eyes open and looked around. She was in a hospital, hooked up to machines. Her hand instinctively grabbed at her throat. If she'd survived, she was surely on life support. But her neck was soft and whole.

No tubes in her mouth or esophagus.

I'm alive. How could I be alive?

Then she remembered the baby, and her hand moved to her abdomen. Surely the tiny life inside her had died in this ordeal. All because Alice wouldn't listen to Benji. Her eyes scanned the monitors and machines around her until she saw the nurses' button. She pressed it and called out at the same time. "Help me! Someone, please!"

An older uniformed woman rushed into the room. "You're awake!"

Panic welled up in Alice's heart and limbs. "I . . . I don't feel well." Of course she didn't feel well. How long had it been since she'd had a fix? "I need . . . I need more."

"Shhh." The woman stood at her bedside. "I'm taking care of you." She put her hand on Alice's shoulder. "You nearly died. Do you know that?"

"Y-y-yes. What . . . happened?"

The nurse hesitated. "I believe it was a miracle." She sat in the chair next to Alice's bed. "What's your name?"

Why should she tell the woman? She needed to get back to her tent, back to Benji. She had survived the heavy stuff, lived through the pepper. She wouldn't push it so hard next time. She started to sit up, but a wave of pain hit her head and slammed her back to the pillow. "I need more . . ."

"You need to rest." The nurse looked straight at her.

"My name is Fran. And you're at a rehab facility just out-side Paris." She was kind and soft-spoken. "We can't get far without your name."

Alice squeezed her eyes shut. The pain in her head was getting worse. Her arms and legs throbbed. She didn't ask for this, didn't ask to be rescued. "Take me back." She had no memory of life before heroin. There was no return-ing to who she used to be.

"You're not going back." The woman stayed in the chair. "Just your first name. Then I'll tell you how you got here."

Her head was spinning now. What would it hurt to tell the woman? "Alice." She pressed her thumb and fingers into her temples. "My name is Alice."

"One more question." The nurse took a chart from the bedside table. "How old are you, Alice?"

She didn't want to say, didn't want the horrified, pitiful look from Fran. But what did it matter? "I'm . . . eighteen."

"That's what I thought." Fran made a note in the chart.

For the first time since Alice started using, she didn't feel judged. She relaxed into the bed. This nurse probably saw people like Alice all the time. Her feet and hands started shaking. Or maybe they'd been shaking. "Please . . . can . . . can you give me a . . . a hit? Just . . . just one."

Nurse Fran stood and touched the side of Alice's head. "You know I can't do that." She smiled, and there was something different about the woman. A light and cer-tainty. "We're going to get you better."

Alice wanted to throw up. No more heroin? She

would have to find a way out of here, slip through a window maybe. She wouldn't feel okay until she got the next needle. The nurse couldn't possibly understand.

"Is there anything you'd like to tell me, Alice?" Fran held Alice's chart to her chest. She waited.

Then Alice remembered and her shaking hand returned to her belly. "I . . ." If the baby had lived, it would've been Benji's. He was the only one. She closed her eyes again. "I was pregnant. Before . . . before I overdosed."

Fran nodded. "You're still pregnant, Alice."

A wave of nausea rushed through her gut and her head pounded. "I'm . . . I'm still . . . ?"

"Yes." Fran put her hand on Alice's shoulder. "You've been here five days, Alice." The woman paused. "Would you like to hear what happened that night?"

Not really, Alice thought. But maybe she should. "Yes. Please."

"Your friend must've known you were overdosing, because he was experiencing the same thing."

Benji had overdosed, too? Alice's heartbeat picked up speed. And how had he gotten a cell phone? Must've been one of those cheap throwaways. "I . . . I remember taking my last breath."

"An officer was fifty feet away, about to check out the homeless camp. He heard your friend yelling and he rushed up in time to give you Narcan. Your friend wasn't doing well, but he pointed at you. He wanted you to have it."

Alice sat up straighter. "What happened to him? To Benji?"

For a few seconds the nurse didn't say anything. She looked down at Alice's chart and then back at Alice. "He didn't make it. I'm . . . I'm so sorry. The officer had just one dose of Narcan on him and by the time backup came . . . It was too late."

"No." Alice was screaming on the inside, but her voice was only a whisper. "Not Benji!" She rolled onto her side and buried her face in her pillow. "Not Benji!"

"He had identification on him. We . . . were able to notify his parents. Benji is home, Alice. He's finally home." The nurse stepped away from the bed. "I'll leave you alone for a bit. When I come back, we'll make a plan to get you better." She hesitated. "Your baby needs you, Alice."

Benji's baby. The child who would never know a father now, all because Benji had asked the police officer to save her life over his own. She pictured Benji, holding her, caring for her. He would do anything for her, and he had. He had given his life for hers. For hers and the tiny baby he had known nothing about. Alice's tears came then, and sobs took over until her sides heaved. Poor Benji. He had never made things right with his family, never found his way past the drug.

But there was something Alice hated even more than that. The man who had been her friend and lover had died without hearing the words Alice had always meant to say. Her true feelings for Benji.

She loved him, she did. But she had never told him.

And now it was too late.

3

Ready or not, Ashley Baxter Blake was finally going to have an art show in Paris. She and her sister Kari had been out shopping for a suitcase, and now they walked up the front porch steps of Ashley's Indiana home and made their way inside.

"All you have to do now is get those paintings shipped and pack." Kari's eyes sparkled. "You must be practically bursting, Ash. Paris! Can you believe it?"

Ashley didn't say anything. She led the way into the kitchen and leaned against the counter. Then she turned to her sister and made a few circles in the air with her index finger. "Yippee."

"No." Kari's smile faded. "Not again, Ashley. Please." She set her purse down and came closer. "You and Landon are celebrating eighteen years. This trip, the art show, it's all happening at the perfect time."

"Yeah. Maybe." Ashley sighed. "Maybe if I get the paintings shipped." She motioned for Kari to follow her. "Come look at my paintings. I have to send twenty of them out tomorrow."

"Yes." Kari sounded optimistic. "That's the spirit. You need this trip, Ash. You do."

Ashley nodded. She'd been dodging the issue of how she felt about Paris ever since the gallery called and asked her to do a show. She could still hear the woman's voice.

This is Emilie Love, owner of Light of the Seine art gallery in Paris. The woman had explained that the shop used to be called Montmartre Gallery, where Ashley had worked twenty-three years ago. Now it was in the Marais district in the fourth arrondissement. *We'd love to showcase your work.*

They were words she hadn't heard since she had lived there. *Montmartre . . . Marais . . . arrondissement.* Ashley had taken the call out to the front porch, so she could catch her breath. The woman continued talking, her English perfect. Something about how the Montmartre Gallery had a different name now. *Light of the Seine.* A nod to the City of Light. "I'd be honored to showcase your work, Ashley. You are very, very talented. I've been through your offerings."

Of the hundred questions that had raced through Ashley's mind, only one mattered. "How . . . did you hear about me?"

"My customers ask about you." There was a smile in the woman's voice. "Several have requested a show." She paused. "You paint from the heart. Everyone can see that."

You paint from the heart? The previous gallery owner had told Ashley that she had no talent, that she'd never make it as an artist. She had been forced to gather her few paintings and take them back to the small room she had rented that year. So they wouldn't mar the good work of true artists.

That's what she'd been told.

"You're thinking about it again." Kari followed her to the basement. "Trying to remember why you said yes in the first place." She tapped Ashley on her shoulder. "Am I right?"

Ashley looked back and allowed the slightest laugh. "Okay . . . maybe."

"You said yes because the people of Paris love your work." Kari reached the basement floor and waited until Ashley faced her. "*Your* work, little sister."

"Right." Ashley nodded, but her anxiety pressed in. She walked Kari to the first of a line of paintings. "This is what I'm sending. At least I think I am."

"These?" Kari looked down the row of art pieces lined against the wall. "Ashley . . . you can't sell these. I want them."

This time Ashley's laugh was genuine. "That's the whole point of a show. You sell the work and start over again."

Kari shook her head. "Please . . . tell me you aren't selling the one of Mom and Erin and the girls."

That particular painting hung just outside the bedroom Ashley shared with her husband, Landon. Where it would always remain. Ashley's tribute to the people she loved, the ones who were in heaven together. "No, Kari. That one's mine."

Ashley had given a version of the work to each of her siblings. Kari and Ryan kept theirs in their office. Brooke and Peter had theirs in a spare bedroom, Luke and Reagan's hung near the front door. And Dayne and Katy kept Ashley's heaven painting in their California house.

Some things would always be too sacred to sell.

"Look!" Kari walked slowly down the line of paintings. "You can't sell these, either. There's the old Baxter house back when Mom and Dad still lived in it." She stopped and touched the framed piece. "I remember when you painted this. When you thought Landon was never coming home again."

"True." Ashley stopped and bent down, studying the work. She could still remember standing in what had been her parents' massive front yard, looking at the pretty house, getting the lighting just right, working on the sky and suddenly feeling someone behind her. And turning around to find Landon there. Home . . . forever home to her. "Maybe I shouldn't let that one go."

"I mean." Kari looked around the basement. "You must have a hundred paintings. How about you only sell the ones that don't make me cry when I look at them."

She had a point. Ashley stared at her work. "But shouldn't they get my best work?"

"Listen." Kari put her hand alongside Ashley's face. "Everything you paint is your best work. Let's pick out the twenty we can actually live without."

And so for the next hour they worked through each of Ashley's pieces until they had a smattering of colors and seasons and subjects. Most of which featured people other than the Baxter family. Already Ashley felt better. "Maybe that's why I've been a little off. Because I was about to sell some of my favorites."

But there was more to her bad feelings. A fear she hadn't ever told anyone—not even Landon. The most terrible part about her time in Paris. Ashley forced the frightening thought from her mind.

"Well then, you should be happy now!" Kari raised her hands high, her eyes sparkling. "You are going with your incredible husband to Paris for your eighteenth anniversary, and you are going to sell your paintings in the one place you never thought you'd sell them." She lowered her arms and grinned. "What could be more exciting than that?"

"Fine." Ashley laughed again. "I'm excited. I can't wait!"

Kari helped her box up the paintings, two per container. But the whole time Ashley couldn't shake the distant memory. What about the darkness in Paris? What if it was still waiting for her? She forced the questions from her mind. It wasn't possible. Kari was right. She should be thrilled about Paris.

As a young girl, she had dreamed of selling her work there. This was a dream come true.

Maybe if she told herself often enough, it would be true.

When the twenty pieces were boxed, she and Kari loaded Landon's old pickup truck and drove the collection to the UPS store in Bloomington. An hour later—after they had provided the gallery information and paid for the boxes to be sent two-day insured shipping—they returned to Ashley's house and Kari hugged her. "I have to go."

"Thanks for your help." Ashley had always been closest to Kari, and today was no exception. "You understand, right? The reason this is hard."

The smile Kari had kept in place most of the day faded. She hugged Ashley once more, longer this time. "Of course. I was the first to hug you when you walked through the front door home from Paris the first time. Remember?"

"I do." Ashley felt tears gather in her eyes, but she blinked them back. "It'll be fine. Landon's always wanted me to go back, to make peace with the city."

"With more than the city." Kari studied her. "It's time."

Ashley nodded. "I know. Thanks again." She stepped back and watched Kari get into her car and drive off. The trip to Paris still troubled her. Maybe if she told Kari the details she'd kept secret for twenty-three years, this conversation would be different. Her sister might even tell her to stay home. But there was no verifying the part she never talked about. How could it harm her now, so many years later? The whole thing might've been only in her imagination.

Something Ashley should've forgotten by now.

When Kari's car was out of sight, Ashley turned to the old Baxter house, the place where she and Landon and their kids had lived for so many years. Ever since her father had married dear Elaine, and the two had bought their own home nearby.

Looking at the house from this vantage point—out front and with time on her hands—Ashley let the happy memories come. She could see herself and her siblings spilling out of the family van the day they moved here when she was ten. Back when she thought home could never be anywhere but the place they'd left in Michigan.

The next morning their moving van had been late, and her father had come up with a quick idea. "Let's paint the porch! We can all work together!"

Dad had gotten buckets of white paint and half a dozen brushes, and they slopped and painted and spilled enough paint over the porch until finally it looked brand new. Then the five of them—Brooke and Kari, Ashley and Erin and Luke—had all run out back to the creek and washed off. But not before they'd found the big rock at the stream's edge. The handprints they'd left there that day were mostly rubbed off from weather and time.

But in her mind, Ashley could still see them as clear as they'd been that long-ago day.

She blinked and the view of the front porch changed, and she could see herself getting into the car to go buy milk . . . and Luke's friend Jefferson Bennett was running behind her. "Can you give me a ride home, Ashley?" There had been no warning, no way to know that Ashley's life and his would never be the same again. That a drunk driver would cross the line and Jefferson would jerk the wheel and take the hit. Or that the sixteen-year-old boy would live just a week longer before leaving them.

Another blink and Ashley pictured herself stepping out of her parents' SUV two summers later with a pair of suitcases and a pregnant belly, home from Paris. Ashley could see the girl she'd been back then. Without faith or hope or a desire to ever come home. Yet there she was, surrounded by the love of her mom and dad. Heading back through the doors of the house she had still loved so well.

And she could see the time Landon walked up the stairs of that porch and into the house after Kari married Tim . . . a million years ago. Ashley breathed deep. Of course she painted what she felt. The memories were a part of her life here at the old Baxter house.

When her dad and Elaine decided to sell, Ashley and Landon were the only adult kids interested in buying it. The only ones willing to live on the ten acres and take care of the place. Of course, the two of them had jumped at the chance.

Ashley would never grow tired of looking at the old house, the white wood siding and pretty gables, the dark roof and white wraparound porch. The solid double mahogany front doors. Their home had gone up in value in recent years, but she and Landon would never sell it. The memories inside those walls and windows were simply priceless.

Ashley took her time walking across the expansive front yard and up the porch steps. She and Landon would be home from Paris before she knew it, back here in Bloomington, where her work came to life. There was nothing to fear in Paris. Those shadowy dark days were decades ago.

She made her way to the kitchen and half an hour later she had whipped up spaghetti with zucchini noodles and homemade tomato sauce. Devin was with a friend and Cole was back at college. His junior year already. Only Amy and Janessa were joining them tonight. At fifteen and nine, they were still home most evenings.

But not for long. All the kids had grown up in a blink.

Ashley set the table, the way she did every night. Dinnertime was as important now as it had been when the kids were little. She was laying out the plates when Landon came through the door. He was fire chief for the Bloomington Fire Department, a prestigious position that no longer required his wearing a uniform.

She heard him walk up behind her. "I must say . . ." He slipped his arms around her waist and kissed her neck. "Has anyone ever told you?" Gently he turned her in his arms and worked his fingers up along her face. "You have the most beautiful hair."

Ashley grinned. They were the words her dear old friend Irvel had said to her many times a day, back when Ashley worked at Sunset Hills Adult Care Home after coming home from Paris. "No . . . No one's told me." Ashley grinned at him. "Not in a very long time."

It wasn't true. Landon said it all the time. But this was part of the game. "Well then"—he kissed her lips—"I'll tell you. You have the most beautiful hair, Ashley." He smiled and his lips met hers. Their kiss lingered, the way it usually did. He stepped back and smiled. "How was your day?"

She hesitated. "It was good. Really." Her smile didn't feel genuine. "Kari and I shipped out the paintings. They'll arrive in time for the show."

"Good." Landon wasn't fooled. He crooked his finger and lifted Ashley's chin. "You're still not sure." He searched her eyes. "I know you, Ashley. Only God knows you better." His voice was soft, his words aimed straight to her soul. "Why so many doubts?"

"I keep thinking . . . maybe it's too soon."

"Too soon?" Landon led Ashley to the kitchen, where he leaned on the nearest counter and pulled her into his arms. "It's been twenty-two years, my love."

"Twenty-three." She managed a weak smile. "But who's counting?"

"Jessie's there, remember. That's another reason to go." Landon raised his brow. "She's got a lunch date all planned for us."

"True." Ashley pictured her sweet niece. Kari and Ryan's oldest, Jessie, was doing a summer in Paris. Studying art, of all things. "Jessie is definitely counting on us."

For a long moment, Landon didn't say anything. Just looked into Ashley's eyes and brushed away the loose strands of hair from her forehead. "Can I tell you a story?"

"Okay." The girls would be home in ten minutes. But for now, they had time.

Landon drew a deep breath. "Once a long time ago, a

group of disciples were crossing the Sea of Galilee when a great storm came up. So great, that the waves threatened to sink their boat." He paused. "And all the while their teacher was in the hull . . . sleeping. His head on a pillow."

Ashley loved when he did this, when he found some Bible story or anecdote from real life and used it to make sense of her world. She lifted her face to Landon. "I think I might know this one."

"Ah, but there's more." Landon paused. "The disciples cried out to their teacher and immediately . . . immediately . . . Jesus woke up. And with two simple words He calmed the storm. Completely." Landon spread his hands as if he could see the glassy water from that long-ago night. "'Be still,' He called out. And I mean . . . the water was glass. Just like that."

A quick laugh caught Ashley off guard. "I love you, do you know that?"

"I do . . . but wait!" He got lost in her eyes again. "Most people stop there. The water was still; Jesus and the disciples carried on and they reached the shore. Just like Jesus had promised from the beginning."

"Thank you, Landon." The roasted vegetables needed to come out of the oven. "You're always a great storyteller."

"No, no!" Landon held up his index finger. "You're forgetting about the other boats."

Ashley blinked. "The what?"

"Aha! I got your attention." Landon smiled. "The other boats. On the sea that night were other boats. It says so right in the Bible. Some versions say there were other *little* boats on the sea."

"Really?" Ashley couldn't tell if he was teasing or not. "Little boats?"

"Yes. Look . . . I'm serious!" He smiled as he held his arms out to the sides. "I mean, I imagine they were big enough to hold fishermen, but whatever. Just more boats than the one Jesus was on."

"Okay . . ."

"This is the whole point, Ash. The other boats . . . they were caught up in the storm, too. And those boats didn't have Jesus in them. But when He calmed the storm for His disciples, guess who also had smooth sailing?"

"The other boats." Ashley answered at the same time Landon did.

He smiled. "Do you get it?"

"We'll . . . see other boats? In Paris? On the river Seine?"

"No." Landon's attention remained entirely on her. "Twenty-three years ago, when He calmed your storm, there were other boats . . . in Paris and back home. Little boats that maybe you know nothing about."

"Hmmm. Little boats." Ashley liked that.

"And I believe . . ." He touched her face once more. "I believe that when we take this trip to Paris, you just might run across some of those little boats."

This time Ashley could do nothing to stop the tears that formed in her eyes. She felt her smile fill her face. "I hope so."

"You have to believe." He touched the spot above her heart. "Here, Ash. Deep inside you."

She went to him again and slipped her arms around his neck. "You're my best friend, Landon Blake."

"And you're mine." He kissed her and when he drew back, he whispered, "I'm one of those boats, Ashley. All you could see was your own situation, the way the storm was about to destroy you. But I was one of those little boats. I would've sunk if you hadn't come home." He brushed his thumb over her cheek. "But there are others. I believe that."

It was a thought that stayed with Ashley through dinner and during their question game with the girls, and long after the dishes were done. Even after Landon had fallen asleep beside her. The idea that Jesus had been with her, in her personal boat when the worst storm in all her life had come up.

Ashley wasn't sure why Jesus had been sleeping during His disciples' worst storm, but she believed it. He had definitely been asleep when she lived in Paris. Where she had made the worst decisions in her life. But when the disciples cried out to Jesus, He was there. Immediately. Just like He had been for Ashley when she came home from Paris. She turned onto her side and put her arm around Landon. The idea that when God had calmed the storm in her own life, He had also calmed the one in Landon's, was something Ashley had never considered.

It was enough to give her the confidence to believe that this trip to Paris was maybe a good decision. Despite her frightening secret. Because now Ashley had a reason to believe she should go back to the place that had almost destroyed her and make peace with it. This trip was about forgiving Paris, once and for all.

And something else. Ashley smiled.

The little boats.

4

The air was just warm enough for John and Elaine to move out onto their small back porch after dinner and watch the Indiana sunset. For a while the two of them sat, side by side, holding hands, taking in the pinks and pale blues and watching the shadows grow longer.

But tonight John wasn't thinking about how they'd spent the day or the dinner he and Elaine had just eaten. His heart was on Ashley, his middle daughter. Finally, he turned to Elaine. "This trip to Paris has to be hard on Ashley. All the planning. Thinking about that city again."

"It is." Elaine carried with her a quiet confidence, a beauty that never tried to compete with the life John had lived before the two married. She had been Elizabeth's friend back in the days when they were raising their children, and years after Elizabeth lost her battle to cancer, John and Elaine had found each other.

Elaine was a very great gift, indeed.

John didn't understand his wife's comment. "You sound sure."

"I am." Elaine set her rocker into motion. "Ashley and

I talked on the phone a week ago. Even then she was still thinking about canceling the whole trip."

"I wondered." John leaned back in his chair. "She mentioned that to me back in the beginning. When the gallery first called." He lifted his eyes to the sky. "Can you believe how good God is? Giving Ashley the chance to go back to Paris and see her artwork on display?" He shook his head. "You can't make this stuff up."

"True." Elaine hesitated. "There's redemption in this part of Ashley's story. But you're right. It won't be easy, John. None of it."

He looked at her again. "I want to join them in Paris. At least for the art show."

A smile filled Elaine's eyes. "That would be nice."

"I'm not sure. I mean it's also their anniversary trip." John stood and walked to the porch railing. Then he turned and stared at Elaine. "I've been wondering what . . . Elizabeth would want me to do." This was something else that made Elaine special. John could talk to her about Elizabeth. Not that he did so very often, but when his first wife came up in conversation, Elaine wasn't intimidated. She understood that John would always love Elizabeth. He would be with her still if he'd had his way.

But he also loved Elaine. Conversations like this were among the many reasons why.

Elaine joined him at the railing. "Elizabeth loved Ashley's paintings. She told me about each one, as Ashley was painting it."

"I didn't know that." John put his arm around Elaine's shoulders and eased her closer to himself. "Tell me . . . what would she say?"

Like she often did, Elaine took her time. As if she could once again hear those sweet conversations with her friend. "When Ashley painted the old Baxter house for the first time, Elizabeth told me that she could see the roof and siding come to life beneath Ashley's paintbrush. How Ashley created with more than the colors on her palette. She painted with memories from a dozen years."

"Mmm." John smiled. "I can hear Elizabeth saying that. How Ashley painted with more than reds and blues. She painted with times gone by."

"In Ashley's paintings, Elizabeth saw family and faith, love and laughter." Elaine turned to John. "I don't think anything could've kept her from being there when Ashley has her first art show in Paris."

Something heavy in John's heart lifted. "You're right." He studied his wife. "So you think I should go?"

"Yes." She shrugged. "Maybe talk to Landon. See what he thinks?"

John turned and pulled her into a long hug. "I love you so much, Elaine. You always have the right thing to say. I'll call Landon tomorrow."

And the next day John did just that. He loved all his sons-in-law like they were his own, but he had a special place in his heart for Landon. The one who had loved Ashley since the two were in fifth grade. Landon was at work when John made the call. "I have a thought." He didn't waste time when Landon picked up. "Do you have a minute?"

"Sure." Landon could've been in the middle of a mountain of paperwork, but he would always make time for the people he loved. "You calling about Paris?"

John laughed. "How did you know?"

"Because . . . she's your daughter." Landon's tone was easy. "You're both thinkers. What's on your mind?"

"I'm wondering . . . if I should go to Paris. Show up for Ashley's art show."

"Really?" Landon's voice lit up. "John . . . she'd love that."

"I'm not sure. I mean . . . it's your anniversary trip and it is a long flight." John stood from his office chair and wandered into the kitchen. He poured himself a cup of coffee. "You don't think it would be strange?"

"Hardly." Landon chuckled. "She'd probably faint . . . seeing you there. It would mean the world. Definitely."

"Okay, then. I'll think about it." John took a sip of coffee and stared out the kitchen window. He was doing telehealth now and had clients every day. The perfect job for a retired doctor. "I'd have to clear my schedule, but to see her face for a surprise like that . . . how could I miss it?"

When the conversation ended, John remembered something and set his coffee down. The box of Elizabeth's letters in the spare bedroom closet upstairs. The kids all had copies of her letters in books John and Ashley had put together not long after Elizabeth died.

But he still had the originals.

How long since I've read those precious letters, Elizabeth? The thought landed on his heart. The letters were separated into bundles, one for each of the kids, all in separate cardboard boxes. So they wouldn't get dusty. The largest box was his, with more letters than all of theirs combined, dating back to before the kids were born. Letters she had written to him when they were separated the year she had Dayne. Others, she'd written just because. When he was at the hospital working and the kids were napping, and she'd had a hundred thoughts she wanted to share with him only.

John moved up to the stairs to their guest room, slower than he had ten years ago, but he still had a spring in his step. He and Elaine walked three miles every day, and he didn't feel the old football injuries in his knees except when he climbed stairs. Once in the guest room, he had Elizabeth's letters spread out on the bed in minutes. Each of the kids' bundles had their names on top.

He took Ashley's stack and moved to the chair in the corner. How blessed were their children to have been loved by a mother like Elizabeth? John opened the first letter and sighed. Elizabeth's handwriting was still so achingly familiar. He ran his fingers over the dark ink and the paper she had poured her heart onto.

Then he started at the beginning.

My dearest Ashley,
    I am writing this to you while you're doing finals. If I could, I'd be there with you, praying over you and whispering in your ear,

"You can do it, Ash. You really can do it!" But I can't be there, so I thought I'd write you a letter.

John smiled. He could picture the scene, the kids at school and Elizabeth at the desk in the office. Thinking of her children. Back then Ashley had been whole and happy and innocent. Before the car accident that took the life of Luke's friend. Before all of life fell apart.

Before Paris.

He kept reading.

Anyway, I bought you a few new canvases. There's something so special about a blank canvas. I know you-of all people-agree, precious daughter. Oh, the things you create on a blank canvas. You see things that aren't, Ashley, and you bring them to life as if they had been there all along. I love that about you.

A chill ran down John's arms. Had he really found exactly what he was looking for here . . . on his first try? Something Elizabeth had written that talked about Ashley's skills as an artist?

He moved on to the next letter.

Dear Ashley,
You're spending the night at Natalie's house. Big sleepover. But here at home, I can't

fall asleep. So, I thought I'd write you a quick letter. I Know I tell you all the time, Ash, but you are such a talented artist. You really are.

Tears filled John's eyes. Two letters! He had actually found a second letter that gave him the answers he was seeking. About whether Elizabeth would want him to go to Paris for Ashley's art show. He blinked a few times so he could see better.

Precious Ashley, I can picture you being old and gray one day and finding these letters and Knowing--to the core of your being--that your father and I believed in you. Truly, honey, one day people will line up to buy your artwork. And all the world will see home and family and faith through your beautiful eyes.

Unbelievable. As if God Himself had led him to these very letters. With the greatest care, John folded up the second letter and started on the third.

Dear Ashley,
Today I was missing the moments when you were in fifth grade. Remember that Peter Pan play you and your friends put on when you were in Mr. Garrett's class? You were

Wendy and you had your own ideas about how things should go at the end. Neverland forever! That was your way of playing the part, and so you did. It was a moment I will remember always, sweet girl. Your love for your life, your determination to never grow old!

John smiled. A single tear fell onto his cheek and he brushed it away. He remembered that performance. How Ashley called for Peter Pan to turn the boat back to Neverland. And how later that month she had her siblings all sign a contract promising to never grow up. He found his place on the letter.

Such good times, Ashley. So, since I was missing those days, I went down to the basement where you keep your paintings. Every one of them. And I was simply breathless, precious daughter. You have been given such a great gift from God. Remember when Dad gave you that art book after we moved here from Michigan? A fresh new book?

Ashley, my dear, look at what your simple drawings have become! I believe that one day, Ash... one day you will have a gallery show in Paris, France. Yes, all the way across the ocean in Paris. Where art is so important, and people expect the very best. And there you will be, among the greats.

*But between you and me, you're
already that good. Even if your gallery is
only here in the basement for now. I love
you always, Mom.*

Three in a row! John had hoped to find even one letter
where Elizabeth talked about Ashley's painting. Then it
hit him. He leaned back in the chair. He hadn't happened
to find the only letters in the stack where Elizabeth encouraged Ashley as an artist. That was something Elizabeth had done as naturally as breathing.

Of course, Elizabeth would want him to go to Paris, to
surprise Ashley at her art show. An hour later, John knew
he was right. Every single letter Elizabeth had ever written
to Ashley involved some mention of her artwork. Even
after she had gone to Paris and given them few ways to
reach her. Elizabeth had only written their daughter even
more letters. Like the one in his hand now.

*Ashley,
    We haven't heard from you in a while. You're
still in France, and I know you're figuring
things out, and that's okay. Your father and
I are praying for you every day. God is with
you, we know that.
    But even though you are struggling, I am
convinced of this. You're supposed to be in Paris
right now. I'm not sure why, Ashley, but I
can feel it every time I pray. God is using*

you there. Maybe because you really are going to showcase your paintings in France— either now or later.

Or maybe He's doing something else with your time away. Whatever it is, I am at peace. Because God is working in your life, sweet girl. I know He is.

I love you always, Mom.

Wow. John could hardly believe it. He wiped another tear and folded the letters. Yes, Ashley had copies in a book somewhere in her bookcase. But had she read them lately? He would put Elizabeth's words together for her somehow and he would give them to Ashley on her big day.

Then, as John set the stack of letters in the bottom of the old box, he felt something hard and plastic. Careful not to harm the item, John pried it from between the flaps of cardboard where it had apparently gotten stuck.

His breath caught as he held it up. "What in the world? Elizabeth . . . when did you do this?"

It was a cassette tape, and in the notes section beneath the plastic cover it said simply, *Messages to my children.* Only this wasn't a series of letters. It was voice messages . . . one for each of them. Words that none of them had ever heard before. John remembered to exhale. Then he set the cassette on top of the pile of Ashley's letters.

An audio message for each of the kids from Elizabeth?

He could hardly wait to tell Elaine . . . and the kids. But without a doubt the first person to hear what Elizabeth had left for them would be him. Alone. But before he could do that, he had to do something practical.

He had to find a cassette player.

5

Love was the last thing Jessie Taylor had expected to find when she signed up for Indiana University's summer semester in Paris. She wasn't like some of her friends, looking more for a husband than a degree. At twenty-two, Jessie had dreams and plans, and she intended to live them out.

Paris was part of that. Gabriel Michel was not.

Their class on French Impressionists was just letting out and Gabriel quickly fell in beside her. "I know I was supposed to be studying all that famous art." He was quite a bit taller than her. Dark hair and tanned skin. "But I couldn't stop thinking about something else."

He stopped and she faced him. "You, ma chérie." He touched her face.

She smiled. "You say that to all the girls."

Gabriel's face fell. "No, mon amour. You know that."

Actually, she did know. Gabriel was a rare diamond of a guy. He was her age, but with the faith and wisdom rare in Paris or anywhere else. "Just teasing." She held her books close. "Let's get coffee."

He looked like he wanted to kiss her. But this wasn't

the time. They'd only been dating a few weeks, and their first kiss hadn't happened yet. Which was how Jessie wanted to keep it. She had no intention of falling for some Parisian boy and then getting her heart broken ten weeks from now when it was time to go home.

Even a boy as incredible as Gabe.

He held the door for her and bought their coffee and they found a sunny table outside, near a flower box of petunias. Their spot, it had become lately. He leaned across the table, his eyes locked on hers. "Now . . . tell me about this dream you had. How you're never going back to the States and how you want to grow old with me here in Paris."

She laughed. He was always making her laugh. "That's a dream for another day."

"Okay." He settled back in his seat, the apple-cheeked college boy once more. "Then tell me about your aunt Ashley. Why is she coming here?"

Jessie loved talking about her aunt. More times than she could count, her mother had given her the greatest compliment. "You're just like your aunt Ashley, Jessie. Just like her." All Jessie knew was that Ashley had an incredible marriage, a beautiful family, and the greatest gift of creating art Jessie had ever seen.

And now that gift lived inside *her*. Ashley had told her so back when Jessie was only thirteen. "You're talented, Jessie. Stay with it. You're going to be a great artist one day."

Words her own mother had often echoed. She grinned

at Gabriel. "Wait till you see my aunt Ashley's paintings. She's so talented. And . . . " Jessie paused for effect. "I just found out. That gallery you like to visit—Light of the Seine . . . she's doing a show there. Right here in the fourth arrondissement!"

"That's incredible." Gabriel set his coffee down and stared at her. "They almost never host American artists."

"I know!" Jessie could hardly contain her joy. "And one day my work will be featured there, too."

Gabriel's eyes softened, but his smile remained. "I believe it will, Jessie Taylor. If anyone can do it, you can."

"Thank you." She thought about Aunt Ashley's life and how it hadn't started out with Parisian art shows. "Ashley was here once before. Did I ever tell you that?"

"No. I thought . . . She lives in Indiana, right?" Gabe extended his hand and took hold of hers. His tone kept things light.

"She does. But she lived here for almost a year . . . when she was twenty."

"Was it a school program?" He drank his coffee, but his attention never wavered from her. "Like you?"

"No." Jessie had never talked about this with Aunt Ashley. But her mother had told her what happened. Most of it, anyway. "Back then, she came here to escape her life in the States. All the bad things that had happened to her."

"Bad things?"

Jessie told Gabe about the car accident. "They were ten minutes from his house when a drunk driver veered across the center line and hit them head-on." Jessie looked down. "The man was driving a delivery truck."

"That's terrible." Gabe set his coffee down. "What happened?"

"Aunt Ashley was badly hurt, but she made a full recovery. The boy was in high school . . . he died a few days later."

Gabe took a few minutes before saying anything. "That's a lot."

"It was. My mom told me no one knew whether my aunt would survive." Jessie's heart ached for Aunt Ashley, for all she had suffered that year. "So, she came here. To try to live again."

"Did things get better?"

"Worse." Jessie took a deep breath. "When she came home, she was pregnant with my cousin Cole."

"Hmm. My mom's story is a little like that." Gabe thought for a moment. "Very terrible beginnings."

Jessie hesitated. "I guess we all have a story. Even me." Her smile felt sad. "I've told you a little about it. And my aunt Ashley's story . . . that can wait for another day."

"Fair enough." Gabriel finished his coffee. They talked about class, and when they left the café, Gabe took her hand. "Jessie . . . do you have a sturdy pair of trainers?"

She felt her smile become a laugh. Gabe was beyond proficient in English, but many times the French word was entirely different from what she would say back home in Bloomington. "Trainers?"

Gabe held his foot out. "Trainers. Shoes."

"Like tennis shoes?" She was wearing a low boot today. But, of course, she had other shoes back at her dorm.

"Not for tennis." Gabriel grinned, but he was serious. "You'll need something sturdy. And jeans. Strong jeans." Clearly, he was struggling to get his point across. "You know what I mean, Jessie. I have a surprise for you. I want to take you somewhere." He gave her ponytail a flick. "Come on . . . it's only ten in the morning."

Jessie's heart skipped a beat. "I think I can figure it out." They walked across campus to her dormitory, and he waited outside. Up in her room she slipped into a pair of jeans and her most sturdy sneakers.

The whole time she never stopped smiling. An adventure that needed a change of clothes? This was another reason she loved spending time with Gabriel. He took her on day trips in the city and outside it. One day they were walking along the Seine, another it was a stroll through the Louvre. Today . . . well, she had no idea what Gabe had in mind, but she was sure it would be unforgettable.

Most Parisians got around by bus or train or the metro. In the few weeks they'd been dating, Jessie and Gabe usually took public transportation. But today they headed south of the city in Gabriel's car. Jessie liked this the most, the chance to be alone with him, side by side on an adventure. So far they'd had their best conversations in the car.

She thought he was going to ask her about her story, the one she had only touched on before. Instead, he kept the conversation light, chatting about their different classes and how quickly the summer semester was going.

"I want to see Indiana." He glanced at her as they drove. "It must be beautiful."

"It is." Jessie stared ahead at the forest land on either side of the roadway. "Not like this. Not like Paris. Obviously." She thought for a moment. "The cities are very different. But Indiana is lovely, Gabe. It is. In spring it smells of lilac and in the fall the colors make an artist know the truth. That only God could create red and orange and yellow and blue. All the hues. It's peaceful and gentle." She smiled at him. "Indiana is home."

"I think I'd like it." He kept his eyes on the road. "As long as you're there, ma belle."

Jessie leaned back into her seat. Her time here was flying by and when fall came, she would have to go home. But how could she leave Gabe? Would he really come see her in Bloomington? Or would she find her way back here? Right now neither option felt like a possibility.

All the more reason to live in the moment. Jessie faced Gabe again. "So, where are we going?"

"You'll see." His eyes shone.

Less than an hour after leaving the city, Gabe took an exit and a few minutes later they pulled into a parking lot. The sign at the front said: AVENTURE FLOREVAL. "We're here." He parked the car and turned to her. "La belle forêt."

Her French was nowhere as good as his. But she'd studied the language in high school and college, so she knew enough to keep up. "The beautiful forest."

"Yes. Very good." He laughed. "Only . . . this time we'll see it from the *top* of the trees."

They climbed out of the car and Gabe met her near her door. The weather was sunny and cool today. Maybe sixty-five degrees. She shaded her eyes and stared at the trees beyond the parking lot. "Wait . . . a ropes course?"

"Actually, many ropes courses." He winked at her. "But don't worry. I'm taking you on the intermediate one this time."

"Oh, good." Jessie's stomach did a flip. "Did I mention I'm not a fan of heights?"

"Which is why we won't go too far up." He took her hand and they headed to the entrance. "Just seven meters off the ground."

"What?" Jessie laughed but she followed him. "Seven meters? And I'm . . . supposed to walk on ropes up there?"

"With me, Jessie." He stopped and touched her shoulder. "You'll be safe with me."

And so she was.

After a quick briefing, she and Gabriel climbed into harnesses and up a series of wooden pegs till they were at least twenty feet in the air. Jessie didn't look down. "So this . . . harness is going to catch me? If I fall?"

He was an arm's length behind her. "*I'll* catch you if you fall." His voice was strong and soft, all at the same time. "The harness is only a backup."

"Nice." She was teasing him, but deep inside his promise made her feel safe. He was there. She wasn't going to fall. "Okay . . . so what's first?"

Gabe looked beyond her. "Looks like it's the chimpanzee swings." They stopped, balancing on a thick branch.

Gabriel read the sign. "For this part of the adventure, hold on to the ropes and move forward from one swing to another."

"Great. Piece of cake." Jessie's legs trembled as she tried to balance herself. "You really think I can do this?"

"You can, Jessie." He put his hand on the small of her back. "Go on. Jump to the first swing!"

Jessie had never tried anything so crazy in all her life. How had she let him talk her into this? Just then she caught a glimpse of the ground. She didn't want to fall, and she couldn't go backwards. Gabe was right. The only way through the course was to do it. Full on, with everything she had.

She held her breath for a few seconds and closed her eyes. When she opened them, she made a lurching motion toward the swing-size platform. With her hands still on the ropes, somehow she landed upright on the swing. "I did it!" Adrenaline pushed through her veins and the shakiness faded. Yes, she could handle this course. She could.

"Watch me, Gabe!" She jumped to the next swing and the next and another. All the while Gabriel kept up behind her. They both had played sports in high school. Gabe had been a striker on the soccer team and Jessie had played tennis. Together, they played soccer on the school's summer intramural team.

"I knew you could do it!" Gabe sounded proud of her. They reached the end of the swings and found a sturdy spot on another branch. "Okay . . ." He didn't sound winded. "Read the sign. What's next?"

A breeze brushed over them and the branch swayed. Jessie held on to the ropes and squinted at the wooden plaque. THE TARZAN LEAP. She didn't want to waste time. They were actually conquering the course. But if the breeze picked up, they'd both be in trouble. She kept reading. "Grab a liana, swing and jump, while grabbing onto a net a few meters away."

Jessie froze, then she looked back at Gabe. "A liana . . . a vine, is that what we're talking about here?"

Gabe chuckled and nodded toward a grouping of tree vines. "Looks like it."

Nothing about the directions seemed possible. Grab a vine and a net at the same time? But again, there was no going back. Something her mother once told her came to mind as she steadied herself and stared at the vine. *God sets our course, but we have to walk it out.* Yes, indeed. "Here goes!"

She lunged for a vine and then threw herself in the other direction. Somehow she had enough momentum to grab hold of the net. Swinging one way then the other she made it to the next tree and a branch even higher off the ground. Instead of looking down, Jessie looked back at Gabe. Again, the wind made the slim platform rock and tilt.

Gabriel let out a Tarzan yell and as he did he easily swung from the vine to the net and back again—mixing it up in a way that could not be called anything but advanced. In seconds he was at her side again. "Mon trésor."

My treasure. Jessie felt her fear dissipate. How could she be afraid dancing up here in the tops of the trees with him? If ever there was a time she wanted to kiss him, it was now. But they had to keep moving. Next was the lumberjack's bridge, a forever-long series of logs with safety cables on either side.

"It's more fun with the breeze," Gabriel called from behind her. The makeshift bridge swayed and bounced.

"Oh, sure." Jessie tightened her grip on the cables that ran along either side of her. "If only I had wings."

"Comme les oiseaux."

Like the birds. "Yes." She steadied herself. "I love when you speak French, Gabe." She took the smallest step forward. "If I haven't told you."

"You have." He was so close, their bodies almost touching. "And do feel free to pick up the pace."

She took another step. "Your French distracted me."

Bit by bit she made her way along the bridge with him right behind her. Next there was a section where they literally walked through the trees. The branch platforms were barely noticeable until she actually felt one with her foot. She was halfway across the treetops when her foot missed a platform and she lost her balance.

Jessie's hands flew over her head and as her body fell backwards, she screamed.

"I've got you!" Gabriel sounded sure.

Before Jessie could drop toward the ground, before her harness had to do its job and stop her from crashing to the earth below, Gabriel had his arms around her. With the strength of three men, he kept his position on his own platform and lifted her back to hers.

She was breathing hard, her knees shaking. "I . . . I almost . . ."

"No . . ." His breath was a whisper against her neck. From his spot behind her, he pulled her close and brushed his cheek alongside hers. "I told you . . . I'll never let you fall. Not ever."

For a few seconds she let her body lean against his. Then she tightened her grip on the cables and stood straight again. With the slightest look back, she smiled at him. "I believe you."

After nearly an hour in the trees, they reached the end of the course. Jessie could still feel the warmth of his body against hers, his hands around her waist, keeping her from dropping. She would never forget this, even if their time in the trees was over.

But as they moved ahead, Jessie saw she was wrong. This wasn't actually the end of the course. She looked back at Gabriel. "Are you serious?"

He shrugged, barely containing his grin. "Two adventures in one. It's your lucky day."

"What?" She stared ahead again. Up next was a zip line that ran through the trees at least fifty yards. And they seemed practically that high up. *Okay, God, I'm going to need Your help on this one.* "That's the way down?"

"It's fast." Gabe chuckled. "Did I tell you this course is for ages eleven and up?"

"Eleven and up. Why am I feeling ten all of a sudden?" She reached the platform where a worker was waiting for them.

"Hope you have enjoyed the course." The man's accent was thick, but his English was good enough. He sounded like he really meant it. Like he was happiest up here in the trees helping customers.

"Yes." Jessie nodded. She wondered if she looked as nervous as she felt. "What . . . what do I do next?"

Gabe patted her back. "He'll switch your hook from the rope to the zip line."

"And I'll close my eyes." Before she could blink, she was connected to the long, black cable.

"Jump." The worker smiled at her. "Have a go."

Jessie's eyes caught the ground a million miles below. If kids could do it, she could. A shrill scream came from her as she leapt from the platform and her feet fell loose. But at the same time the cable caught her and she began speeding down the line. Fast, but not too fast. Slow enough that she could appreciate what was happening. She was flying! Flying through the prettiest treetops and filled with an exhilaration she'd never known before.

Too soon her feet touched the ground, and another worker unhooked her. The woman helped Jessie out of her harness and moved her a few feet so Gabriel could land. A minute later he was at her side, both of them still breathing hard, walking along a path through the trees. "Well, Jessie . . . what did you think?" He stopped and faced her. "Good adventure?"

She looked at him and the moment shifted. They were alone here on this part of the trail. He put his hands on her shoulders and then he worked his fingers into her hair and touched his lips to hers. The kiss didn't last long, but it was warm and full and it took Jessie's breath more than anything up on the ropes course.

"Yes." Her voice was soft. All she wanted was for him to kiss her again. "The very best adventure, Gabriel."

He brushed the tips of his fingers against her cheek. "Tu es belle, Jessie."

You are beautiful, Jessie. Again his words filled her heart. She did a slight curtsy. "Merci."

They held hands back to the car, their fingers woven together, skin to skin, and she remembered once more falling into his strong arms up in the trees. The warmth of his embrace. The feel of his lips on hers. And only one question consumed her.

How was she ever going to say goodbye?

6

Alice Arquette felt the brush of her husband's elbow against hers as the two peeled potatoes for tonight's dinner, the smell of his day-old cologne familiar and warm. Fifteen years had come and gone since their wedding day, but she still felt like a schoolgirl around Paul.

"So . . . this girl Gabriel is bringing home, she is special, then." Paul caught Alice's eyes and kept peeling. "Has he talked about her?"

"He has." Alice felt the familiar concern in her heart. A twinge that reminded her of the truth—Gabe was growing up. He could do as he pleased after college. Even move to the States. "It's new, but . . . he likes her very much."

"Hmm." Paul turned his attention again to the potato. "He can't move to the United States for her. I'll forbid it."

An ache stirred in Alice's heart. "Please do." She smiled. If only it were that simple. "Can I tell you something?"

The corners of his lips lifted in a way that betrayed his stern tone. "Are you saying . . . I can't stop him?"

"Exactly." She rested her head on his shoulder for a moment. "But I'm grateful that you care. So grateful, Paul."

"I love him, Alice." He put more effort into the potato. "More than my own life."

That was the beauty of Alice's story in a handful of words. God had brought her a man, strong and intelligent and willing to overlook her past. And though the two of them hadn't been able to have children, from the beginning Paul had taken on Gabriel as if the boy were his own. Some children never get to be loved the way Gabe was loved by Paul.

Of course her husband didn't want Gabriel to fall in love with an American girl and leave France. Neither of them did. But if that happened, if their only child did leave the country, all would not be lost.

Because they had each other. Their beautiful days. Their early coffee Monday through Friday and their quiet Scrabble games every Saturday morning. Their walks along the narrow streets near the Seine and their love for cooking.

And they had their undying faith.

Alice would never want for anything because of Paul Arquette. Because God had—in His limitless kindness—given her the man beside her. The cell phone in his pocket rang and Paul winked at her. "Be right back."

After he stepped out, Alice finished the potatoes. Then she wiped her hands on her apron and moved into the dining room. There on the grand mahogany buffet that ran along the far wall, were a dozen framed photos. Moments that had defined Alice. One of them was the picture that never should have been.

The one of Alice and Gabe, when he was just six months old. Her mother had found a church by then and Alice had gone with her. It was dedication Sunday, the day the church brings new parents up to the front with their little ones. On that day Alice had publicly promised to raise Gabe to the light, to the love of Jesus. And their new church family promised to do all they could to help.

Both had kept their promises, and now here they were. Gabe was grown, still drawn to the light of God every hour, every day.

Alice studied the photo. Neither of them should be alive, not with the way Alice had lived her life all those years ago. They had been headed for the darkest, most destructive ending when suddenly everything changed. It was a miracle. Alice was sure of the fact. What other explanation could there possibly be?

The doorbell rang, and Alice untied her apron. This would be her first meeting with Gabriel's new friend. Jessie Taylor. "Coming," Alice called out. Her voice sounded young like a song. The way it had sounded these past two decades. Like the new life she'd found was still bubbling up inside her.

Paul met her in the foyer and they opened the door together. Alice knew two things from the moment she saw the beautiful brunette on the front step that evening. First, her eyes shone with the same light that lived in Gabriel. And second, Gabriel was in love with her.

"Do come in." Alice stepped back and Paul did the same.

A warmth came from the girl as she hugged Alice. "Nice to meet you, madame."

Alice took the girl's hands as she stepped back. "Yes. *Enchanté.*" She smiled. "Gabe has told us so much about you."

"And you." Jessie grinned. Then she held up a brown paper bag. "We brought blueberries. Gabriel said they were your favorite."

It was Paul's turn, and he kindly shook Jessie's hand. "Dinner is ready. We have so much to talk about."

Never mind that Paul was one of the most powerful lawyers in Paris. He was gentle with people. His guiding principle—at work or at home—was that all people had worth. Everyone had a story. And always people deserved kindness. Alice had heard her husband say those words often.

The group headed for the kitchen and Alice opened the bag of berries. "They smell delicious."

"Just picked. Got them at today's market." Gabriel kissed her cheek and took a deep breath. "Mmm. Your famous steak frites." He glanced at Jessie. "I told you she was the best cook!"

When they were settled at the table with the meal spread out before them, Gabriel prayed over the food. "And thank You, God, for Jessie. In all the world, that You might lead her here, to me. In Jesus' name, amen."

Alice caught the hint of a smile on Jessie's lips. The depth of her son's feelings for this girl was matched by hers for him. No question.

They talked about the art class Gabe and Jessie were taking, and how Jessie wanted to be an artist, like her aunt. "She's having a show here in Paris. At that little gallery, Light of the Seine."

"An artist." Alice sat her fork down. "That's interesting, Jessie. Not many American artists are celebrated here." She hesitated, not sure if she should continue. Maybe this wasn't the time. "I knew an American artist once. A long time ago."

Gabriel spoke up then. "Jessie and I were talking about that. How we each have such interesting stories. How God spared us through really hard times." He winked at Jessie. "Same with her aunt. I'm sure I'll hear those details eventually."

"Yes. I was about to tell your son her story when he whisked me off on a trip through the tops of the trees."

"Oh, my." Alice looked from Jessie to her son. "Do tell."

"Aventure Floreval." Gabe laughed. "Jessie was quite good at it."

"Except the time when Gabriel had to catch me." The girl's eyes lit up and her cheeks grew pink.

"You were harnessed." He looked at her, like they were the only two in the room. "Nothing would've happened to you."

"Because you caught me."

Gabe turned back to Alice and Paul. "Anyway, about our stories." He hesitated. "There are similarities between Jessie and me, Mère." He looked at Jessie. "She should tell it."

"We've only just met your sweet friend." Alice smiled at the girl. "We can save deeper conversations for another day."

"Honestly . . ." Jessie took a sip of water. "I don't mind sharing. Redemption isn't redemption without the broken path that took a person there."

"See?" Gabriel seemed to reach for the girl's hand under the table. He grinned at Paul and then Alice. "This is what I like about Jessie Taylor. She speaks like a poet."

Again Jessie's cheeks darkened. "Gabe."

"She paints like one, too." Once again, her son seemed to remember his parents. "Even the little I've heard, her story is like a movie."

"Well, then . . . I'd love to hear it, Jessie."

"Me, too." Paul dabbed a napkin at the corners of his mouth. "Your story starts in Bloomington, Indiana?"

"It does." Jessie took a quick breath. "My father was a professor at Indiana University. My mother had spent all of high school loving her boyfriend, a football player named Ryan Taylor. But they had a misunderstanding and things fell apart between them." She glanced at Gabriel.

Alice doubted her son and this girl had gone through any fallings-out of their own. Not according to the way they looked at each other.

"Anyway, my mom and Ryan ended things . . . and my mother fell in love with a young teacher's assistant. A man studying to be a professor. Tim Jacobs. The two married, but a few years later my mother learned Tim was having an affair with one of his students."

This was a lot. Alice didn't take her eyes off Jessie. Next to her, Paul was also riveted.

"My mom begged Tim to stay in her life. Begged him to break things off with the student." Jessie didn't hide the pride in her voice. "My mom didn't believe in divorce. She still doesn't. She forgave her husband and prayed he would come back home." She hesitated. "Which he did."

"That couldn't have been easy." Alice felt for the girl's mother.

"It wasn't. But they made another attempt and they found love again. And my mom got pregnant." Jessie smiled, despite the sadness in her eyes. "With me."

Gabriel put his hand on her shoulder. He looked like he might stand up and take her in his arms. His desire to protect this college girl was palpable.

"What a gift you must have been for them after their near breakup." Paul set his napkin by his plate.

"Yes." Jessie nodded. "But there was a complication. Tim—my father—still had to deal with the female student. She didn't want to end things, and so she invited Tim back to her apartment one more time."

"Oh, no." Alice leaned in.

"It wasn't like that. My father went only to tell her things were over. He had no intention of returning to her. He wanted to stay with my mom forever. And with me." Jessie paused. "But the student had another admirer. An athlete at the school, a young man on steroids. He had been stalking the female student."

"This is the part I do know." Gabriel still hadn't taken his eyes off Jessie. "It's so sad."

"It is." Jessie nodded. "That night my father stopped at the store and bought a pink rabbit for me. Then he drove to the student's apartment to tell her things were over and not to call ever again. But the stalker was waiting outside her apartment and . . . when my father stepped out of his car and walked up to the front door, the young man shot him."

Alice gasped and put her hand over her mouth. "Your father?"

"Yes." Jessie looked from Alice to Paul. "He died there on the sidewalk. Before he could give the student the letter saying it was over."

"Oh, Jessie." Alice stood and went to the girl's side. She hugged her shoulders and pressed her face against the girl's. "I'm so, so sorry."

"Me, too." Jessie's expression was sober. "When I was five, my mom gave me the pink bunny. I still have it." She took a full breath. "A year after my father's death, Ryan Taylor came back into my mom's life. The two fell in love and got married. When I was two years old, Ryan adopted me. He's the only dad I've ever known . . . and one of the best men on the planet. For real."

Alice gave Jessie another quick hug and then took her seat again. They had definitely gone deep tonight. "Thank you, Jessie. For sharing that."

Gabriel looked proud of his friend. "See?" He kept his eyes on Jessie. "There is no redemption without brokenness."

"Talk about poets. Gabe needs to be a writer." Jessie's smile was back. "Your son has a way with words."

"He always has." Paul smiled at Gabriel. "If he doesn't become a lawyer, I think he'll be an author one day. He sees life through a different lens. His beautiful heart."

Gabe put his hands up and chuckled. "Okay, okay." He looked at Alice. "Jessie says her aunt's story is powerful, too. She suffered a terrible car accident, and then came here to paint." He turned to Jessie. "What happened to her?"

Jessie slid her plate back a bit. "Here in Paris . . . she connected with a man who did not have her best interest at heart." She hesitated. "My aunt came back to Indiana pregnant. The man . . . he was a married artist here in Paris."

"Oh, my. I'm sorry." Paul's eyes were warm with sympathy. "Much brokenness."

"And much redemption." Jessie's expression held a deep peace. "Today my aunt is married to the only man she ever loved. They have four kids and her dreams of being an artist came true." Jessie paused. "God is so good."

"He is." Alice was quiet for a moment. Was this the time to talk about her own story? Maybe it would help Jessie know her better.

Gabriel looked at her, like he could read her mind. "What about you, M'man? Share your story."

"Okay." Alice took another sip of water. "My mother raised me by herself and at first our life was beautiful. The two of us took trips on the weekend and frequented the zoo when the weather was nice." She smiled at the memory. "But in my early teens I hurt my ankle in a footrace. The doctor put me on pain medicine for a short while." She allowed a small shrug. "I wanted more. At a party one weekend I found the answer in a small vial of heroin."

Shame came over her the way it hadn't in many years. How could she have given herself to that monster drug? She had lost so many years, and almost her life. Gabriel's life.

Paul put his arm around her and kissed the side of her head. "You don't have to tell us, Alice. It's okay."

"It's behind me. But it's part of my life." She looked at Jessie. "Do you have time?"

"Of course." Jessie was clearly rapt. "They say heroin is addictive from the first time you take it."

"They're right." Alice heard the sadness in her voice. "It didn't take long before I would've killed for my next heroin hit. When I wasn't high, I was in pain. At first the drug offers the greatest euphoria of your life. But you only get that once. Then heroin takes away your normal." She paused. "You spend the rest of your days trying to feel like you did before your first hit, trying to keep from feeling drug sick."

The four of them were quiet for a few seconds.

"Soon I began breaking into my mother's house and stealing things, whatever I could pawn for a few francs so I could get more of the drug. Finally . . . I broke more than the window. I broke her heart. She called the police and changed the locks on our small flat.

"I ran through the night feeling lost and alone. I could never go back home, and I couldn't survive till morning without more of the drug." She shook her head. "That night . . . I overdosed. I was with my friend when it happened, and somehow a police officer came upon us. He had Narcan." She looked at Jessie. "I've heard of it." Jessie nodded. "It reverses the effects of a heroin overdose."

"Yes. Anyway, when I woke up, I was in a hospital bed and the nurse told me the bad news. My friend Benji was dead. He had asked the officer to help me . . . instead of him. So there I was, alive and pregnant. And it was my friend's baby."

Jessie's expression was frozen. Like she could hardly believe any of this. "I can't imagine . . . how hard that must have been."

"I got help and eventually I got a job at a boulangerie . . . a bakery." Alice hadn't told the story in years. The worst part was just ahead. "Even then, all I wanted was the drug. Every hour. Every day. It called my name and screamed at me to go back to the homeless tents near the Seine. At least then I could have peace." She looked at Gabriel. "The baby inside me stopped me from doing that. But still I fought my addiction with every breath."

"It's okay, Mère." Gabriel's tone was protective, the way it often was with her. "You don't have to tell this part."

"I don't mind." She felt the hint of a smile on her lips. "It's in the past." She turned to Jessie again. "I came up with a plan to end my life. I was going to jump off the Pont du Garigliano—the highest bridge along the Paris stretch of the Seine. It's eleven meters above the shallow water."

"That's more than thirty-six feet." The look on Jessie's face said she understood. A person couldn't survive a jump like that.

"But that day I came to work and there was a new girl behind the counter. She . . . she was pregnant, like me. We went for a walk after work, and we talked about our stories. The girl was angry at her family and angry at God. But she was sure about one thing." Alice smiled. "Babies deserve to live."

"Mmm." Paul took her hand. "I love when you say that. It is the most lovely truth."

"Yes, it is." She drew a sharp breath. "The conversation we had that day, it saved my life."

Jessie's eyes were watery. "That . . . that's beautiful."

"Things changed after that. I went home and apologized to my mother. I worked long shifts and had my baby." She grinned at Gabe. "And he turned out to be the best son any mother could ever have."

Paul nodded. "Also, true." He looked at Gabriel then at Alice. "I met Alice years later and over a single cup of coffee I knew I was home. I never looked anywhere else again."

"We married a year after we met, and Paul has always been Gabriel's father." Alice looked at Jessie. "Redemption from brokenness." She took a moment. "I always wanted to find that girl, the one who talked me into choosing life. For both me and my baby. But my next shift back at the boulangerie, she was gone. I never found her."

Jessie set her napkin on the table and asked just one question. "What was the woman's name, the one from the bakery?"

"I've tried to remember her whole name, but it never comes to me. All I can recall is her first name." Alice picked up her fork.

Gabriel turned to Jessie. "The young woman's first name was Ashley." He smiled. "Just like your aunt."

Alice felt a slight skip in her heart. "Your aunt, the artist from Indiana . . . her name is Ashley?"

"Yes." Jessie looked at Alice. "You don't think . . ."

"No." Alice uttered a sad laugh. "There's a thousand Americans wanting to be artists in Paris."

"True." Jessie shook her head. "And my aunt wasn't here very long."

"Anyway . . . enough of my story." Alice stood and grinned at her family and Jessie. "Who wants dessert?"

Somehow the question seemed to break the intensity of the moment, and everyone laughed. The heaviness faded as Alice went to the kitchen and dished up her homemade apple tarte. But she was sure of one thing. After tonight, Jessie would forever be more than a casual friend.

She would be family.

7

·········

The pressure made it hard for Ashley to breathe. In ten minutes they were boarding an early morning flight to New York City's John F. Kennedy Airport and from there a second plane to Charles de Gaulle Airport in Paris. She had to get her breathing under control.

Ashley stared out the window at the streaky sunrise painting the sky. Was she crazy, going back to Paris? It wasn't just the terrible things she had done there, it was the danger she had been in. The pieces of her past she still hadn't told anyone. Paris was the last place she wanted to be. Better to put Paris and what happened there forever behind her. Hadn't she always wanted that?

She should've told the gallery owner no.

But now there was no turning back. To make matters worse she'd had the most terrible nightmare a few nights ago. An absolutely awful dream.

"It'll be okay, Ash." Landon nudged her. "A week from now we'll be home and you'll be so glad you went. Trust me."

She nodded, but her next breath was as tight as the last. Just then her cell phone rang. *Good*, she thought. *A distraction*. Her niece's name flashed on the screen. *Jessie Taylor*. Ashley answered it. "Jessie. Hey!"

"Aunt Ashley!" The girl sounded practically giddy. "Are you in Paris? I can't wait to see you."

"Not yet." Ashley tried to focus. "We're about to board the first flight."

"Okay. Good." Jessie laughed a little. "I want you and Uncle Landon to have lunch with me and Gabriel and his mother. Remember, I told you about Gabe?"

Gabe . . . Gabe. "Yes, of course. The boy from your art class." Ashley squeezed her eyes shut. Everything in her screamed, *Don't get on that plane. Don't do it. Don't go back to Paris. You nearly died there.* Her niece was still talking. "Anyway, Aunt Ashley, we'd love to have lunch with you."

"Sure. We were planning on it." Wherever Jessie was, the background noise made it hard to hear her. "And hey, Aunt Ashley, I have a question for you. Gabriel's mother . . ." The call started to break up. "I figured . . . if that was . . ."

"Jessie?" Ashley tried hard to hear her. "I'm losing you."

"I'm just asking if . . . I don't think it could be . . ."

The call failed.

Ashley tried to call her niece back, but it went straight to her voicemail. Whatever the girl wanted to say, it would have to wait until their afternoon together in Paris. If Ashley survived that long.

The gate attendant called their boarding group and Landon took both her bag and his. He looked deep into her eyes. "You okay?"

Why couldn't she draw a full breath? Her heart pounded against the wall of her chest. "I'm . . . I'm fine. I am." This was ridiculous. She had survived more than most people. Of course she would make it through this trip to France. No one was waiting to harm her on the other side of the ocean.

Besides, saying yes to the art show had been her choice, her decision. She had agreed to every detail, and she had promised Landon that the two of them would celebrate their anniversary while they were there. In the city that made her physically sick to think about.

Ashley stood by Landon as they moved toward the Jetway. Every few seconds Landon turned to her, worry heavy in his eyes. She forced a smile. "Really, Landon. I'm fine. I will be."

He didn't look convinced. When they were on the plane, he slipped her carry-on into the compartment above their seats. She took the window and after he was buckled in beside her, he reached for her hand. "You know where I was?" Something in his tone soothed her anxiety.

She faced him. "Where you were . . . when?"

"Back then, when you were in Paris the first time. When I heard the news that you were . . ."

"Pregnant."

"Yes." He held her eyes. People were still boarding the plane and the flight attendant was asking passengers to find their seats. But Landon's voice filled her senses.

"Tell me."

"I was playing basketball with my roommates. Baylor

had an intramural gym with four courts. Every court had a game, with people lining the walls watching." He hesitated. "The place was packed but in the middle of the mass of people I spotted Jalen."

"Your best friend."

"Right. His eyes were locked on me . . . and his face looked pale. Like someone had died." Landon shifted so he could see her better. "I subbed myself out of the game and met Jalen just off the court. He told me my mom couldn't reach me. But she wanted me to know. You were home, and . . . you were pregnant."

In a single heartbeat, his story shifted Ashley's narrative. Why hadn't she thought about this before? What happened in Paris didn't only hurt her. Paris had also affected her parents and her siblings. And clearly it had deeply affected Landon. They were taxiing to the runway, but Ashley stayed focused on her husband. "You never told me."

"I didn't want you to feel bad." His voice was soft, kind. "You thought going to Paris was about you getting away from everything here. Remember?"

"Nothing felt right. After the accident." Ashley remembered the way her heart hurt, how it seemed God had abandoned her. "I couldn't get far enough away."

Ten minutes later when they were in the air and leveled off on their flight to JFK, Landon turned to her again. "You could've gone all the way to the moon, Ashley. But you could never go far enough away that I wouldn't have thought about you, prayed for you every day."

For a minute or so Ashley looked out the window at the clear blue sky. Then she faced Landon again. "Can I ask you something?"

"Anything, Ash. You know that."

"What did you think? When you heard I was pregnant?" It was a question Ashley had wanted to ask her husband since the day she saw him again after having Cole. Sometime after she had returned to Bloomington. "I've . . . always been afraid to ask."

"Always?" Landon looked wounded. "Are you serious?"

The plane shuddered a bit, but Ashley barely noticed. "I guess . . . I never wanted to know the answer. How you really felt."

He brushed her hair from her forehead. "How I *really* felt?" He took his time. "I was devastated, Ashley."

A rush of tears stung her eyes and she nodded. Her voice was so tight, the next words were difficult to say. "See? That's why." She looked away. "I . . . I didn't want to hear . . . that you saw me differently. I still don't want to know that."

"Ash." His voice was the softest touch against her heart. "You think I was upset . . . because you'd stepped out of some perfect box? Honestly?"

"Of course." She worked to keep her voice at a whisper. "I was Ashley *Baxter*. You fell in love with me when we were in fifth grade." A tear fell onto her cheek and she let it be. "You thought I was perfect, Landon. A Baxter girl. And that I'd always be perfect."

"No." He didn't hesitate. "I knew you weren't perfect.

No one's perfect." He shook his head. "I was upset back then *because* I knew you. I knew how important your family was to you and I knew that for you to come home from Paris pregnant and alone . . . after what had happened the year before with the accident . . . I was worried you'd never be the same again. That I'd lose you for good."

"Wait . . ." Another switch flipped. "You . . . you weren't disappointed in me?"

"No. I was terrified. I wanted to run to you and take you in my arms and tell you that whatever had happened, wherever you'd been and whoever had broken your heart in Paris, it was all going to be okay." He leaned close and kissed her. Just long enough so she could feel the familiar passion. "Like I said . . . because I knew you, Ash. Then and now."

Ashley's understanding of the past, the way she'd always assumed Landon had felt after hearing the news, began to change. It no longer fit her longtime narrative. "And . . . that day. What happened after Jalen came and told you?"

Landon hesitated, but then he shook his head. He put his finger to her lips. "Let's save that . . . for another day."

"A Paris day?" Ashley thought she understood. This trip wasn't only about her laying to rest what had happened all those years ago. He needed to do the same. Something she had never considered before.

"Yes. A Paris day." He leaned back into his seat and smiled at her. "Now . . . let's try to sleep. Last night I barely closed my eyes and it was morning."

"Same." Ashley turned to the window again. Of course, he hadn't judged her. That never would've been Landon. If she'd thought about it, she would've realized long ago that she didn't need to worry about asking him that question or anything else.

Another thing . . . she should've told Landon her secret. Enough time had gone by that the whole dark situation felt like a figment of her imagination. Like another bad dream. Better to tell her husband, so he could assure her that the evil she had seen and heard and felt back in Paris was not a danger to her. Not now and not back then.

That would be one more conversation to have in Paris.

The pilot found smooth air again as they prepared to land in New York. Ashley looked at Landon. He was asleep, so she closed her eyes. Everything in her wanted to go back in time, back to her first trip to Paris. She would have done everything differently if she'd had the chance. She could feel the memories of that time building in her heart, demanding to be replayed.

There was no point going back. Remembering her time in Paris would help nothing.

Instead, she did something she hadn't done often lately. She pictured her mother. Her beautiful mother, forever young and gone too soon from cancer. What would her mom think of her going to Paris now? An actual accomplished artist. Ashley smiled.

She had been ten years old, and her parents had gotten her a sketchbook before the move from Michigan to Indiana. One late afternoon, Mom found her sketching the backyard tree house. For a long while, her mother just sat next to her, watching Ashley work. Her mom looked from the drawing to the tree house and back again.

After a while Mom leaned in close. "You are such a gifted artist, Ashley. One day everyone will know your work. I believe that."

Ashley's heart had swelled almost to bursting. She looked up. "Really?"

"Yes!" Mom ran her finger over Ashley's drawing. "You know where famous artists display their best work?"

Even then Ashley had known. "Paris!" She had bounced a little in her seat. "Near the awful Tower."

Mom had smiled. "Eiffel. The *Eiffel* Tower. Not awful." She patted Ashley's head. "So, what do you think, Ash? About Paris?"

Ashley had stared at her drawing and then up at her mother. "Mom . . . one day you can go with me to Paris . . . and I'll paint pictures there."

The memory faded and Ashley stared out the window again. *Mom, you would be so proud of me. Going to Paris again. Having a show at the very gallery . . .* The very gallery where the previous owner had called her paintings American trash.

The thought of Paris still made her feel terrible about herself. Like nothing she did or ever could do would be good enough. Not for her family or God or the art community or her son Cole.

And definitely not for Landon Blake.

Ashley took the magazine from the seat pocket in

front of her. MAKE THIS THE YEAR OF TRAVEL, the cover suggested. It was the same thing Landon had told her when they thought about their eighteenth anniversary. *Let's make this the year. Agree to the art show and travel to Paris. It's time.* Why in the world had she agreed?

She leaned closer to her husband. A Bible verse came to mind, one she had relied on often, especially in the years after Cole was born. *Do not be anxious about anything, but in everything, by prayer and petition, with thanksgiving, present your requests to God. And the peace of God, which transcends all understanding, will guard your hearts and your minds in Christ Jesus.*

The words ran through her heart over and over and over again. And finally, Ashley felt her nerves settle. She had made this decision and she would stand by it. The time had come to make new memories in Paris, to take her rightful place among the artists whose work was displayed in the famous capital city. Landon would be at her side and the two of them would come home stronger because of their time together in France. She would walk in the grace of God and know once and for all that no one was chasing her, no one was trying to kill her. Yes, she would embrace this trip and all it involved.

Everything was going to be okay.

• • •

A CHILL HUNG in the Paris air that early July afternoon as Albert Arnaud crossed Rue de Turenne toward Rue Quincampoix. He held a steaming hot latte from Neighbours a kilometer behind him. The Australian coffee shop was his favorite. The familiar white-and-blue cup gave him a good feeling about the day. About his future.

The mistakes he'd made before, he would not make again.

He'd given his word.

The latte was too hot to drink, so he stepped inside a men's clothing shop. "Bonjour." Albert smiled at the shopkeeper. She was young and pretty, easily half his age. "I need a brown leather belt." He glanced at the nearest rack. "Would you have that?"

"Oui." She was flirting with him. His shoes were the finest Italian leather, his designer sweater, cashmere, his beard well trimmed. Albert was under no delusions. The girl wasn't interested in his looks. She motioned to him. "Follow me."

Fifteen minutes later Albert had a new leather belt. He had refused the slip of paper with the girl's phone number. He wasn't interested. Besides, if she knew the type of person he was, she wouldn't have offered.

Back on the street, he sipped his latte and took his time. His work happened in the dead of night. The days were his, time to do what he wanted. And usually that meant walking the streets of the Marais in the fourth arrondissement. He couldn't get enough of it.

Sometimes it felt like he'd only been home days, and not a decade. Every season of his thirteen years in London, he had longed for home. But the move had saved his life. There hadn't been any way around it. Not after the murder-for-hire went wrong. He had failed the greatest modern-day artist of all time.

A man Albert still loved. Albert hated himself for that.

Lonely as it was, his sojourn in London had bought him time. Paris police weren't looking for him now and he didn't frequent the Montmartre District anymore. Jean-Claude Pierre wasn't there, so the thrill was gone. Instead, Albert was left with these two terrible truths: His previous boss was dead and he had died angry with Albert.

While in London, Albert had lived under a different name, but there was no need now. This time around, he was one of the most elusive trained killers Paris had ever known. He covered his tracks better than anyone. And people he interacted with—like the shopgirl and the barista—knew nothing of his line of work.

Another sip of his coffee and Albert savored the taste. Sometimes he got his morning latte from the closest Terres de Café, the Paris original with their high-grade beans from all over the world. But Albert loved how the Australians brewed a cup of coffee. And Neighbours was a more vibrant atmosphere.

Albert glanced over his shoulder, then up ahead and behind him. The way he did every minute or so. He was expert at knowing if he was being followed, if this was the day his secrets would be exposed and his life would come to an end.

At Rue Quincampoix, Albert turned right. No one was following him. Not today. He finished his latte and was passing the small art gallery on the right—Light of the

Seine—when something caught his eye. He stopped and his heartbeat doubled. What was this? After all these years?

He walked the few steps to the gallery window. Posted to the inside of the glass was an advertisement for a show later that week. A few of the artist's works dotted the large bulletin. But that's not what stopped him. At the center of the ad was the face of the artist and her name.

Albert would've known her anywhere. In a crowded train station or at a café, walking a city street, or here . . . on an ad for a gallery show.

The face of an American artist: *Ashley Baxter.*

Back then, being hired to kill the girl was the biggest job Albert had ever been given, he and his buddy Guy Peters. The two had done odd jobs before that, drug dealing, gun smuggling. Whatever Jean-Claude Pierre had needed. But when the artist wanted someone harmed or threatened, he had always used a different pair of guys.

Until Ashley Baxter.

That was the secret no one had known about Jean-Claude Pierre. People saw him as a handsome, famous artist, but his family fortune had come from a long history of criminal activity. He let few people into his inner circle, and Albert had been one of those.

Albert thought about Jean-Claude constantly, even still. He would have died for the famous artist or spent a lifetime in prison. He narrowed his eyes and stared at the woman's familiar face. He could hear Jean-Claude's urgent voice on the phone more than two decades ago. "She didn't get rid of it."

At first Albert hadn't known what his boss meant. "Get rid of what?"

"The kid." Jean-Claude had been seething. "I heard from the receptionist at the clinic. The American left before having the abortion."

Albert hadn't been sure what Jean-Claude wanted him to do. "You want me to take her back to the clinic?"

"Stop talking." Jean-Claude had never sounded so angry. "You're my A-team now. You and Guy. Don't ask questions. Just . . . take care of her."

Albert remembered feeling a slight thrill work its way through his body. Had he moved up Jean-Claude's criminal chain? "Okay. So . . .?"

"So . . . I don't want a kid, Albert." Jean-Claude was seething. "Kids grow up. Ashley Baxter will want money." He lowered his voice. "I'm not giving away my inheritance. You and Guy . . . kill her. Throw her body into the Seine."

The order seemed out of character for the artist. Jean-Claude was with a different paramour every few weeks. But as far as Albert knew, this was the first time he had ordered a hit on one of them. "How are we supposed to pull that off, boss?"

And Jean-Claude had explained.

He would pay Albert and Guy more money than their criminal activity typically earned them in a year. Albert was given the code to a lock box where he would find a loaded gun, gloves, and a deadline. Everything Albert and Guy needed to pull off the job.

They did everything right, Albert and Guy. The pair stalked the American girl morning and night for three days, looking for the perfect opportunity. But the moment never came, and the deadline passed. Albert and Guy had failed. Completely.

In the wake of that, Jean-Claude must have brought in outsiders because twelve hours later, Albert's friend Guy was dead and Albert was on a flight to London.

Running for his life.

Albert didn't blame Jean-Claude. The missed hit was his fault. His and Guy's. It remained Albert's one regret in life. He had let Jean-Claude Pierre down and he would do anything to change the fact. Even with no one paying him for the job. Albert had always been sure of one thing. If he ever had the chance to finish the hit on the American artist, he would.

Because that's what Jean-Claude had wanted from him.

And Jean-Claude Pierre meant everything to him. Even now.

Albert stared at the ad once more. Yes, the artist would be at this exact location Thursday at seven o'clock. Which could only mean one thing. After all these years, Albert was going to see Ashley Baxter again. And he would have one more chance to do Jean-Claude's bidding.

No matter what it cost him.

8

Ashley and Landon were headed east over the Atlantic Ocean on the nighttime nonstop to Paris. Once Landon was asleep again in the seat beside her, there was nothing Ashley could do to stop the memories.

She leaned her head against the window and closed her eyes. Seconds later she was no longer on a flight to Paris to celebrate her first French art show and her eighteenth wedding anniversary. Instead, she was twenty years old and packing a pair of suitcases in the upstairs bedroom she had still shared with her older sister Kari.

Their conversation came to life once more.

"This is all because of the accident. That's why you're leaving." Kari had sounded afraid. "I think you should wait, Ash. Get more counseling."

Ashley didn't want to get angry with her sister. She and Kari were best friends. "Of course it's because of the accident." Ashley dropped a pair of shorts into the suitcase and turned to Kari. "Don't you get it? Everywhere I go it's the same thing. People see me coming and their expressions change."

"What?" Kari slid to the edge of her bed. "What's that supposed to mean?"

"Just what it sounds like." Ashley had waved her hands in front of her, like she was clearing invisible smoke from the room. "They stare at me like I'm this . . . this horrible person."

"That's crazy." Kari stood. "Is that what you think?"

"Of course." She shrugged and grabbed two T-shirts from her closet. Her tone rose a notch. "I was driving. I should've veered the other way or seen it coming. It's my fault Jefferson is in that cemetery instead of living his life."

"Hey." Kari had lowered her voice. She waited until Ashley stopped moving and finally looked at her. "No one . . . not one person . . . thinks that accident was your fault. You were both victims, you and Jefferson." Kari took a step closer. "Don't run to Paris because of that."

Tears had blurred Ashley's vision and the fight left her. She slumped to her bed and covered her face with her hands. The accident wasn't her fault, Kari was right. The truck was already over the line by the time she saw it. They were on a curve, so she couldn't possibly have noticed him sooner.

Ashley was still sitting on her bed, hands over her face, when she felt Kari's hand on her shoulder. "Go to Paris some other time, Ash. You have so much here."

Ashley lifted her head. "I have nothing."

"You do." Tears had filled Kari's eyes, too. "You have us,

all of us. And me . . . your best friend. And you have Landon."

Before Ashley could respond, before she could sort through her feelings, their mother's voice called from downstairs. "Ashley . . . Landon is here."

Landon.

Ashley felt a surge of panic. She'd already said good-bye to him at her going-away party, the one she hadn't wanted in the first place. Every minute in his presence made her less likely to get on that plane.

Kari was staring at her. "Go. He needs you, Ashley."

Nobody needs me, she wanted to shout. Ashley ran out of the room, and down the stairs to the front of the house. Landon was there in the entryway, wrapped in a gray winter parka. There was snow in his hair. For the first time he didn't look sad about the situation.

He looked angry.

"Can we talk?" He spoke through gritted teeth. "Please, Ash."

It was one of the coldest days of winter, but Ashley didn't want this conversation here inside the house. Where her family could listen to every word. She grabbed her warmest coat and hat from the nearby closet and wrapped a scarf around her neck.

He led the way to the porch swing out front. The cold had given way to a blizzard, and snow swirled across the covered porch. Landon waited till she sat down on one side of the swing, before taking the opposite.

The space he allowed between them was definitely intentional.

"It's cold." Ashley's teeth chattered. "And I need to pack."

"You can pack later." Landon slipped his hands into his jacket. "It hit me this evening, you're really going. You're leaving tomorrow and you have no plans to come back."

Ashley blinked the snow from her face. "You already knew that. We talked about it at my party."

"Yeah, about that . . ." Landon was so angry he didn't look cold at all. Like he couldn't see or feel the snow all around them. "I dropped a dozen hints that I wanted time alone with you. Down by the stream, near the rock. Or out here after everyone was gone." He released a single laugh.

There was nothing funny about it.

"There I am in the living room talking to the friends we grew up with and you breeze in and say you're turning in early. At ten o'clock, Ashley. With five people still at the party." He knit his brow together. "Including me." He stood and paced to the porch railing before turning and staring at her. "What was that all about?"

"I was tired." Ashley could only keep this up for so long. He was onto her, of course. She could never lie to Landon and get away with it. "It wasn't my fault those guys stayed so late."

Landon uttered another sad laugh and shook his head. He turned and faced the snowy front acreage of the

Baxters' property. The snow was coming down harder now, flying in every direction. When he spoke next, he had to yell so she could hear him. Especially with his back to her. "If this is how you want it to be, Ash."

That was the problem. Ashley didn't want things like this, distance and discord between Landon and her. Yes, she was moving on, and true, she had no plans to return. But that didn't mean she wasn't aching for Landon Blake. Even then.

Ashley stood and closed the distance between them. She slipped her hands around his waist and laid her head on his back. Even through his thick winter coat, she could feel him breathing, feel his hot anger trembling through his body. Her voice was a whisper against the wind. "I'm sorry, Landon."

He turned and searched her eyes. "Say it again. Look at me and say it."

She did as he asked, and it was almost more than she could take. Her eyes lost in his, she repeated herself. "I'm sorry! I . . . never meant to hurt you."

His anger eased. In its place was a quieter desperation. "Me?" He worked his arms around her waist and held her close. "What about you, Ash? You're hurting us both with this . . . this stupid trip to Paris." He tugged on her hat, bringing it a bit lower on her forehead. "Don't you see? You're not ready. Leaving Indiana . . . your family . . . me . . . That won't make the accident go away."

He was right, and she hated him for it. Especially now, fourteen hours before heading to the airport. Being here in his arms made her doubt everything about going. Which was not at all how she wanted to feel. She slipped free of his arms and sat on the swing again. "At least in Paris no one will know."

Landon studied her and after a few seconds he did a slow nod. "So that's it? That's what this is all about?" He moved back to the swing and sat, facing her. "You want to be where no one knows you as Ashley the girl who had the accident?"

She didn't want to cry. It was too cold. Her tears would freeze on her face. "Sounds pretty good right about now."

"It doesn't work that way." His voice softened for the first time that night. "You're supposed to go to Paris with a plan to paint . . . to chase your dreams. You don't go so that people won't see your past."

"I have a plan, Landon. You know that."

"But the accident will be in here." He put his hand over his chest. "You can't outrun it, Ash. All you can do is let God heal you from it. So you can live again." He shook his head and again he stood and walked to the railing.

The snow was letting up a little. Ashley could see the road at the end of their front yard. But it was still cold and this was going nowhere. She wanted to tell him to go home, that she'd made up her mind and she was leaving in the morning. Which was true. Nothing he could say would change her decision now.

But her heart wouldn't let her speak. She stood and went to him once more. This time she came up next to him and slid one arm around his waist. Since their first date when they were sixteen, Ashley had loved being at Landon's side, tucked in close against him.

At first, he didn't move, but then he eased his arm around her shoulders and held her. Tighter than before. After a minute, he faced her. With the soft snow falling around them, Landon brushed a few flakes from her cheeks.

Then he did the only thing she wanted him to do. He brought her face to his and kissed her. His lips barely touched hers at first, as if he didn't want either of them to leave this moment more hurt than they already would be.

But after a while, his kiss changed, and the passion and intensity were there for them both. Or maybe it was the impossibility of it all. He pulled back first, breathless in the freezing air. "Don't leave, Ashley." He kissed her again, her lips, then her cheeks and forehead, like he couldn't get enough of her. "Please . . . don't leave."

There was no stopping her tears. All she wanted was to stay right here forever, in Landon's arms, his lips on hers. But even this moment couldn't change her mind. She kissed him, then. She held on to his face and kissed him the way she had wanted to at the party the other night. When they couldn't find a minute alone.

Finally, she caught her breath, and she could feel her tears ice cold on her face. "I can't stay." Her voice sounded broken. "My teacher has everything set up. The flat where I'll be staying. The job at the gallery."

Gradually defeat colored his eyes and his expression.

He nodded and once more he kissed her, but this time everything about it was sad. When he pulled back, he let himself get lost in her eyes one last time. "Come back to me, Ash. When this . . . running away is behind you. Please . . . come back."

Ashley knew what he was going to say next, even before the sound left his lips. He lowered his face to hers once more and this time his kiss was brief. Final. As he eased back, he looked all the way to her soul. "I love you, Ashley Baxter. Don't you ever forget it."

They had never said the words to each other. Before the accident they had been in a relationship, and many times the moment had seemed almost right. But always Ashley had a way of keeping things light. Like she wasn't sure she was ready to trust Landon with her whole heart. Even after so many years.

But especially not now. Her tears had dried, and she reached up and dusted a few snowflakes from his face. "I could never forget you, Landon Blake. Never."

That was it. She couldn't say anything more, couldn't admit to having the same feelings—even if deep inside her the words were screaming to get out. Of course she loved Landon. She had loved him since he defended her to the rest of the kids in Mr. Garrett's class. The day she came to school with her hair hacked off because some kid got his gum stuck in it.

Yes, she loved him. But she wouldn't tell him now. He deserved someone better than her. Someone who would stand by him and believe in God the way he did. Someone carefree and young and happy, without the struggles and painful memories of the accident, memories Ashley faced every hour of the day.

She took a step back and the cold engulfed her immediately. If only she could stay in Landon's arms forever. Never be cold again. She smiled at him. "See you, Landon."

He walked her to the door. There he kissed her one last time and then he moved back a few feet. "See you, Ashley."

Her tears didn't start again till she was inside the house. She shut the door and leaned against it, almost as if she could feel Landon's presence through the thick wood. After a while, her father found her there in the dark foyer.

"Did Landon talk you into staying?" He stopped a few feet from her. Like everyone who loved her, Ashley's dad hadn't wanted her to go to Paris, either.

"He tried." She shook her head. "But I'm going. He knows that."

Her dad sighed. "You don't have to go through with it, Ashley." He pulled her into his arms and stroked the back of her head. "No one would think you failed if you stayed here. For now, at least."

Ashley thought about all she had waiting for her in Paris. The room she was renting, her position at the gallery. The chance to take her four precious paintings to Paris and see if someone there saw what she saw. What her dad and mom saw. She clung to her father. "I have to go. It's all I want to do."

"Sweetheart." The tenderness in his voice warmed her freezing heart.

She looked up.

"Please . . . tonight, pray about whether you should go." He smiled, but that didn't ease his obvious concern. "You can still get a refund on your ticket."

"Thank you." Her father meant well. Just like Kari and Landon. Just like her mom in the conversation they'd had earlier that morning. Everyone wanted her to reconsider— now, at the last minute. She took a deep breath. "I'm going, Dad. I have to try." She shrugged. "I'm an artist. Or at least I think I am."

"You are." His smile deepened. "You always have been."

"Right." She looked off for a few seconds. "Everything's lined up. If it's going to happen for me, it's going to happen now."

"Okay." Her father took his time, but eventually he nodded. "I wanted you to know how I feel. That I think this trip to Paris can wait. And I'd like you to pray about it." He paused. "But if you've made up your mind, then your mother and I will take you to the airport tomorrow."

She waited, her emotions swirling through her. Finally, she nodded. "Thanks, Dad." She leaned up and kissed his cheek. "I need to finish packing."

Her dad hugged her once more and Ashley jogged up the stairs. The feel of Landon's kiss was still on her lips.

When she reached their room, Kari was asleep. Just as well. What would she know about Ashley's feelings? Kari and her boyfriend, Ryan Taylor, were the perfect couple. Ryan played college football on TV and Kari's work in design here at Indiana University had made her top of her class.

Of course, Kari didn't understand. Her faith had never been tested. As for Ashley, every day she felt further from God. More removed from the Ashley Baxter she used to be before the wreck.

If God loved her, why had He allowed that truck to cross the line? Just as she had been approaching? And how come Jefferson had died? Why should she trust a God who had not prevented any of that?

Believing in Him, praying to Him, trusting Him . . . it all used to be so simple. Like waking up every morning. Faith was part of being a Baxter. But the truth was, the foundation Ashley had built her life on wasn't crumbling.

It was gone.

9

They were an hour into the flight to Paris, but Ashley was still lost in the past.

That night on the porch in the snow, she had practically changed her mind about going to France. Ashley narrowed her eyes and looked across the vast ocean. If only she had done that. She could've held on to Landon and never let go . . . told him that she loved him and stayed with him forever.

But then . . . then she wouldn't have Cole.

She would go through the pain of Paris all over again to have her oldest son. She pictured him. Tall and blond with tan skin and the fine features of the father he'd never met, never knew. Cole was a junior at Liberty now, dating his high school friend Carolyn Everly. Yes, Cole was golden. He loved God and his family, and he would've laid down his life for any of them.

For a stranger, even.

If she could keep her eyes on Cole, on God's gift of her oldest son, she could survive any of the memories and moments ahead. Ashley smiled. She reached over and took Landon's hand, sliding her fingers between his. They had always fit together so well. He was sleeping, but not so deeply that he didn't notice her hand in his. His eyes stayed closed, but he squeezed her fingers and the hint of a smile tugged at his lips.

Even after being married to Landon these past eighteen years, Ashley still couldn't believe God had led her back to him. Together they had raised Cole and Devin, Janessa and now Amy—her sister Erin's daughter. Erin and her husband and three of their kids were killed in another horrible car accident just outside Bloomington. They had been coming home for a surprise birthday party for their dad when they were rear-ended by an eighteen-wheeler. Only Amy had survived, and Ashley and Landon had taken her in like one of their own.

And together she and Landon had lost little Sarah Marie—just after birth.

Yes, they had been through much, and always God was the constant. God and Landon. Because even when Ashley had turned away from the Lord during her time in Paris, He had never turned away from her. Landon hadn't, either.

The seasons and years slipped away, and Ashley was back in time again, landing in Paris twenty-three years ago, sitting in a window seat much like this one. Rain had been falling that day, but Ashley didn't mind. She collected her two suitcases from the baggage area and stood for a minute in the bustling concourse. The place where the various trains and metro lines intersected.

Ashley had purchased a book to help with some simple French phrases, and she knew which metro stop to look for. There was something exhilarating about standing there, in the heart of Charles de Gaulle Airport. She had done it! She had left Bloomington and her family and the wrestling match she'd been having with her faith.

Now it was just her.

A dark-haired man at least ten years her senior walked by and smiled. "You need a ride, ma chérie?"

She almost said yes. Why not? She could meet people in the city and get immersed from the first hour. But she remembered what her father had said. Not everyone who smiles at you has good intentions. She shook her head. "No, merci."

The man gave a sideways nod of his head, as if to say her loss. But his smile remained. *People are friendly in Paris,* Ashley thought to herself. She was going to love this city. As she boarded the metro she realized something else. She hadn't thought about the accident since she'd gotten off the plane.

Anna Martin was the woman Ashley's teacher Helen Barr had connected her with. Decades ago, her teacher had been college roommates with Ms. Martin. Now the woman lived in the third arrondissement in a fourth-floor flat just fifteen blocks from the gallery where Ms. Barr had arranged for Ashley to work. The job was good for up to a year. That was all Ashley's visa allowed for now.

Ashley felt like an entirely different person as she stepped off the metro twenty minutes later. She was not far from the flat where she'd be living, and just across the river from Notre Dame Cathedral. The fringe of the Marais. Ashley had studied the map of the twenty districts that made up Paris. She'd read that each arrondissement had its own personality and flavor.

That wasn't completely true for the third and fourth districts. Most of the historic buildings, quaint art galleries, and favorite tourist spots were in the third and fourth arrondissements. The Marais was most famous, but the third was in walking distance, alive and eclectic and charming, with colorful boutiques and a hundred sidewalk cafés.

Ashley hadn't wanted to get off the metro any closer than this. From here she could see a long stretch of the Seine and now that the storm was letting up she wanted only to walk along the river and convince herself she was really here.

Her suitcases were large and cumbersome, but Ashley didn't mind. She pulled them behind her as if they weighed nothing. She was in Paris! That was all she cared about.

The metro had dropped her off near the famous Pont des Arts that crossed the Seine near the Louvre. Ashley could barely breathe as she stepped onto the footbridge and stopped along the metal railing. Straight ahead she could see the world's largest museum. She pivoted to the right and there again was magnificent Notre Dame. A turn to the left and in the distance she could clearly see the Eiffel Tower.

Just like one of the drawings she'd made when she was in fifth grade.

A quiet laugh escaped Ashley. She was really here.

A light rain fell on her cheeks and hair, but that didn't matter, either. She had her red umbrella if she really needed it. For now all she wanted was to take in the sights and sounds and breathe the smells of the city. One of the girls in her art class back in Bloomington had warned her that Paris had a bad odor. "Between the catacombs and the public urinals . . . the romance will wear off quickly," she had said.

The girl's words hadn't discouraged Ashley, and now that she was here, she could tell for herself. Her classmate had been wrong. Ashley could smell hot sweet beignets from a nearby food truck and even in the rain the aroma of a dozen different types of flowers wafted from an overflowing cart at the end of the bridge.

Her heart felt free and full and light. Ashley raised her hands over her head and twirled in two full circles. She might as well have been in her own movie scene, dancing here on the famous bridge. She had studied this. The Pont des Arts had been built in 1804 and during wartime, the base of the bridge had survived two bombings.

The one Ashley was standing on had been rebuilt in 1984.

A redheaded teenage boy on a bike rode by and tipped his navy beret to her.

Ashley nodded in return, then she laughed and stared straight up at the rainy sky. Two more twirls and she held her hands out to her sides. French guys were so friendly! People were kind and they liked her. No one felt sorry for her or looked the other way.

Ashley was going to love Paris.

The rain fell harder again, and dark clouds moved in overhead. Ashley watched the way the raindrops danced along the Seine and for a quick moment she thought about taking off her tennis shoes, hurrying down the bank and jumping into the water. Just for a few seconds, so she could say she had immersed herself in Paris culture from the moment she set foot here.

She smiled at herself.

Was swimming even allowed in the Seine? Probably not here. Another quick glance at the sky and she picked up her pace. She still had two suitcases to take care of, so she hurried across the bridge, through the fourth district and on into the third.

The rain was falling still harder, and there was no holding her umbrella while she was pulling her things behind her. The pace about killed her. Not because she couldn't walk a mile or so, but because she couldn't stop and take in the sights. Everything demanded her attention.

By the time she reached the correct address, Ashley was drenched. But she almost liked it. *This is where I'm meant to be*, she thought. *With the Paris rain on my skin.* She felt giddy, even more than before. Because the city was beyond anything she had imagined. She looked up. Anna Mae Martin lived three floors above a café. Of all things! The artsy sign was black with fancy white script lettering. BON CAFÉ. *Good coffee.*

I'll spend an hour here every day, Ashley told herself. *Dreaming up my next paintings.* On the long flight here, ideas had already formed in her heart. Next might be a painting of a young woman, short, stylish dark hair and pretty features. And next to her a mysterious stranger, handsome and tall. The two of them standing on the Pont des Arts staring at the Eiffel Tower. And the man would have his arm around her, like he never wanted to let go.

Because they were young and in love and in Paris.

Yes, maybe she should get coffee first. She could finish the sketch she'd started on the plane, since all she had done so far was the faintest basic outline. The placement of the couple and the height of the bridge. Ashley hesitated but then she shook her head. That could wait.

Anna Martin was expecting her.

The building had no elevator. "You'll have to walk up," Ms. Martin had told her over the phone. "But you're young. The stairs won't be a problem."

Not normally. Ashley laughed under her breath as she heaved her two suitcases up a few steps and then repeated the process. Two floors later, a pretty blond girl about her age rounded the corner. She was skipping lightly down the stairs, but she stopped at Ashley. "Oh. Can I help you?" She spoke English, but her French accent was thick.

"Really?" Ashley was out of breath.

"Sure. I was just heading down for coffee. It's the best in the city." She smiled. "And welcome to Paris. I'm Celia."

"I'm Ashley." Her heart soared. *I have a friend!* "Well, then." Ashley lifted one of her suitcases up a step to Celia. "Yes, I'd love the help. Please! I'm moving in on the fourth floor."

"With Anna Martin? She told me about you!" Celia took hold of one bag and together the two began making their way up. "You're the artist."

Pride filled Ashley's heart. *I'm in Paris and I'm an artist.* "Yes. That's me." Every step was an effort, but Ashley barely noticed now. "I have a job at the Montmartre Gallery."

"Oooh, I love that place!"

Both girls struggled to move the bags, but the job was easier with two of them. Ashley glanced at Celia. "What about you?"

"I'm interning for a publishing house. I want to be a writer." The conversation was broken up only by the effort of lifting the heavy bags. "We're dreamers, you and I." Celia giggled. "One day when we're famous we'll laugh about today, dragging your suitcases up to the fourth floor."

With every step, the troubles of home faded. By the time Anna Martin let them into her spacious flat, Ashley had all but forgotten Bloomington, Indiana. Celia made plans with Ashley to have coffee the next day, and when she left, Ms. Martin went over the house rules. "Keep your room clean, and no boys allowed." She raised her brow. "Boys are trouble. Focus on your work, Ashley. The rent is cheap, it's a gift. As long as you have a job at the gallery, you have a place here."

"Yes, ma'am." Ashley's hair was still wet, but that didn't bother her. This was quickly becoming one of the best days in her whole life.

"Your teacher says you are talented." Ms. Martin smiled at Ashley. "I do think this will be a good arrangement."

According to Ashley's teacher, a few decades ago Ms. Martin had been quite the artist, herself. Galleries sought her for her impressionist landscapes. Ashley looked around the grand living room. The stunning pieces gracing the walls had to be Ms. Martin's.

"Your work." Ashley was in awe. "It's beautiful."

"Thank you." Ms. Martin smiled, humble. "I hear the same thing about yours."

She showed Ashley to her room. The space was small, but one wall was all windows. Even on this rainy day, the light streamed across the twin bed. Ashley had to check to see that her feet were still on the floor. "This is perfect. Thank you."

The woman looked out the window for a long moment. "Artists need light. I think you'll be happy here."

Indeed. Ashley was still beaming long after Ms. Martin left her alone in her new room. The storm was passing, so Ashley put her things away and then changed into a navy dress, one that came down nearly to her ankles. A lightweight pink cardigan made the perfect finish for the outfit. Next she applied foundation and blush, eyeliner and heavier mascara than usual. She wanted to look her best.

She checked the mirror and grinned. Yes. She tossed her shoulder-length dark hair and blended the blush along her high cheekbones. "You are definitely an artist, Ashley." She did another quick twirl and laughed. "You almost look French."

Sleep hadn't been easy on the flight and she was hours off her schedule. But the gallery would be open till dark, and Ashley couldn't wait another day. She opened the big suitcase with her paintings. Each of them was a glimpse of home, her life back in Bloomington. She laid the pieces out across her bed. Her work wasn't solely landscape style, the kind where paintings looked like a snapshot of reality. No, Ashley painted landscapes with a flare of impressionism, not unlike Ms. Martin's work.

Pride welled up in her heart. She'd been drawing since she was a little girl. And today . . . today she would step into the future she had dreamed about. The gallery would display her work under a heading that read something like "Up and Coming." And she would stay in Paris for three years or five, maybe, visiting the parks and cafés and finding a hundred different images to capture on canvas.

Yes, her life was about to begin.

The first painting in her suitcase was of Lake Monroe on a cloudy day. A little boy and his father fished at the water's edge. They were her dad and her brother Luke, of course, side by side each of them holding a fishing pole. The way Ashley would always see them.

Another of her paintings was of her high school football field. A single player knelt in the end zone—his final moments before finishing his playing career. The third was of the creek behind the Baxter house, five children playing at the water's edge. And the last, a depiction of downtown Bloomington, with a mother and daughter strolling the nearest street.

People in Ashley's paintings were almost always seen from the back. There was a reason for this. Though Ashley saw her own family members, other people might see theirs. That way she didn't have to create details of the faces or get too specific. The people could be whoever the viewer wanted them to be.

Her parents had agreed, these four represented a perfect mix of her work. She returned them to her suitcase, careful to layer the white packing paper between each piece. Twenty minutes later, Ashley pulled her suitcase through the front doors of Montmartre Gallery, the place she had dreamed about for nearly a year.

Ashley took a deep breath and looked around. An older couple was browsing a wall of modern art. At the sound of her entrance, they turned and studied her. Neither of them smiled. Suddenly Ashley was very aware of herself. Her pretty dress felt cheap and Bohemian now, clearly not the elite vibe of the gallery.

She was about to say hello when a thin woman with a tight face approached. She looked Ashley up and down—much like the couple had. "You are Ashley Baxter?"

"Yes, I am."

"You do not know the dress code at Montmartre." She wrinkled her nose, like she'd gotten a whiff of old milk. "You will wear a black skirt and white blouse. Black heels. And your hair . . ." She looked like she might say something mean. Instead she rolled her eyes. "Your hair is fine. It's too short to wear in a bun—like the other girls."

Ashley's head began to spin. What was happening? Who was this woman and how had they gotten off to such a bad start? Ashley straightened herself. This was her best day ever. No one was going to ruin it. She cleared her throat. "I'm sorry, who are you?"

"Marguerite." The woman looked ready to walk away. "I own the gallery. You work for me."

Perfect. Ashley felt her heart sink. "Yes . . . well, thank you for hiring me."

"You will work the front desk and help our English-speaking customers." Her expression looked frozen. "The other girls are French only."

So that's why she was here. Ashley felt her shoulders slump a little. Suddenly Marguerite seemed to notice her suitcase.

"What in the world is that atrocious bag?" She stared at Ashley. "I would have thought you'd leave your belongings with Anna Martin—who was kind enough to let you live with her."

Ashley had no idea what to do. A part of her wanted to turn and run, get back to Ms. Martin's as fast as she could and figure out a different gallery. But she'd come this far, and since Marguerite knew Ashley's landlord, honesty was her best option. "I brought my work." Ashley tried to manage a smile. "Four of my best pieces." She hesitated. "I'm . . . I'm an artist."

"You are not an artist." Marguerite folded her arms. "You are *trying* to be an artist. There is a difference."

Ashley felt the life being sucked from her. She nodded

and looked over her shoulder toward the door. "Then . . . maybe, I should . . ."

"Fine." The woman turned and motioned for Ashley to follow her. "Best to get this over with."

Pulling the suitcase behind her and aware of the looks from the elderly couple and another patron, Ashley followed Marguerite into a smaller room at the back of the gallery. Light flooded in from the windows and easels were set up in each corner. Marguerite put her hands on her hips. "Open your . . . bag."

Ashley did as she was told. Her heart pounded in her chest. One at a time she removed her paintings and set them on the floor near her suitcase. She didn't want to look at Marguerite's expression or see her reaction.

But she had no choice.

"This?" Her expression made the previous ones seem pleasant. "This is your work?"

For a quick moment, Ashley studied her paintings spread out on the floor. She was still proud of them, no matter what this woman thought. She lifted her eyes. "Yes. These are four of my favorites."

Marguerite stared at the canvases and then glared at Ashley. "This is not art. This . . ." She waved her hand at Ashley's paintings. "This is American trash."

Ashley felt like she was sinking, like a hole had opened up in the gallery floor and it was swallowing everything that mattered to her. Her art and her hope of selling it and even her dream of being an artist. She couldn't find her voice, couldn't think of what to say.

So Marguerite said it for her. "You will put that garbage back in your bag. And you will take the pieces back to Anna Martin's home. Then you will hide them in your room and never bring them out again." She leveled her gaze at Ashley. "Your work is a disgrace, Ashley Baxter." She said just one more thing before leaving Ashley alone with her paintings. "Be here tomorrow at ten a.m. We have a big show tomorrow night. I will need you all day."

And just like that Ashley knew the truth. She should've listened to Landon, should've heeded her father's wisdom. She never should've gotten onto the plane. Because she was not talented or promising—the things her teacher had said. In fact, she was not an up-and-coming artist, at all.

She was a fraud.

10

Mia Barrons balanced an ice cream cone in one hand and three shopping bags in the other. Today was her birthday, and she had spent it the way she dreamed. With her oldest daughter, shopping and laughing and eating their way through Paris's famous third and fourth arrondissements.

She had three girls now, and all of them lived in Normandy with Mia and her husband, on a working dairy farm.

A far cry from the life Mia had lived when she was trying to be an artist here some twenty-three years ago. She put the thought out of her mind.

"Look at this, Mama." Estelle was twenty-two and the thrills of Paris beckoned her much as they had Mia all those years ago. Her blond daughter pointed to a window display. "Those heels! If only I had a reason to wear them!"

"Your graduation, maybe?" Mia took a closer look. "You'll be a doctor one day, Estelle. Passing your baccalaureate may be just the first step, but it's worth celebrating."

"True." Estelle's green eyes sparkled as she looked back at the pair of shoes. "They're expensive."

"Let me get them." Mia linked arms with her firstborn. "Come on."

They walked inside the boutique even as Estelle shook her head. "Mama, it's your birthday. I can't."

"My precious Estelle." Mia stopped and smiled at her daughter. "Seeing you happy, that is my favorite gift."

The shoes were a perfect fit, and no surprise. Estelle could have been a model with her height and striking looks. Instead, she wanted to help people. One day soon, she would be the very best doctor.

When the shoes were packaged and they had set out again along Rue Quincampoix, Mia turned her face to the sun. The weather was balmy and breezy. Perfect for their trip to the city.

"Let's stop here." Estelle walked ahead to what looked like an art gallery. Light of the Seine, it said on a colorful sign above the door.

Mia smiled. She and her husband, Harry, had been searching for a piece to go in the dining room. He and the other girls were meeting them in Paris tomorrow, then the family would stay for a week. Harry had meetings with dairy buyers, and Mia and the girls would visit the museums. And they'd do more of this, of course.

The gallery seemed warm and inviting with two walls of windows. The light brought out exquisite colors in the various pieces.

"Hello." The woman at the counter looked to be in her forties. She had clear eyes and a kind expression. "Welcome to Light of the Seine."

Mia understood how the gallery got its name. "Your place is beautiful, madame."

"Merci." The woman smiled. "I'm Emilie. Did you hear about our show this Thursday night?"

"No." Mia looked at her daughter. "We're from Normandy. I'm afraid we're just visiting."

Estelle spun around and grinned at her. She mouthed the words: "A gallery show!"

Mia shook her head. "No . . . We have plans for our evenings." It was true, Harry had dinners lined up with their family and his clients every night of the week.

"Well, here." The woman took a flyer from her countertop. "Just in case."

The minute Mia took the flyer, she stopped. Everything around her slipped into slow motion. She stared at the face of the artist at the center of the paper. "Ashley . . . Baxter."

"Yes." Emilie looked pleased. "You know her work?"

Mia's heart began to race, and she held on to the counter so she wouldn't drop to the floor. "I . . . no. It's just . . ."

"Mom?" Estelle was at her side. "Are you okay?"

"I . . ." *Pull it together,* she told herself. She clenched her jaw and worked to stay strong. "Ashley . . . she used to live in Paris. Is that right? A long . . . long time ago?"

Emilie looked more closely at Mia. "Why, yes. She did." A slight pause told Mia much. The shopkeeper knew at least something about Ashley Baxter's past. "The gallery used to be called Montmartre. It was in the third. I bought it a few years ago. Changed the name and moved it here."

Mia could barely focus on the woman's words. "You . . . you knew Ashley back then."

"She was young. Maybe twenty." Emilie hesitated. "An American. She worked the front desk."

There was more to Ashley's story, and Mia knew it. The American had dated Jean-Claude Pierre. Mia was sure. Because she, herself, had dated the man at the exact same time.

* * *

MIA NEEDED A minute.

Her daughter wanted to talk to her boyfriend, so the timing was perfect. They left the art gallery and stopped at Mia's favorite Paris spot—Terres de Café. They sat at a table near the window and ordered from the waiter.

"Mama, you sure you're okay?" Estelle had looked worried since they'd left the gallery. "You looked white as a sheet back there."

"I'm fine . . . I just . . . I believe I know the American woman, the artist being featured at Light of the Seine." Mia felt more composed now. "I saw her for a brief time when we were both in Paris, twenty-three years ago."

"Okay." Estelle looked at her for a long moment. Gradually her worry turned to possibility. "Does that mean we'll go to her show?"

Mia laughed. The first time in ten minutes. "No, your father has plans for us."

"Yes, Mama." Estelle stood and held up her cell phone. "I'll step outside for my call. Is that okay?"

"Of course." Mia watched Estelle leave through the front door and find a place at one of the tables outside.

Alone now, Mia pulled the piece of paper from her purse and stared at it again. *Ashley Baxter.* For a brief moment, Mia closed her eyes. The only reason she knew the American's name was because the woman at the clinic had called it out from the front desk.

But she had known Ashley's face long before that.

Back then Mia had been so jealous of Ashley she thought about her morning and night. The pretty American had gotten a job at Montmartre, one of the finest art galleries in Paris. Weeks before they hired her, Mia had worked there. But Marguerite had dismissed her without warning. "We have enough French girls." That's all the woman had said.

By then, Mia had done more than work the front desk at Montmartre Gallery. She had taken up with one of the most famous painters in the city—Jean-Claude Pierre. Mia had known the man was married, but she hadn't cared. When she was at his side, she actually felt like an artist— even though she'd never completed a single painting.

Without a job, Mia took a position across the street at a jewelry shop. More than the money or the hours, the thing Mia liked most about it was she could keep an eye on the gallery. On Jean-Claude. And she could see first-hand the face that had replaced her at the front desk.

The face of Ashley Baxter.

Since the girl was obviously an American, Mia told herself Marguerite had only hired her for her English. Because Mia was obviously the better gallery girl. But with her front-row view of the Montmartre, within a week Mia picked up on something else.

The American girl was also seeing Jean-Claude.

Betrayed and angry, Mia tried to break things off with the famous artist. But the man wouldn't hear of that. "You have my afternoons, ma chérie." He took her face in his hands. "She has my nights. There is room for both of you."

Mia felt sick at the memory. How could she have allowed herself to be caught up in Jean-Claude's web? Not only that, but she had learned by then that Jean-Claude Pierre was a very dangerous man. He had a crew of criminals doing his dirty work. Mia knew because he would take calls from them during the day.

When Mia was with him.

Even so, Mia continued her seedy lifestyle. And when she wound up pregnant, weeks after Jean-Claude had started dating Ashley Baxter, Mia wasn't surprised at the artist's reaction.

"You will get rid of this child," he told her. There had been a dark and evil chill in his voice. "Get rid of the child . . . or I will get rid of you." He smiled then, as if maybe he was having a little fun with her. *Surely, he didn't mean what he said*, Mia had told herself.

At first Mia ignored Jean-Claude's order. But after a few weeks, she began to notice men following her. And it occurred to her that perhaps Jean-Claude was not joking.

Fine, she had thought to herself. She would do what he asked. After all, why would she want Jean-Claude's baby? The man clearly didn't care for her.

Mia looked out the window at Estelle. Her daughter was still on the phone, laughing and gesturing. Her boyfriend was a good man. The two would be married soon.

And though they wouldn't be going to Ashley's show on Thursday, Mia would write the American artist a letter. She would do that tonight and leave it with Emilie Love at Light of the Seine. That way Ashley would know the impact she had made.

Yes, Mia had to at least do that.

A wave of nausea came over her. Her daughter shouldn't even be alive, shouldn't be twenty-two and in love and planning a wedding. And she wouldn't be except for one thing.

The courage and conviction of Ashley Baxter.

• • •

A DAY HAD passed since Albert Arnaud spotted the advertisement on the outside window of the small gallery in the fourth district. Since then, he had hidden the fact from his superiors. They paid him well for his criminal work.

Ashley Baxter wasn't their business.

And so, Albert had created a plan, and that afternoon he entered the gallery much like any other patron. He had done his research on the place so he meandered his way up to the owner, Emilie Love. After several minutes, Albert stopped at a pretty impressionist piece. "I like this." He looked over his shoulder at Emilie. "Tell me about it."

He waited until Emilie was at his side and minutes into her explanation of the artwork, before he stopped her. "That is not why I am here, Ms. Love."

"Do I know you?" Concern filled Emilie's eyes. She began to back up. "What . . . what is this about?"

"I am a reporter from *Style* magazine. You know the publication?"

"Oui." The woman's expression relaxed some. "Okay."

Albert motioned for Emilie to come close again. "I need to know more about Ashley Baxter. What time she will be here on Thursday, and what door she will enter through."

The woman told him all he needed to know. She absolutely believed him. Albert smiled as he left.

The gallery owner had no idea what was about to go down.

11

Ashley and Landon arrived in Paris and got through customs with little delay. Once they had their bags they connected with their private driver. Ashley was glad. She didn't feel like sharing a ride today.

"You stayed awake." Landon had slept most of the flight, but he was alert now.

"Yes." She forced a smile. "I . . . kept remembering."

"That's what I thought." Landon took her hand. "Tell me about it."

Ashley shook her head. "Maybe later, Landon. Is that okay?"

"Sure." He looked slightly hurt. "I have to believe all this remembering is good for you."

"I'm not sure." She wanted to ask what he had expected. Of course being here was bound to stir up the worst memories. "I'm sorry, Landon. It's not about you. You know that, right?"

"I do." He kissed her hand. "You'll find your way through this."

They stopped for salads near the Seine and before they reached their hotel, they drove past a street Ashley recognized. At the stoplight, she checked the sign and her heart skipped a beat. This was where Jean-Claude Pierre had owned a private studio. A place where Ashley had been far too many times.

She thought about telling Landon, but it didn't seem right. By the time they checked into their brownstone boutique hotel it was two in the afternoon, and Ashley had been awake for more than twenty-four hours.

"I have emails to answer." Landon kissed her forehead once they were in the living room of their suite. "You go lie down and get some sleep. If you feel rested, we'll go out for dinner later."

Ashley welcomed the idea. "Sorry. I should've slept on the plane."

"Don't be sorry." He took her in his arms and held her for a long time. "Go sleep and you'll feel better in a few hours."

But even with the sun-blocking shades and the comfort of the soft linens and pillows, Ashley still couldn't sleep. She could see herself walking her suitcase back up the stairs to Ms. Martin's flat, fighting tears every step of the way.

Her new friend Celia was not here to help this time around. Besides, what would Celia think of Ashley now? Her dream of being an artist at the Montmartre Gallery had lived exactly ten minutes. So much for dreams.

Ashley had been honest with Ms. Martin about Marguerite's reaction to her artwork. "She said it was trash."

"No, dear." Ms. Martin sat at her kitchen table across

from Ashley. "It's a matter of taste. Marguerite does not like Americans."

The woman's kindness stirred a spark of hope, and it stayed with her the next day when she showed up at the gallery, wearing a black skirt and white blouse. *Marguerite doesn't like Americans. That's all. I'm an artist, no matter what that woman says.*

Marguerite stationed Ashley at the front desk. When an American customer came through the doors, it was Ashley's job to lead them around. No, she wasn't an artist, but at least she was working in a gallery. Still, she had no training, no idea what to tell the customers, and she told that to Marguerite an hour later.

Again the woman looked at her like she was brainless. "Read the card, Ashley. Just point at the painting and read the cards. I'll take it from there."

The gallery was quiet most of the day. Ashley was so bored she began to long for her family and Landon and even her junior college classes back in Bloomington. But as evening approached there was a spark of excitement. "You are comfortable in your job, yes?" Marguerite approached her just after six. "What is it you Americans say . . . Trained? You are trained, yes?"

A day on the gallery floor wasn't much training, still Ashley felt she had no choice but to agree. "Is something happening tonight?"

"Not just anything." Marguerite literally looked down her nose at Ashley. "Jean-Claude Pierre has a show tonight. He is the most popular artist in Paris." She pointed to the young men moving paintings from the gallery floor and setting up new ones. "The place will be very crowded tonight." She paused. "I will need you to stay till the end."

The end? Ashley had been on her feet since ten that morning. "What time will I be done?"

Marguerite looked surprised that Ashley had asked. "When I *say* you're done."

That was all Ashley could take. Tomorrow Ashley was going to look for a new gallery, a place where they liked Americans. Maybe another gallery owner would take a look at her work and love it. But for now, she couldn't leave. Ms. Martin would hear about Ashley's hasty exit, and everything would spiral out of control from there.

She had to stay, and though she was still jet-lagged from just arriving in Paris the day before, Ashley found herself looking forward to the show. Jean-Claude Pierre was a new name to her, but based on the crowd already gathering outside, clearly the man was popular.

Marguerite allowed the earlier customers to finish their shopping and leave the gallery. Then she locked the doors for thirty minutes while Ashley set up a table of hors d'oeuvres and wine. At 6:30, the doors opened and dozens of people filed inside the gallery.

Jean-Claude's work was abstract, but some pieces tended toward realism. Especially a few of the nudes. Ashley wasn't impressed. She thought her art was prettier than the art of this popular painter.

Not until Jean-Claude Pierre walked through the back door did Ashley's opinion of him change.

Instantly.

Jean-Claude had an aura about him, a physical presence that was evident the moment he entered. He had short blond hair and a chiseled face, and his eyes were steel blue. The muscles in his arms and legs showed through his thin Italian button-down and dress pants.

Ashley couldn't take her eyes off him.

The artist had to be in his late thirties, much older than Ashley. But she had never felt more drawn to a man in all her life.

A few minutes later, a small woman with hair even blonder than Jean-Claude's walked in through the back door and found her place next to the artist. *His wife*, Ashley told herself. Of course. Ashley positioned herself so she could see Jean-Claude's left hand. Indeed, he wore a ring. So that was that.

He was a married man.

Even still, Ashley caught herself watching him. Once when she was in middle school, her family had gone to Destin Beach on the Florida Panhandle. The wind had picked up on the third day, and Ashley had gotten sucked into a riptide. Her dad was right there, and in a display of strength the whole Baxter family remembered, he snatched her from the current and helped her back to the beach.

Ashley never forgot the intensity of the pull that day. Which was what she felt now, standing in the same room as Jean-Claude Pierre. At first the artist didn't seem to notice her. He was obviously caught up in the questions and praise from the many patrons. With Marguerite on one side of the man and his wife on the other, Ashley hardly expected him to notice her.

She was wrong.

Half an hour into the show, Jean-Claude excused himself from the other women and made his way to the desk. "Chérie. I cannot take my eyes off you. What is your name?"

Her knees shook and her palms felt suddenly sweaty. She struggled to find her voice. "Ashley. Ashley Baxter."

"My paintings pale in comparison to your beauty, Ashley." He moved closer and she could smell his cologne.

Her heartbeat quickened. "Thank you."

"You are my American beauty, oui?"

Ashley didn't hesitate, didn't think for a single moment about what she was saying or what it would mean to a man like Jean-Claude. "Oui, monsieur."

"Very well. Forgive me, belle, if you catch me looking. You are by far the most beautiful thing here tonight."

Ashley couldn't draw a breath, and she couldn't exhale. What had he just told her? An older female patron approached her not long later. "Jean-Claude has many girls," the woman said. She kept her voice quiet. "Stay away from him."

But Ashley couldn't.

Later she would wonder who that older patron was, and whether God had sent the woman to warn Ashley, to keep her from making a tremendous mistake. Ashley would never know.

That night when Jean-Claude's paintings had all been sold and after his wife had left with their driver, the artist approached Ashley. "I will be waiting for you out back, ma chérie. Don't be long."

Ashley couldn't focus on counting the receipts or helping return the other paintings to the gallery floor. Marguerite must have known something was going on between Jean-Claude Pierre and her new American gallery girl. Because before Ashley left, the woman walked up to Ashley and looked her in the eyes. "Don't get caught, Ashley. Jean-Claude is married and highly respected." She paused. "Just make sure he favors Montmartre. He is our favorite artist."

In other words, go ahead and have an affair with the man, as long as he doesn't move on to a different gallery. That's what Marguerite had basically told her. Ashley should've been sickened, should've run back to her room at Ms. Martin's. Maybe never shown her face at the Montmartre Gallery again.

Instead, she was practically breathless when she finished her work and walked out the back door of the gallery. Jean-Claude was waiting for her, leaning up against a white Mercedes. No one else was in sight.

"Ma chérie." He took her hand. "Marguerite says you do not work tomorrow."

That wasn't true, but Ashley nodded. "Okay." If Marguerite said so.

"Then . . . beautiful girl, let me show you Paris."

Jean-Claude's tour of the city began that night with drinks at a nightclub in the Marais. Ashley was only twenty

and she'd never drank before. She felt heady and sophisti-
cated, sipping a martini and looking into the artist's blue
eyes. "Tell me about yourself." His words were a caress.
Only one guy had ever treated her with more respect. But
he wasn't in Paris.

"I'm an artist," Ashley told him. "That's why I'm here."

"I'm sure you are." Jean-Claude kissed her hand. "Tell
me more."

Ashley didn't want to tell him about her life. She had
left Bloomington because she didn't want to talk about
that. She felt the flirtatiousness in her eyes. "Instead . . .
tell me about you."

"I am a man who grew up loving art." He was so close
she could smell the mint of his breath. He never once
looked away. "I am still that man today."

The message was clear.

In this situation, he was the patron and she was the
painting.

•   •   •

THAT NIGHT WHEN Jean-Claude brought her back to Ms.
Martin's, he walked her to the door. She leaned against
the red brick wall and he moved close. So close he was
almost touching her. For the longest time he just looked
at her. Then he ran his thumb over her brow and came
closer to her.

But instead of kissing her, he brushed his face against
her cheek. His whisper felt like a physical touch. "Until
tomorrow, belle. I will see you at ten tomorrow morning."

"Are you sure . . . Marguerite said I don't work tomor-row?" Ashley wasn't supposed to have a day off for weeks.

"I'm sure, mon amour." Jean-Claude shook his head, and a sly sort of smile lifted his cheeks. "You have tomor-row off."

Ten in the morning. "Okay, then . . . demain . . . tomor-row. Bien." She spoke French before she could stop herself, and Ashley could see that her effort made Jean-Claude smile.

His words stayed with her as she made her way up to the fourth floor, quiet so she didn't wake up Ms. Martin. With every step up to Ms. Martin's front door, with every pounding heartbeat, shame covered Ashley like a suffocat-ing piece of plastic. What was she doing? Yesterday she wouldn't have considered even talking to a married man, let alone going to a bar with one.

Now, though, she was a worldly Parisienne. An artist. She would've kissed him if he'd tried. Never mind her family or her upbringing, her faith or her prior convic-tions. Never mind Landon Blake. Ashley was the softest clay in Jean-Claude's talented hands.

But when she looked in the bathroom mirror that night, the spell broke. *What am I doing?* "You are not going to have an affair with Jean-Claude Pierre," she ordered herself. "That's not who you are, Ashley Baxter. No."

She reminded herself of this again and again, every few minutes that night. By the time she was ready for bed and had slipped between the covers in her new room, she had convinced herself. Jean-Claude was a fellow artist, nothing more. He wanted to show her Paris, and why not? No way Ashley was going to cross lines with a married man.

Even so, the last image she saw as she fell asleep that night was the handsome face of Jean-Claude Pierre.

12

If this was a dream, Ashley couldn't wake up. The past was as alive as she was and the memories kept coming.

The next day Ashley was on her guard. She wore a white denim skirt, white tennis shoes, and a modest red blouse. *There is nothing special about today,* she told herself. *I'm allowed a day in the city with a new friend.*

She would keep the boundaries between them. No more walls down, no doe-eyed smiles in his direction. He held the door for her as she stepped into his Mercedes. The car smelled of leather and expensive cologne. *You are not having an affair, Ashley Baxter.* She closed her eyes for a brief moment. *You are not.*

"I wish to show you the captivating arrondissements of Paris, ma chérie." He pulled away from her building and turned his eyes to her. "Ashley . . . you are even more beautiful in the daytime."

And every promise Ashley had made to herself fell like a house of cards.

By the time they reached the next traffic light, Ashley had all but forgotten her name, let alone her convictions. She swallowed hard and stared straight ahead. Just one thought pierced through the intoxicating sensation of his presence.

God, help me. Please.

He started the tour in the sixteenth district. "Tourists find this arrondissement less interesting." His eyes met hers again. "But it is where the wealthy retire."

Ashley glanced at the pretty street and the old French architecture. The people walking the sidewalks looked wealthy. Even the dogs looked rich. What did Jean-Claude mean by telling her the wealthy retire here? Was that a hint, a foreshadowing of what he saw with her? That somehow they would share their lives together? Maybe even living in this beautiful section of the city?

"I'm taking you higher now, Ashley." He kept his hands on the steering wheel. "Do you trust me?"

"Yes. Oui." She felt young and immature. Not ready for a man like Jean-Claude. "I trust you."

He drove her to the fifteenth district, and he left the car with a valet. As they stepped out, he kept an appropriate distance. *Just friends*, Ashley told herself. *He only wants a friendship with me.*

Jean-Claude held the door open for her. "This is the Montparnasse Tower. One of the tallest buildings in Paris. More than a million tourists take this elevator ride every year." He winked at her as he pushed a button. "I have privileges. I will take you where others cannot go."

Her head was spinning as the elevator whisked them to the top of the building. Jean-Claude told her that the place where they were going offered a 360-degree view of

Paris. They stepped off the elevator and he directed her to a small room at one end of the rooftop. Clearly some sort of VIP area. Inside were comfortable chairs, cold water, and pastries.

"I prepared this for you, chérie."

Here it comes, Ashley thought. He was going to try to kiss her or take advantage of her. She was ready to stop him, ready to tell him to take her home. She wasn't some cheap American affair. But instead of making any sort of move, Jean-Claude took the seat opposite hers and sipped a glass of water. "I am intrigued by your artwork, Ashley. You will have to show me sometime soon."

Ashley could barely catch her breath. "Merci, Jean-Claude. Merci."

They finished a plate of strawberry eclairs and chocolate macaroons, and he led her outside to the edge of the viewing area. "It is almost like heaven up here. You can see my city . . . all of it."

His city. Ashley was consumed by the words he chose and the way he said them. The dizziness she felt had nothing to do with how high up they were. In no time they were back in his car. "You know Hyde Park in London?"

Ashley had never been there. "I've heard of it."

"There is a hidden diamond of a park much like it in the seventeenth arrondissement. Square des Batignolles. We will walk there."

Was she in a dream? Ashley had never heard of these places, never imagined she'd get to visit them in her first few days in Paris. And how was it that Marguerite had given her the day off? Just so she could see the city with Jean-Claude? Did he have that much power with the woman, with his good standing at Montmartre Gallery?

Ashley didn't have time to sort through the answers. At Square des Batignolles, they parked in an empty lot and Jean-Claude helped her out of the car. He wore black jeans and a white T-shirt and between his cologne and his strong arms, Ashley had to work to keep her distance.

She wondered if he would take her hand as they strolled the meandering path past bubbling streams and picturesque ponds. Grassy knolls cropped up on either side of the trail. "This is only a preview, mon amour. I will bring you back someday. Picnics in the park are quintessentially Paris."

Ashley could barely walk a straight line. *Quintessentially Paris?* Who talked like that? How had she found this wonderful man and what was she doing allowing herself to fall for him? Back in his sedan, they breezed through the thirteenth arrondissement. "Here you will find street art and Butte aux Cailles, a popular neighborhood with the young people. Like yourself." He grinned at her. "We will go to the eleventh. I have found the perfect patisserie for us."

For us. Ashley tried to remember to exhale. He asked her about her art, why she had started painting and where she saw herself with it in ten years, twenty. "Still painting." Her words were breathy, dreamy. As if everything she'd told herself last night had never happened. "Selling my work. Making a living at it."

"And so you will." Again his voice was a physical touch. They stopped at a charming white-brick café and he led her to a private patio. Again they were expecting him, a fact that made Ashley feel heady and important. Jean-Claude had done his homework. He had planned and made phone calls and prepared the day in great detail.

All for her. Which had to mean something.

Maybe he was divorced, and the woman had only been with him last night because they were still friends. He clearly didn't care for the woman. Jean-Claude had only had eyes for Ashley from the moment they first saw each other. So maybe this was love? A love at first sight that could only happen in Paris.

Ashley dared to dream it was so.

Over coffee, Jean-Claude reached across the table and touched his fingertips to hers. But only for the briefest few seconds. Then, as if he remembered himself, he drew back. "My love of art happened very young," he told her. "I saw a tree outside my bedroom window. And I wanted to re-create it." He laughed. "I couldn't do anything else until I found paper and sketched that tree. I have what they call a natural talent."

Somehow his story didn't sound arrogant. Who could argue with him?

"You like lakes, chérie?"

A picture of Lake Monroe flashed in Ashley's mind. She blinked and it was gone. "I love lakes. So peaceful."

"I will take you to a lake like none other." He winked at her again, and she felt her heart flutter. "Bassin de la

Villette is in the nineteenth. It is situated in the fifth largest park in Paris. It is another place I will take you again."
He touched her shoulder but only briefly. "When we have
more time, mon amour."

The lake was everything Jean-Claude had said. Grassy
hills and people sitting on blankets talking and eating,
soaking in the sun. He was explaining that the park was
more than sixty acres in the northeastern part of the city,
but all Ashley could think about was him. Was he going to
hold her hand? Would he try to take her in his arms? What
was this? What were they doing?

She was practically desperate for him to kiss her. And
what did that say about her? Who had she become just
days after landing in Paris? Her mouth was dry as she tried
to focus on his explanation of the area.

In the twentieth district, Jean-Claude showed her the
grave of Oscar Wilde. Her new friend put his hand alongside her face. "People often kiss this grave." He looked puzzled. His thumb eased across her lower lip and his touch
sent chills down her body. He came closer to her again.
"That's a waste of a kiss. Would you agree, mon amour?"

He was doing it again. Talking in code. She practically
cried out for him to stop the pretense and kiss her. But she
held her tongue. Instead she only let herself get lost in his
eyes. "Yes, Jean-Claude. A complete waste of a kiss."

In the fourteenth arrondissement, he took her to a private entrance of the famous catacombs. Ashley had read
about the underground tunnels. In the late 1700s Paris
had grown so much that the boundaries of the city came

up against the cemeteries once far removed from civilization. After a terrible rainstorm, the wall of Saints Innocents cemetery collapsed, spilling more than a million corpses into the streets of Paris.

Officials quickly decided on a solution. Sixty-five feet belowground, nearly two hundred miles of tunnels lay dormant, in what used to be limestone quarries. Over the next twelve years, every corpse was moved to the catacombs and stacked along the underground pathways.

They began their descent down a chilly set of stone stairs. "People say the catacombs smell of death." Jean-Claude stopped and smiled at her. "I think it smells rather pleasant."

A shiver ran down Ashley's arms. Something sinister seemed to hide behind the man's charm and debonair exterior. Ashley let it go. No point letting her imagination get away with her. He was still talking. Apparently, Jean-Claude knew much about the catacombs. "They keep the temperature fifty-seven degrees in your Fahrenheit. Through summer and winter." He stared at her. "Bodies and bones do best at that temperature."

A strange sensation came over Ashley. It was a feeling she didn't like.

As they walked to the first tunnel, Jean-Claude stopped at a sign over the entrance. ARRÊTÉ! C'EST ICI L'EMPIRE DE LA MORT!

The words sounded like a love song coming from her new artist friend. Ashley found herself moving ever closer to him, drawn to his warmth. "What does it mean?"

He didn't hesitate. "Stop! This is the empire of death."

Her expression must've shown her concern, because a quiet chuckle came from him. "Do not be afraid, mon amour. This is Paris history. That is all."

Of course, she told herself. And how lucky she was to have someone like Jean-Claude show her places like this. Deep in the catacombs the smell was a dusty mix of decaying remains and incense. Ashley tried not to think about it. They turned a corner and she gasped. Human bones were stacked on both sides of the narrow walkway, laid in the most meticulous fashion.

"The femur bone makes lovely art, yes, ma chérie?"

She had no idea what to say to that. And because she stayed quiet, Jean-Claude must've gotten the hint. Death did not enthrall Ashley like it did Jean-Claude. She looked back toward the entrance. "We should go."

"Oui." He smiled at her. They'd spent enough time in the catacombs. "Come, mon amour."

He followed her up the stairs, and something about his nearness now made Ashley feel more than attraction. Like maybe she really was in danger. *Ridiculous,* she told herself. *He's in love with me. There's no danger in that.*

Except Jean-Claude was married. Or it seemed like he was. Ashley refused to think about it. He took her to the twelfth arrondissement next, to one of the most famous restaurants in Paris—Le Train Bleu in the Gare de Lyon train station. The walls were encased with gold trim, and crystal chandeliers hung from the ceilings. Countless exquisite paintings decorated the walls and ceilings.

From the moment she walked inside, Ashley felt like a child, gawking at every detail.

Jean-Claude touched her face, and his fingers were like velvet. "It is not as beautiful as you, Ashley."

Her face grew hot under the desire in his eyes. People didn't just waltz into Le Train Bleu, Ashley knew that much. Again, Jean-Claude had wielded his power to give her the most unforgettable experience.

They shared a dinner of arugula salad with pecans and wild yams, fresh-caught fish, root vegetables and organic herbs. When Jean-Claude ordered a bottle of champagne, Ashley did nothing to stop him. She could drink. She was old enough in Paris.

After dinner the sun was about to set. "I have more for you, ma belle." He took her to an elevated walkway above the city. And at a spot so beautiful Ashley could only soak it in, Jean-Claude stopped and she did the same.

The champagne made her feel like she was floating, and with the most natural ease, Jean-Claude turned to her and leaned his back against the railing. Pinks and blues streaked across the sky and the fading sunlight shone in his piercing blue eyes. "Today . . . has been a dream, ma chérie."

"Oui." Everything about her past life disappeared. So what if he was married? She was with him now, and he wanted her. She could see that clearly here. He wanted her more than his next breath.

And she felt the same. *Kiss me, Jean-Claude*, she wanted to say. She ached for him, wanting him more than anything in all her life. They were inches apart, the smell of him leaving her defenseless.

"Ashley . . . ?" It was the gentlest question. And though he didn't say more than her name, she understood.

"Yes, Jean-Claude. Oui." She felt herself drawn toward him, and before either of them could say another word, his hands were on her shoulders and in her hair. And in a moment of passion greater than Ashley had ever experienced, his lips were on hers.

She had no idea how long they stood there kissing, lost in the glow of the sunset and the haze of the champagne. Somehow they made their way back to his car, and then to his studio, and a hunger filled Ashley. An otherworldly hunger that felt dark and forbidden. But that didn't stop her.

Nothing did.

And before she knew what was happening, she was in his bed, twisted up in his sheets and it was morning. She sat up with a start and her breath caught in her throat. What had she done? She pulled the covers up to her chin as Jean-Claude stirred and opened his eyes.

"I . . . I have to get to work."

"No, mon amour." His laugh was as seductive as his kiss. "You have today free." He pulled her into his arms. "You are mine, ma chérie. Today we finish looking at Paris. We will see the Eiffel Tower and the Louvre. But not yet."

Ashley couldn't say no as he pulled her close. She didn't want to. And again she was trapped in his gravity, unable to stop herself or do anything but whatever Jean-Claude asked of her.

Later that day, he took her sailing down the Seine in the seventh arrondissement, and he snuck into her room at Ms. Martin's to see her artwork. "These are so very beautiful, Ashley." He drew her to himself. "You are a wonderful artist."

A week later she was working at the gallery when Jean-Claude came by with his wife and two young children. Ashley had to pretend she barely knew Jean-Claude. She even gave his daughter one of the lollipops the gallery kept for small children.

What am I doing? Ashley felt sick to her stomach and a terrifying thought pressed in on her soul. Something her mother had told her a long time ago.

The devil doesn't always look like a devil, she had said. *Sometimes he masquerades as an angel of light.* Ashley couldn't agree more.

Jean-Claude was living proof.

13

Landon was beginning to think maybe the trip to Paris wasn't a good idea, after all. They'd been in their hotel room for three hours, and still Ashley was asleep. He had checked on her a few times, and always she looked restless, muttering under her breath.

Was she still caught up in the memories of the last time she was here? Worse, was she trapped there? Maybe they should've held the show in Bloomington. She didn't owe the people of Paris this time to display her work.

Whatever the situation, he let Ashley sleep. They could see the city tomorrow.

In the meantime, he sat in a chair by the window and watched the sun set over Notre Dame and the Seine. He could see the historic landmarks clearly from the window. If only Ashley could understand how her time here hadn't hurt only her. How it had damaged him and drawn him to her all at the same time.

A memory came to mind. That same year when he was at Baylor, he'd been out walking across campus late one night with Jalen's sister, Hope. The girl was dark-skinned with hazel eyes and a happy heart. She skipped ahead of him and then turned and walked backwards, facing him.

Hope had a spark that had drawn Landon, for sure.

But even after an hour talking to the girl on a bench at the center of the quad, all Landon could think about was Ashley. Where was she? What was she doing? There was no real way to reach her. No email or cell phones back then. He had only the phone number of Anna Martin, Ashley's landlord.

So that night after Landon said good night to his beautiful new friend, he stood outside the door of his own dorm room and did the math. It would've been morning in Paris. Why not call Ashley? Maybe he could catch her before she went to work. He could tell her he was thinking of her and just hear her voice.

That would be enough.

Never mind that she had asked him not to call, or that she had told him she needed this time. Before he could stop himself, he went back inside and sat at the small table in the common space. A few minutes after he used his credit card to pay for the charges, the phone was ringing. A woman with a thick French accent picked up.

"Bonjour." She sounded pleasant.

"Uh . . . hello. Bonjour." Landon felt stupid. Why had he done this? Ashley wouldn't want him checking up on her. He clenched his fist and tried to think about what to say. "I'm . . . Landon Blake. A friend of Ashley's. Is . . . is she there?"

The connection wasn't great, but after a few seconds the woman spoke. "You have reached the right place, Landon." She hesitated. "But Ashley is not here. She . . . has been gone much."

Gone much? What was that supposed to mean? Landon remembered the sick feeling in his stomach. "Is she . . . working?"

"Yes . . . and seeing the city with a friend."

Who was she seeing the city with? he wanted to ask but he couldn't bring himself to say the words. "Okay. Can you please . . . can you tell her Landon called?" He thought for a moment and changed his mind. "Actually, don't tell her. I'll . . . I'll try again another time."

"Very well." The woman didn't sound like she cared one way or the other. "Have a nice day, Landon. Bonjour."

"Bonjour." Landon had hung up the phone and walked outside again. For the next hour he sat alone under the night sky. Who was Ashley palling around with? And how come she hadn't tried once to call him at his dorm? He had no answers, but an idea hit him.

Maybe she had called home. Her parents must've heard from her. They would know about this new friend and the places Ashley had been seeing. After class the next day, he called Elizabeth Baxter. She had been like a second mother to Landon. Surely, she wouldn't think it strange that he wanted to know.

But the moment he heard Elizabeth's voice on the other end of the phone, Landon felt the sick feeling again. When he brought up Ashley, Elizabeth seemed more than discouraged. She sounded distraught. There was no hiding the fact.

"Landon . . . we haven't heard from her." Elizabeth sighed. "I'm sorry. I wish I had better news."

He stood and paced as far as the phone cord would let him. "You mean . . . she hasn't called this week?"

Elizabeth waited a few seconds. "We haven't heard from her since the day she left."

Panic welled inside Landon. "The day she . . . ? It's been three weeks."

"I know." Elizabeth sounded tired. "John and I have called every few days. We always leave messages with Anna Martin. We keep it light, so the woman won't think we're worried."

Landon wasn't sure about mentioning the next part, but he couldn't help himself. "I guess she's been seeing the city with some new . . . friend?"

"We've heard that, but we know nothing more. Ms. Martin tells us she passes our messages on to Ashley." She paused. "But still she hasn't called."

The conversation ended and Landon felt sick. Where was the girl he'd known since the fifth grade? What was happening to her in Paris? Could she be in trouble or was she turning into someone none of them would even recognize?

Landon didn't want to think about the answers, but a few hours later, the anxious feeling had moved beyond fear to something else. Frustration. And by the time he met up with Jalen and Hope that night, he was more angry than anything else. Fine. If Ashley didn't want to talk to him or her parents, so be it.

He had better things to do than wonder about her.

And so it was that Landon and Hope began hanging out. They were friends first, but a month later after dinner and a walk across campus, Landon kissed her. He didn't feel about her the way he did about Ashley. The way he still felt. But maybe he would in time.

Because as far as Landon was concerned, he probably wouldn't see Ashley ever again. And one way or another he had to get on with his life. Even if he missed her till his dying day.

The memory lifted and Landon blinked a few times. The sun was down, and the lights of Paris replaced the colorful sky. Somehow, tonight he felt like that college kid again. Alone and sad and a million miles away from Ashley Baxter. With no way to reach her.

Even with her lying asleep in the next room.

• • •

ASHLEY SLEPT IN fits and starts, but she couldn't find her way out of the memory. Finally she realized she had just one choice. She needed to see her past through to the end. Only then could she open her eyes and make this trip about her and Landon . . . and not Jean-Claude Pierre.

Spending her days and nights with Jean-Claude made time stand still for Ashley. One afternoon he took her to lunch in the elegant eighth arrondissement. Over vodka and tonic, she leveled her gaze at him. "You are married, Jean-Claude."

"Oui, ma chérie. I am committed to another."

Ashley knew this. But in that moment she felt the floor begin to tilt. "But . . . you are in love with me. Every night . . . you tell me you love me. That I'm . . . all you want."

"It is true." Passion blazed in Jean-Claude's eyes. "I want only you, Ashley, mon amour. We have today."

What was that supposed to mean? She had given her heart and soul, her mind and body to this man. And now he was telling her they had today? "You mean . . . only today?"

"Oui. That is all we will ever have." He slid his chair closer to her and kissed her on the lips. A kiss that rocked her senses. "That is enough, yes?"

She didn't have to think about her answer. "Yes." Her eyes were lost in his as she nodded. "That is enough."

Her time with Jean-Claude was wrong, but it was magical all the same. He would take her hand in his and she would forget her very soul. The affair continued every day when she got off work. And if Jean-Claude talked to Marguerite, then she would have an entire day with him.

And at night . . . at night the fire between them was otherworldly. He was a temptation she was powerless to resist. It was the same for him. They were hungry for each other, neither could get enough.

Their time might have continued indefinitely if Ashley hadn't started feeling sick. Not just in the morning but at night, too. A week passed before she realized that maybe, just maybe, she was experiencing more than a stomach bug.

A trip to the local pharmacie and Ashley found a test. She took it the next morning and she had her answer, the one she feared more than anything in all her life.

She was pregnant.

Like that, her passionate, forbidden Paris days with Jean-Claude came to an end. As if somehow he knew about the baby before she said a word. She took a cab to his studio that night, but before she could climb out and head for his front door, Jean-Claude walked out of the building with a young man.

The two were arm in arm like lovers.

Ashley had the driver take her a few streets away, where she threw up in the gutter. How could he cheat on her? How long had he been seeing other people?

The next day she was walking to work at the gallery, fighting nausea and wondering who she had become, when she saw Jean-Claude again. This time he was with a blond girl, the same age as Ashley. Maybe younger.

Jean-Claude kissed the girl's hand.

The overnight change was more than Ashley could grasp. Had Jean-Claude been seeing other people the whole time? Whenever he wasn't with her? Ashley worked that day in a fog, and by the time she walked home the reality set in. Of course he'd been seeing other people. He was a married man who spent his days and nights chasing whatever conquest he could charm into his bedroom.

A week passed and on a rainy Tuesday while Ashley was working the desk, Jean-Claude finally walked through the front doors. He smiled at her as if no time had gone by and immediately he was at her side. He took her hand and tried to kiss it.

This time she pulled it away. The masquerade was over and she could see Jean-Claude for who he was. Ashley took a step back. "We need to talk."

He looked surprised, but his smile remained. "Very well, mon amour." He nodded toward the back room. The one where Marguerite had called her artwork American trash. "We will talk there."

Ashley followed him and when they were in the small room, she shut the door behind her. She was hurt and angry and her heart was breaking. But more than all that she was disgusted with herself. What had she done? Who had she become?

"You are angry, ma belle?" Jean-Claude approached her. His mouth was on hers before she could stop him.

Despite all she knew about the man, at first Ashley returned his kiss. The feel of him close to her was that intoxicating. But then she remembered the situation. "Stop!" She pushed him away. "Don't." Her breathing was fast and uneven. What sort of spell had he wielded on her?

For the first time, Jean-Claude did not smile at her. His eyes turned cold. "Say what you have to say, Ashley."

Her fear doubled. Gone were the days when she had thought he would leave his wife and marry her, raise their child together and retire with her in Rue de Passy. Things were over between them. But where did that leave the child inside her? She summoned her strength and stared at him. "Jean-Claude . . . I'm pregnant. I'm going to have your baby."

His expression became hard and unyielding. "You, ma chérie, are not going to have my child." He spat the words at her. "Only my wife will have my children."

"Your wife?" Ashley couldn't believe this. "You don't love your wife. You love me. You told me so."

Jean-Claude's laugh sounded mean, different than at any time since Ashley met him. "Indeed, I love my wife. She is respectable, refined. I care about her and my children very much." He sneered at her. "You . . . you are American trash." He lifted his chin, arrogance personified. "Like your paintings."

Ashley backed up till she was against the wall. "Don't say that. You . . . you loved my paintings."

"No." He dusted off his hands and checked his cuff links. As if this matter was over. "There is a clinic down the street. You will take care of this situation." He scowled at her. "I would have thought a tramp like you would be on the pill."

Ashley felt her knees buckle. In slow motion, she began to slide down the wall to the floor. *No . . . this couldn't be happening.* Jean-Claude had loved her, she had seen it in his eyes. She was willing to look past the other people in his life, as long as he committed himself to her. "How . . . can you say that?"

"Easily. It's true." He uttered a single, condescending laugh. "Bonjour, chérie. I will not see you again."

She wanted to scream, wanted to order Jean-Claude to stop this game and be the person he was before. The man who exuded passion and seduction and romance. Her lover who had called her his personal work of art. What happened to him?

But before she could say another word, Jean-Claude was gone. The next day when she reported to work, Marguerite found her at the desk. "I have heard . . . about your situation." Clearly Ashley made the woman sick. "Get it taken care of . . . or you do not have a position at Montmartre."

Ashley couldn't eat or drink or sleep. Her entire world had imploded, and there wasn't a thing she could do about it. She had been tricked, played. No matter how smooth Jean-Claude had been or how he had seemed, it was all a lie. He didn't care about her.

And now that she was pregnant with his child, he loathed her.

She missed work the next day and went to Square des Batignolles. The park where Jean-Claude had promised future picnics and long walks. On a bench near a quiet pond, Ashley let the tears come. She cried until she was sobbing, until she thought she'd pass out from the horror and shame and sorrow.

There, bit by bit, Ashley remembered who she had been back in Bloomington. She was an awful person now, a tramp, just like Jean-Claude had said. She wasn't sure which part of her situation was the most devastating. The fact that she'd been played or that she'd so willingly walked into an affair with a married man?

Her family would disown her after this.

And what about the baby inside her? The child would never know his father, that much was sure. If she didn't have an abortion, she would lose her job. Ms. Martin would know, of course, and then Ashley would be sent home overnight. Whether her family took her back or not.

If she did find a way to live life on her own, and if she kept the baby, then the child would grow up knowing how cheap and promiscuous his mother was. *Ashley Baxter, American trash.* Not only that, the child would know she had failed in every possible way. Morally and professionally.

What sort of mother would she be given that truth?

She had just one choice. Her sickness built and grew and she dry-heaved into the nearest trash can. There was nothing in her system. She hadn't eaten for days. *How could you let this happen? You're the worst person ever, Ashley Baxter. No one is more terrible than you.*

The accusations came, one after another.

Finally, when her tears had dried and she was no longer gasping above the sound of her sobs, Ashley pulled herself up off the bench. What she was about to do would help her baby. The child would be in heaven—much better than living with someone like her.

She took a cab to the clinic a block down the street

from the gallery. At the desk she signed in. "Name?" The desk clerk gave her a compassionate look.

"Ashley Baxter." She felt dead inside. This was the only way . . . the only way out. The abortion was for her baby's good, she was convinced. It wasn't because of her job. She would find another place to work. No way she was stepping foot back in the Montmartre Gallery. Never again.

The woman handed her a clipboard with two pages of questions. "Have a seat, Ashley. We'll be right with you."

Another girl was already in the waiting room, and as Ashley sat down she practically gasped. It was the blonde who had been with Jean-Claude. Did that mean . . . was she . . .

Ashley couldn't think about it. She sat down, her back to the girl, and filled out the paperwork. Name. Date of last period. And then a box to check, giving the clinic permission to put instruments inside her and scrape her uterus clean. The procedure was called a D & C, the document explained. Harmless, but with occasional rare side effects.

Yes. Ashley checked the box. Yes, she was willing to take the risk, willing for them to rip her baby apart and throw it in the trash can so she never had to think about Jean-Claude Pierre again.

She finished the paperwork and signed her name at the bottom. Then she returned the clipboard to the woman at the desk. But as she sat down something began to happen. She could hear a voice. A child's voice. *Mommy . . . don't do this. You don't want to hurt me.*

Ashley shook her head and put her hands over her ears. What was this? Who was talking to her? But even with her hearing muffled, the voice spoke. *Leave this place, Mommy. Run! Don't do this.*

Stop! Ashley ordered the voice. "Stop!" She spoke the word out loud, but it did nothing to silence the sound in her head, the childish words filling her heart.

I love you, Mommy . . . I already love you. Even if no one else does, I love you.

And Ashley could picture her baby. It would be a boy, she knew. With every cell in her body, she knew. As if God Himself were telling her it was so. He was alive and whole and his heart was beating inside her.

But not for long.

And suddenly . . . as if her own life depended on her next move, Ashley stood and ran for the door. Fast . . . like someone escaping a charging lion.

"Ashley Baxter?" the woman called after her.

"No!" Ashley was at the door now. She looked over her shoulder at the woman. "I won't do it. I won't!"

She raced out the door and down the street, away from the clinic. Away from the Montmartre Gallery. She didn't stop until she was at a café, and she tore through the front door. Two minutes later she was eating a muffin and drinking a glass of milk. Not for herself.

For her baby.

With one hand on her still flat stomach and the other gripping her napkin, Ashley hung her head and closed her eyes. *God, I'm a failure. If You're there, if You're real . . . You know that.* She had nowhere to turn, no one she could tell. Ms. Martin would kick her out as soon as she learned the truth. And she would.

Jean-Claude had eyes everywhere. Ashley was beginning to understand that.

She remembered his comment about the dead bones. They were beautiful, he had said. She shuddered. Suddenly she felt sure about something. Jean-Claude might kill her for keeping her baby, and if he did, so be it. This child would not die at her hands.

Life would be nothing but hard roads and lonely valleys from this day forward. Her family would not want her back, and she didn't want to return, anyway. She would find a way here in Paris, maybe in one of the residential arrondissements she had visited with Jean-Claude. But one thing was certain. She would not be alone. Not ever again. Because she would have her baby boy.

And no one would ever take him from her.

Not ever.

14

·········

Cole Blake was walking back to the dorm from a meeting with the other resident assistants when he got the call from his grandpa Baxter. This was the summer before Cole's junior year, and classes hadn't started yet.

It would be months before he'd be home to see his family. He smiled and took the call. "Hey, there."

"Cole, my boy!" His grandpa's smile was practically visible over the phone line. "It's good to hear your voice!"

"You, too." Night had fallen, and fireflies danced on either side of the path. "Everything okay? With you and Grandma Elaine?" It wasn't often that he got a call from his grandfather. Texts came every few days. But not phone calls.

And not this late in the evening.

"Well." His grandpa laughed. "I have a wild idea. I thought I'd share it with you."

Cole reached his dorm. He sat on the outdoor stairs. "Okay . . . tell me."

"All right. So you know your parents are in Paris for the week."

"My mom's show." Cole stared at the starry sky. He

would've given anything to be there. "I wanted to go. Maybe next time."

His grandpa hesitated. "Actually . . . maybe this time."

For the next few minutes his grandfather explained how he had checked flights, and if Cole could get home by Tuesday, then they could fly to Paris the next day. "We would get there in time for her show. If everything goes just right we would check into a hotel near the gallery, and when the show starts, we walk through the door and surprise her!" He sounded like a kid, he was so excited. "What do you think?"

Cole's mind raced. He didn't have more meetings till next week. "You know what . . . I think I could do it."

"We'd stay another day and see the sights. Then we'd come home. You could be back at school a week from today."

"Hold on." Cole put the call on speaker and checked his calendar. "My next appointment is on that Monday. That would work!"

"So you'll join me?" Grandpa Baxter laughed. "Come on, Cole. Let's go surprise her. It'll be the greatest gift."

Cole was laughing, too, now. "I love that about you, Papa. You always have the best ideas."

"This one's crazy, I know. But why not? Life isn't a dress rehearsal, right?"

"Definitely. Let's do it!" Cole talked specifics with his grandpa and after a few minutes the call ended. He couldn't believe it! He was actually going to Paris!

Cole didn't know all the details about his mother's

time in the City of Love, except for what everyone in the family knew. She'd had a brief relationship with a married man and come home pregnant with him.

But now he was twenty-two, and he'd never been to the city where he came from. The place where his birth father had lived. No, the man wasn't a good guy. And he was dead now, anyway. But Cole had always wanted to visit Paris. He had long wondered if a part of him would feel at home there.

Of course, he had always pictured taking the trip with his mother. The woman who had kept him and raised him and loved him with her whole life. But this would be even better. The trip wouldn't be with her, it would be for her. A gift for the best mom any kid could ever have.

The gift of a lifetime.

• • •

ASHLEY LIFTED HER head from the pillow and blinked. Where was she? She sat up straighter and let her eyes adjust. Then it hit her. She was in their Paris hotel room, she and Landon, here in the Marais.

This was their anniversary trip. Her first Parisian show.

The details were all coming back to her. She put her head in her hands and winced. Her temples throbbed, her headache still holding on like a vise grip. She wasn't sure if it had been a dream or a long and terrible memory, but she had just replayed every awful detail of her last time in Paris. Right up until the best part.

The part where she kept Cole.

She slipped her feet over the edge of the bed and grabbed her phone from the bedside table. Nine o'clock already. Poor Landon. Had he gone out for dinner, or was he still in the other room? She made her way to the sink and grabbed a bottle from her bag. Tylenol. Yes, that's what she needed. She peeled the plastic from the hotel glass at the edge of the sink, filled it with tap water, and downed two pills.

There. That would help.

She looked at herself in the mirror and made a face. Her mascara was streaked down both cheeks, so she must've actually been crying. Not just remembering the tears from those far-off days. When the water from the sink was warm, she drenched a fresh washcloth and pressed it to her face. Was this how the entire trip was going to be?

Before she could figure out an answer, the door opened and Landon stepped in. "Ashley . . . you're awake."

"How long did I sleep?"

"Four hours." He came to her and put his hands on her shoulders. "How are you?"

She dried her face and turned to him. Then she slipped her arms around his neck and rested her face on his chest. "I couldn't stop remembering. It was like . . . like I was in a trance. Or a coma. I'm sorry, Landon."

He kissed the top of her head. "It's okay, Ash. Maybe it was good for you to remember."

"It wasn't." Tears filled her eyes again. She lifted her

face to his. "I hate everything about my first time in Paris, Landon. Everything but the most important part."

"Our son." Landon's eyes were kind. He understood her so well.

"Yes. Cole."

"How about you brush your teeth, and we go to bed?" He took a step back. "Doesn't sound like you got much rest."

She sighed. "Sleeping sounds good. Tomorrow is a new day." She wanted to believe it. The whole week couldn't possibly go like this.

Like so many times, Landon was right. Before they fell asleep, he prayed for her and recited Philippians 4 over her. "*Do not be anxious about anything, but in everything, by prayer and petition, and thanksgiving, present your requests to God. And the peace of God, which transcends all understanding, will guard your hearts and your minds in Christ Jesus.*"

And finally, in the shelter of that timeless truth, safe in Landon's arms, Ashley fell asleep.

The memories would be back, because there was more to the story. But for now, they left her alone, and when morning came, her headache was gone. They were meeting Jessie and her new boyfriend today.

Ashley dressed in her summer capris and a white T-shirt. *Help me, God, to take every thought captive today. The past is gone. Protect me from it, please. Give me back my joy, please.*

She prayed until she was with Landon in the living

room. "It's going to be a great day." By then she believed it. She smiled at him and kissed him. A kiss that lasted longer than she intended. "Tomorrow is our anniversary."

"I've been thinking about that." He kissed her again. "I love you, Ashley. You're the greatest gift God's ever given me."

"I love you." Her heart danced. Yes, today would be good. She was ready.

They stepped outside and a black SUV pulled up. They had a private driver today, someone who would wait for them while they had lunch with Jessie and as Landon took her to Palais Garnier, the opera house in the ninth district, a place Ashley had never visited before.

The driver helped them out of the car near an outdoor café in the eighth arrondissement near the Champs-Elysées. Ashley saw Jessie right away. Her niece ran to them, a handsome young man standing by the table where the two had been sitting.

Landon squeezed Ashley's hand. "She looks happy."

"She does." Ashley felt so much better. This was her life. Not the memories that had haunted her yesterday. And now they would have a beautiful lunch with Kari's oldest daughter.

"Aunt Ashley! Uncle Landon!" She reached them, breathless. "I can't believe you're here." She was in their arms in a rush. "Seeing you here, it's like a piece of home."

The innocent joy in Jessie's eyes was the same as Ashley's had been when she stepped off the plane here twenty-three years ago. If only she hadn't gotten pulled into the world of Jean-Claude Pierre. Ashley banned the thoughts. "You look marvelous, sweetheart." She glanced back at the table. "Introduce us to your guy."

Jessie's eyes lit up. "He's wonderful, Aunt Ashley. You'll love him."

Together they hurried to the table and Jessie introduced them to Gabriel Michel. The young man was twenty-two, the same age as Cole. He was polite and well spoken, and his English was beyond fluent.

When they were all seated, and after the waitress had brought them their salads, Gabriel looked at Ashley. "I see Jessie in you. The two of you are very alike."

It was true. Ashley smiled at Jessie. "One day soon the gallery show will be hers."

Jessie beamed beneath the compliment. "I hope so." She looked at Gabriel and then back at Ashley. "So what do you think about Gabe's mother?"

Ashley wasn't sure what her niece meant. "His mother?"

"Yes . . . the story I told you when you were boarding the plane." Jessie bounced a little. "Do you think it's possible?"

Landon chuckled in Gabe's direction. "I'm in the dark on this one."

Gabe laughed. "My mom told Jessie a story a few days ago. In fact . . . she's meeting us here in a few minutes. If that's okay."

"Of course." Landon set his fork down. "We'd love that."

Clearly, Jessie wanted to get back to the story. "I tried

to tell you the other day." She could barely contain her enthusiasm.

"Oh, right . . ." Ashley remembered. "You were saying something at the end of the call. But it broke up. We lost connection."

"Got it." Jessie settled back in her chair. "I wondered how much you'd heard." She looked at Gabriel and back at Ashley and Landon. "I'll let Gabe tell you."

Jessie's boyfriend grinned. "Sure. I don't think there's a connection." He paused. "Twenty-three years ago, my mom worked at a boulangerie with an American artist. Someone who meant a great deal to her."

Ashley felt the slightest uneasiness. She had, indeed, worked at a bakery before returning to Bloomington. But she didn't want to think about twenty-three years ago. Not today. A forced laugh slid between her lips. "There are many young American artists here in Paris."

"Definitely." Gabe nodded. "That's what I told Jessie. But she thought we should ask you anyway. Because of the other detail."

"Yeah." Jessie leaned in close to Gabriel. "Tell her."

Ashley tried to dismiss the strange feeling building in her heart. She remembered to smile. "Tell me what?"

"Her name." Gabriel slipped his arm around Jessie's shoulders. "My mom's friend. Her name was Ashley."

At that moment, Ashley looked up. A woman was coming their way, one with Gabe's brown eyes and chestnut hair. Twenty-three years might have passed, but Ashley would have known the woman's face anywhere. A drug addict who had been pregnant and desperate and hopeless. She still remembered the girl's name from that awful time in her life.

Her name was Alice Michel.

•   •   •

THEIR EYES MET and Alice stopped. She put her hand to her mouth and tears filled her eyes. How was it possible? After all this time how could she have actually found the Ashley she'd looked for all her life?

The American woman was on her feet, moving toward her. Tears flooded her eyes, too. "Alice?" They met up and stared at each other. As if they could somehow see through the years to the young women they had been back then.

"Ashley." It wasn't a question. Alice was sure, now. This was the woman she had always wanted to find. "What . . . what was your last name, Ashley? I couldn't remember, not for the life of me."

"Baxter." Ashley wiped a tear from her cheek. "I was Ashley Baxter. Now Ashley Blake."

"And I'm Alice Arquette." Alice held her arms out and Ashley did the same. The hug lasted a long while. Not like two long-lost friends. Alice and Ashley hadn't had time for friendship. What they had shared was deeper than that.

Because Alice's life had depended on her connection to the girl this woman had been.

Alice stepped back and looked into Ashley's eyes. As if everything else around them had disappeared. Then Alice told Ashley the words she'd always wanted to say. "I have looked for you, Ashley . . . and prayed for you. For twenty-three years." She laughed, but the sound was more of a cry. "I asked God that I might sit across from you at a café like this and tell you what happened back then."

Ashley looked confused. She didn't break eye contact. "I knew . . . your story. What you were going through." She paused. "I still remember."

"But there are parts you don't know." Alice released Ashley's hands and dried her eyes. "You saved my life, Ashley. I'd like to tell you about that."

"Of course . . ." Ashley led her back to the table and they took their spots. Ashley sat next to a man who she introduced as her husband, Landon.

And Alice sat next to Gabriel. She greeted Jessie and then she took a deep breath and began to tell the story. The very one she had prayed she might tell Ashley one day. And now she could only pray for something else. That her story would matter to Ashley, that maybe the woman across from her needed to hear the story.

As much as Alice needed to tell it.

15

Ashley was gripped by Alice's story from the moment she started to tell it. Until now she hadn't remembered the girl from the boulangerie. But here those memories were alive again for her, too. At her side, Landon also was quickly caught up in the story. Same with Gabe and Jessie.

From the beginning, Ashley had the feeling she was on holy ground. Like there was something in the pieces of Alice's story that God wanted her to hear.

"I was a heroin addict." Alice didn't sound ashamed of the fact. That was her old life, clearly. "Do you remember that?"

"I remember you'd battled drug addiction. We both needed the job." Ashley had been sent away from Ms. Martin's house and had found a hostel in the neighboring district. The place had just one shower and most guests stayed only a night or two. Backpackers seeing Paris on a budget.

Every night Ashley would slip into her bunk and pray no one would hurt her. She had no privacy, nothing to call her own except the two suitcases under her bed. But it was a place to stay. And working at the bakery had been a way to keep food in her mouth. A way to help her baby.

She had to look out for her little one.

Alice was saying how bad things had gotten for her before she took the job at the boulangerie. "I used to steal from my mother. So I could buy heroin." Her expression was more serious now. Clearly they both had regrets. "Then one night I overdosed. Do you remember me telling you that?"

The details were becoming clearer. "Yes. Your . . . your friend died that night."

"He did." She took hold of Gabriel's hand. "My son's birth father. He was a very kind man. He asked the police officer to give me the Narcan. So I could live."

Gabe looked down at the table for a minute and then back at his mother. "I wish I could've met him."

"He saved my life the first time." Alice looked at Ashley. "You saved it the second time."

Alice went on to say that she would've gone back to the drugs, back to hating her mother and scrounging for scraps on the street. She would've lost her baby for sure. "But instead, God led me to you."

Under the table, Landon ran his thumb over Ashley's hand.

The two young women only worked together for a few weeks. "But every day you would talk to me in the back room." Alice smiled. "If you could call it that. The space was just a closet, really."

"I can picture it."

"We both felt the same about our lives." Alice took her time. "Remember, we talked about how we could never go back to our families. We thought we'd be terrible mothers." She hesitated. "But my situation was worse than that because of my addiction. I craved another hit of heroin every hour of the day back then."

Ashley could see herself, skinny and pregnant, talking to Alice in that break room. The girl had been a French version of herself—all except for Alice's addiction. The only addiction Ashley had ever known was her addiction to Jean-Claude. And by the time she met Alice, she was over that.

Alice continued. "Every day I thought about going back to that spot under the bridge near the Seine. A bunch of drug addicts lived there in tents. Everyone shared needles." Alice teared up again. "I thought that was love. I told you that."

"Yes." Ashley nodded. "I remember."

"And every day you took my hands, Ashley, and you told me that wasn't love. It was a sickness. You told me my baby deserved more than that." Alice's voice was thick with emotion now. "Some days I only returned to work for one reason. To hear you say those words again. That drugs weren't love. That the people under the bridge didn't care about me. They cared only about the next hit."

That's right. Ashley had indeed said that. "I told you that even if your mother never forgave you, God loved you."

"Yes, you'd just come back to believing in God. You

had the same faith my grandmother had. But my mother had never taught me about Jesus." Alice hesitated. "Because of you, I began to wonder if maybe God was real."

Alice explained that she had been living in a halfway house, a place for recovering addicts. When Ashley spoke to her about God, Alice no longer felt alone and desperate for more heroin. She felt like maybe there was hope, after all.

"But I still struggled. You didn't work for a few days, and I decided everything you'd said wasn't true. There wasn't a God and no one loved me. I told myself I'd be crazy sick for a hit of heroin until the day I died."

Ashley glanced at Gabriel. This was hard for him to hear, that much was obvious. He had hold of his mother's hand again. "I still can't believe this, M'man. It sounds nothing like you."

"I know." She smiled at him. "But it *was* me. And the story of my redemption is important. Because everyone has a past. Everyone comes from some background. The place where God found them and picked them up and dusted them off. The day they first understood how loved they were."

"Yes." Gabe nodded. "It doesn't have to be drug addiction. We all have something."

Alice turned to Ashley. "Without you to talk me into living those few dark days, I made a plan." She paused. "I . . . I was going to take my life. Mine and my baby's." She looked at Gabriel for a long time and she kissed his cheek. "I'm sorry, son. Sorry I ever considered that."

He put his arm around her and held her. "You're here. I'm here. That's all that matters, Mère."

"Thank you, Gabriel." Alice was quiet for a while. "The truth is, I was going to jump off the Pont du Garigliano. There would have been no surviving that."

"This is the part she told Jessie the other night. When we all had dinner." Gabriel looked concerned for his mother. "It had been a long time since I'd heard the story."

"It'll be a long time till you hear it again." Alice smiled at him but pain filled her eyes. "I have to tell Ashley. I've begged God for this chance."

Ashley wondered if maybe she and Alice should've had this conversation alone. But they never would've met if it wasn't for Jessie and Gabe. "Was that the night . . . when you came into the bakery? When you weren't sup-posed to be working?"

"It was." Alice angled her head. "I was there to say goodbye, Ashley. It would've been my last hour. If I'd had my way."

"I could tell something was very wrong."

Alice nodded. "Right." She explained how she couldn't stop shaking, and Ashley took her into the back room. "You asked me if I was going to do something stupid. Find more drugs or . . . you didn't say it, but I think you knew."

Ashley had known. She could see the past vividly now. The girl, shaking and desperate. Her eyes wide with fear. And then Ashley saw herself, what had happened that day. "I took you in my arms and hugged you."

"No one had hugged me like that for years." Alice

shook her head. "I had lost so much, but in that hug . . . in that single hug I felt hope."

Landon tightened his gentle grip on Ashley's fingers. He kept his eyes on Alice, like he couldn't get enough of this story. Across the table, Jessie looked the same way.

"I think I pulled an old Bible from my backpack." This was something Ashley hadn't thought about since she'd come home more than two decades ago. She had actually had a Bible with her.

"You did." Alice sounded like she was lost in that long-ago moment. "That's exactly right. You said you'd bought it at a secondhand store a few days earlier. And you pulled another book from your backpack. A book for expecting mothers."

"Yes." Ashley was there again, sitting at a dingy table in the stuffy back room of the old boulangerie. "I opened the book and showed you what our babies looked like. Because we were both at about the same stage of our pregnancies. Four months, maybe."

"Exactly." A cry came from Alice and she covered her mouth. "I . . . I still can't believe it. Until that moment, I hadn't really thought my baby was real. Just a problem, a reason I couldn't live any longer."

"I remember feeling like that." Ashley needed to be honest, too. "There was one day when I thought an abortion would be the best thing for my baby. Because at least then he'd live in heaven with God." She shivered. "I told you that, right? How I ran out of that clinic that day."

"Yes." Alice smiled. "But that day when you gave me

the Bible and that book, you put your hand on your belly, and then on mine. And you read me Psalm 139. About how God knits babies together in their mothers' wombs."

"That Scripture is on a plaque in my parents' home." Gabriel sounded proud of the fact.

Ashley remembered something else. "After we read that psalm . . . you looked different."

"Hope took root inside me that day. A divine hope." Alice sniffed, but she couldn't stop smiling. "I had a life inside me. I wanted to live. I was going to live. When I left the bakery that day, I was sure."

A heaven-sent rescue. That's what it had been. A picture of God's living grace and mercy and redemption. "I told you that day that I was going home. Right?"

"You did." A sad laugh came from Alice. "You said you had to make peace with your family. That you believed they would take you home again even with the baby. They would love you no matter what. You had to believe that."

Ashley was amazed at the details Alice recalled. "I had talked to my parents by then. They didn't know I was pregnant. But they were thrilled that I wanted to come home."

"Yes. And your situation made me wonder . . . maybe I could contact *my* mother. Maybe it wasn't too late." Alice hesitated. "But I didn't know I wouldn't see you again, Ashley."

"My plans to go back to Indiana came together quickly." Ashley could see herself packing her bags, making sure her paintings were in the large suitcase, and her filthy clothes in the other. "They booked me on the next flight out."

"If that had happened any sooner, I'm not sure what I would've done." Alice shook her head. "Without that final conversation with you." She sat back, more relaxed now. "You know what I did when I left the bakery that day?"

Ashley already felt chills on her arms.

"I went back home." Alice nodded. "I walked up to the front door of my mère's flat and knocked. Like a regular person. Like someone who believed in second chances." Her voice cracked and she took a moment. "And when my mère answered the door, do you know what happened?" Alice took her time. "My m'man took me in her arms and held me. Rocked me like when I was a little girl. No judgment, no angry words, no demand for an explanation. She loved me then and she loved me while I continued to get help and when I brought my baby boy home. My mother loved me."

There were tears in all their eyes now, picturing the moment, imagining the scene. Ashley struggled to find her voice. "That's . . . that's incredible, Alice. A beautiful story."

"Now you know." Alice reached across the table and squeezed Ashley's hand. "You saved my life. God used you that day. And because of that, here we are. Here we all are."

It was a story Ashley would hold dear as long as she lived. A good moment from her time in Paris. When the lunch ended, and they had promised to have breakfast one morning before the week was up, Ashley and Landon walked back to their car.

Landon asked the driver to take them someplace different. "Not the opera house. Not now." He checked his phone. "Maybe later." Instead, Landon had the man drive them to the Sacré-Coeur Basilica. A church that sat in the midst of a small, gated park.

From the moment Landon gave the driver their destination, Ashley knew why her husband had picked that place. She sat back, drained from Alice's story, and she held Landon's hand.

"You know what they call the eighteenth arrondissement, right?" He leaned closer.

"Hmm." Ashley wasn't sure. She hadn't seen Paris as a tourist destination since she was young. "Tell me."

"The artists' eighteenth." Landon kissed her cheek. "And you, my love, are an artist. You always were."

When they reached the park, Landon took her to another of the most famous spots in Paris. Someplace Ashley had never been. Tucked in behind the basilica, at the summit of the Butte Montmartre, was a wall that stood nearly three hundred feet high. The tallest point in the city.

And on it, in every single language known to man were three simple words.

I love you.

Landon pulled Ashley close as they stared at the towering wall. "I love you, Ashley Baxter Blake. Do you know how much?"

She smiled and lifted her eyes to the wall. "You love me in every language, is that it?"

"In every language. Through every season of every year of our lives." They stood back from the crowd of tourists gathered at the attraction. He kissed her the way she had wanted him to since that morning in their hotel living room. "I love you forever, Ashley."

"I love you." She kissed him this time. "Happy anniversary."

Their anniversary wasn't until the next day, but that didn't matter. This was an anniversary trip, after all. Despite every horrible memory and the awful things she had done here. A smile caught Landon's lips and a sparkle filled his eyes. "You know what I'm going to say, right?"

Ashley had no idea. She didn't need fancy words or poetry at this point. She only needed him. She slid her cheek along his and allowed herself to get lost in the feel of his arms around her. "What are you going to say, Landon?"

He moved back half a step and searched her eyes. "The story of Jesus and the storm. Remember?"

And just like that another chill came over Ashley, because Landon had told her there would be moments like this while they were in Paris. Times when God would show them how Ashley's choices and heartache when she was lost in this city must've held some redemption. Even for someone else. And so they had. Ashley felt a warmth fill her heart and soul. Landon didn't have to say the words. Ashley already knew.

Because in the greatest storm of her life, today's lunch was something God wanted her to notice. He had made good out of Paris, after all. And today's lunch brought them the one thing Landon had hoped they would find when they came to France.

People like Alice Arquette.

The little boats.

• • •

WITH THE INFORMATION he'd received from the gallery owner of Light of the Seine, Albert had a number of ways he could kill Ashley Baxter. Twenty-three years ago, the American artist had been his first paid hit and he had failed.

But he was better at his job now.

Albert settled into his leather recliner and stared at the walls of his expensive flat. He had completed thirty-three hits since returning to Paris. Businessmen who stood to make great financial gain, small-time politicians with too much information. Spouses threatening public divorce.

His boss made the connections. Albert did the dirty work.

He picked up a newspaper from the table near his chair. WHISTLE-BLOWER REPORTER TAKES HIS LIFE, the headline read. Albert smiled. Few whistle-blowers ever really took their own lives. But Albert knew many ways to make it look like they had.

His victims died of suicide and food poisoning, car accidents and accidental falls. At least that's how it seemed. Occasionally a body would show up in the Seine and the police would suspect something more than an accidental drowning.

But Albert was good enough to elude authorities.

He surveyed the small, windowless room. On occasion, Albert brought people to his flat in the sixteenth arrondissement. Men or women he'd met on the street or in bars. But no one ever came into this room. The door was locked from both sides and for good reason.

Albert scanned the space. Every inch of the four walls and ceiling was covered with photos of Jean-Claude Pierre and his work. A shrine to the man who had given Albert prestige and power. His idol.

His obsession.

"I'm about to make you a very happy man, Jean-Claude." He talked to the artist here. It was their place, for just the two of them. "You and me, both."

Yes, it wouldn't be long now and Albert could do one last deed for Jean-Claude Pierre. He tried to imagine how good it would feel to know he had finally finished what the artist had asked of him. He stared at a photo of himself with Jean-Claude. Happier times. "Soon, Jean-Claude," Albert whispered. "Very soon."

He had lived for this moment, dreamed about it.

Every day since seeing the ad in the window at Light of the Seine, Albert had been planning. The gallery used the same caterer for every show. Albert knew that now. If all went well, he would deliver a poisoned piece of cheesecake especially for Ashley Baxter. A treat for the night of her show. If that didn't kill her, Albert had other ideas.

He knew which hotel Ashley was staying at and which car service her husband was using. From the table next to his chair, Albert picked up a handgun. One way or another, the American artist would not return home in coach beside her husband.

But under the plane in a body bag.

16

The next day, lunch with the gallery owner and her husband took place at a restaurant not far from Light of the Seine. Ashley had to keep reminding herself that this was really happening, that she was back in Paris about to see her paintings sold at a professional gallery.

Never mind what Marguerite had said about her work twenty-three years ago.

This time the gallery owner didn't despise Ashley. Emilie Love adored her.

They had ordered chicken confit with roasted potatoes and parsley salad. Landon must've enjoyed the food because he was nearly finished with his plate. Same with Emilie Love and her husband, Edward. Ashley was trying, but she wasn't hungry after what had happened earlier. Her heart was too full to eat much.

"I thought it'd be warmer in Paris this time of year." Landon set his fork down and looked from Emilie to her husband. They sat outside at a table near a busy sidewalk. "The weather is perfect."

"Paris in July is the stuff people write songs about."

Emilie smiled at Landon and then at Ashley. "I've checked, and Thursday looks to be the same. Sunny and clear. Perfect for your show."

Her show. With Emilie going on about her reasons for buying the gallery, Ashley drifted. No matter what awful things she had done in Paris, it was right for her to be here now. This was where her mother had always pictured her, selling her paintings in Paris. Only God could've allowed such redemption.

Landon turned to her. "Why don't you tell us, Ash?"

She had missed something. "Yes . . . of course."

"Like Emilie said . . ." Landon smiled. He wasn't going to leave her hanging. "Her favorite of your paintings is the one of the Baxter house in the fading sunlight. Right?" He smiled at the gallery owner.

"Yes." A dreamy look came over Emilie. "There's something so ethereal about that one. I feel like I'm living in that house every time I look at it. What about you, Ashley? Which one is your favorite?"

"Mine is about to be sold." Landon patted Emilie's hand. "I'll need to bring my checkbook to the show."

Ashley laughed as she considered the question. Her favorite? "I can't choose one." She smiled at Emilie. "They're like kids in a way. You spend all that time with them, creating them . . . and a piece of your heart is in every stroke of the brush."

"Mmm." Emilie nodded. "I like that."

Their meal together ended far too soon, but Emilie and Edward had to get back to work. He was a loan broker a few blocks away. Landon grinned as the meal ended. "It's our anniversary today. Eighteen years."

"What?" Emilie practically jumped out of her chair. "I did not know this." She looked at Ashley. "We cannot keep you a minute longer. I'm sure you two have plans."

"We do." Ashley looked at Landon. "He has the afternoon all figured out."

"And the evening." He put his arm around Ashley. "Lots of surprises."

Emilie and Edward paid the bill and they parted ways. "Two days till your show." Emilie looked back as she and her husband walked off. "Happy Anniversary, you two!"

Ashley and Landon were still smiling as they headed the other direction. They took their time, slower than the other tourists and locals. Landon glanced at her as they strolled toward the next intersection. "Look at that." He nudged her, teasing her like he often did. "A happy day in Paris, Ashley. That has to be a good thing."

"It is." Peace flooded Ashley's heart. Alice's story would forever change the narrative of her time here. The information was a gift from God, no doubt. And now their time with Emilie and Edward. "I like those two."

"They're great." He stopped walking at the light. "Okay. Our car will meet us a block from here."

"Another car?" She loved this. "You make every anniversary so special."

"Just wait." He kissed her. "We're about to find some new memories in this city."

Once they were in the car, Landon turned to her. "Do you know what a flaneur is, Ash?"

"Hmm. It's French." She smiled at him. "Oui?"

"Oui. Nice." He angled his head and looked deep into her eyes. "Some people think it means idle. But it goes deeper than that."

She raised her brow, flirting with him. This was how they were together. How they always had been except for a few bad years before they found each other again. "Do tell."

"Okay." He grinned. "A flaneur is someone who enjoys an easy walk, a stroll. And that's what we're going to do first."

He took her to the fifth arrondissement, the busy Latin Quarter, to the Arènes de Lutèce—the place where gladiators fought thousands of years ago. "I can't imagine gladiators were actually real." Ashley stood next to Landon as they read a plaque telling more about the history. "America feels so young."

"It is." He raised one eyebrow. "Come on . . . we have more to see." They walked like true flaneurs down Rue Mouffetard, a market street frequented by tourists. But today it was calm, quiet.

"I could actually get lost here." Ashley took her time, looking at the architecture of the buildings on the street, and checking the occasional market booth. "It's like time has stopped." She looked at Landon. "Do you feel it?"

"Mmm." He crooked his arm around her neck and brought her face to his. "The way I always feel when I'm with you, my love."

She was glad he didn't say it in French. She didn't ever want to hear those words in French again. They didn't stop at the famous Shakespeare and Company bookstore. The line was out the door. "Our car should be here any minute."

"Did you call the driver?" Ashley hadn't noticed Landon on his phone.

"I told you . . . don't worry about a thing, Ash." He pointed to a nearby bench. "Let's sit for a minute."

Not until they were seated did Ashley realize how close they were to the Seine. "Wow . . . this view."

He was watching her, smiling. "Yes . . . breathtaking."

"Landon." Even now, eighteen years his wife, Ashley felt herself blush.

He turned and faced her, and as he did he pulled a small box from his pocket. Then he opened the velvet lid and held it out for her to see.

"What's this?" Ashley put her hand to her mouth and took the box from Landon's hand. Inside was the smallest pendant of a sunburst, covered in crushed diamonds. "Landon . . . it's beautiful."

"It's light." He put his hand alongside her face and kissed her. "Like you."

The piece was stunning. "I've never seen anything like it."

"It's custom. I had it made for you before we left Indiana."

Ashley's heart soared. There was nothing she could ever have done to deserve him. "Thank you. What can I say?"

"This is the year of light, Ash." He eased the necklace from the box and slipped it around Ashley's neck. "Like your art show—Light of the Seine—here in the City of Lights." He searched her eyes. "Like God's Spirit, living inside you. His redemption. Light like you." He slipped the empty box back into his pocket. "Happy Anniversary, Ash. I love you forever and always. More than you could ever know."

Their car pulled up and he held the door as she stepped inside. She felt the tiny necklace and knew she would wear it always. A reminder of the light, indeed.

They traveled across the Seine now and up into the tenth arrondissement. Ashley hadn't been here last time she was in Paris, though Jean-Claude had told her he'd take her to each of the districts. That was only one of the promises he had broken. She pushed the thought from her mind.

"I wondered about taking a boat ride, but the Seine seemed like something everyone would do." Landon peered through the windshield and grinned. "Up ahead is a place most Parisians don't even know about."

A thrill ran through her. "How did you find all this? And the wall the other day?"

"I have my sources." They exited the car and Landon took her hand in his. Again his pace was slow. "I figured with all the excitement yet this week, today we could take an hour and really slow down."

This was so much better than how she'd felt the first day. "Sounds like heaven."

They reached a sign that read CANAL SAINT-MARTIN and just beyond it a slim winding river that ran through the heart of the district. "This way." The joy in his eyes reminded her of how he had looked as a boy. Back in middle school.

Ashley wasn't sure what was better . . . this tour he had put together for her, or the way he looked leading her through Paris. They reached a boat dock and Landon pulled out his phone. The woman at the gate scanned a barcode that must've been in an email receipt. And like that, they were seated, side by side, across the wooden plank of a boat that looked as old as the arched bridges overhead.

"See those?" Landon pointed at the thicket lining the canal. "They're chestnut trees. More than a hundred years old."

"So pretty." She pulled out her phone and snapped a photo. Then she took his hand. "I'll paint them later."

A few times they stopped the boat to visit one of the colorful shops. Boutiques each unique in their offerings. After an hour Ashley had souvenirs for each of the kids and something special for Landon.

They had dinner that evening at La Marine overlooking the canal and the setting sun. There, Ashley pulled out the special gift for Landon. "Here." She wished she would've brought something from home, like he had done. "I have a card for you back at the hotel. And that new drill you've been wanting."

They both laughed.

"But . . ." Ashley figured this would redeem herself. She'd been too busy worrying about Paris to actually plan for their anniversary. "I did find this at one of those shops." She handed him a small bag. "Open it."

Landon took the gift. "You didn't have to, Ash."

"You'll see." She watched his eyes as he pulled an old wooden frame from the bag. "It's made from the wood of one of the canal boats. Apparently, when they take them out of circulation, they make gifts out of them."

"Really?" Landon studied the piece. "And what's this?" He held it up and studied the writing at the bottom. "Paris. Pour toujours. It's in French."

Ashley had asked one of the clerks. "It says *Paris. Forevermore*. We'll have someone take our picture before it's too late. And I'll put the photo in that frame."

His eyes told her that he understood. "Forevermore. Paris will not be ruined by some evil man from your past." Landon put his hand alongside her face. "We'll remember Paris for this. For us."

"Yes." Ashley looked at the sky, the way the fading sunlight streamed through the ancient chestnut trees. "Okay . . . now's our chance." She stood and he did the same. Then she found someone to take their photo as they stood with their backs to the canal, the trees and light and old wooden boats all in the picture.

Paris. Forevermore.

Their anniversary tour ended in the first arrondissement, and Landon had the driver drop them off at a place Ashley remembered all too well. The Pont des Arts. The sky was dusk now, just dark enough for the moment to feel surreal. Like something from a dream.

He walked with her to the start of the footbridge, and she stopped them. She faced the Louvre and then Notre Dame. Then she turned to look at the distant Eiffel Tower. "I've been here. Hours after I landed the first time."

"I wondered." Landon was patient, not rushing the moment.

"I thought . . ." She leaned against the metal railing and Landon took the spot beside her. "I thought Paris men were so romantic. Smiling at me, tipping their hats." She allowed a sad laugh. "I wanted to live here forever."

Ashley doubted this was on Landon's itinerary, but it had to be said. "Jean-Claude Pierre was not romantic. I actually think he was dangerous, Landon."

There it was. The part of her past Ashley never talked about. The possibility that maybe she had actually been in more trouble than she knew.

Landon put his arm around her. "Tell me."

Ashley steadied herself. *I have to do this,* she told herself. *He deserves to know.* "It isn't like . . . I kept it from you, Landon." A cool breeze came off the Seine and she shivered. "I didn't think about this part. I didn't want to think about it."

For a long minute, Ashley said nothing. Fear circled her and pressed tight against her throat.

"I'm here." Landon ran his fingers through her hair. "Whenever you're ready."

"Thank you." She drew a slow breath. If she told him,

maybe she could move past this. Finally let it go. "It happened after I decided not to have the abortion. After I ran out of the clinic."

Landon eased his hold on her and faced her. "You must have felt so alone."

"I did." Her palms felt clammy. "A few nights later I was reporting to work at the gallery. I thought I might still have my job, and earlier Marguerite—the owner—had asked me to be there. They were hosting another show."

In the distance a siren pierced the night air. Ashley clenched her jaw and then forced herself to relax. "Needless to say, Marguerite did not want me. Not ever again. It was like everyone connected with Jean-Claude knew about the baby, and that I had decided not to have an abortion."

"I'm sure you're right. He had a lot of power in the art circles back then, from what you've said."

"Yes." Ashley gripped the railing, so tight her fingers turned white. "He was very powerful." She hesitated. "That evening I was walking back to Ms. Martin's flat, and I realized I was being followed."

"You saw someone?"

"Two men. They were dressed in black. All black." She closed her eyes, but it didn't take away the image in her mind. When she blinked again, she looked at the Seine. Lights from Paris were sparkling on the water. "The men—they looked familiar. I kept checking over my shoulder and they got closer and closer. They had their hands in their pockets like . . . like maybe they had guns. Or knives. And they were staring at me, Landon. Straight at me."

Anger flashed in Landon's eyes. If he could've, he would've gone back in time and taken care of the guys himself. With his bare hands. Ashley could see that.

She faced him and linked her arms around his waist. "The street was dark. No one seemed to notice the trouble I was in. And then, for no reason . . . they stopped. They just stopped following me and turned around. The next time I looked over my shoulder, they were gone."

"So, you never found out who they were?" Landon searched her eyes. "No closure on this story?"

"Not really." She looked out at the river for a long while, and then back at Landon. "I saw them a few more times. They were definitely following me. I could tell. Then I had coffee with a friend I met the first day. Celia. She wanted to be a writer . . . I'm not sure if she became one or not."

"Hmm. What about her?" Landon seemed edgy. "I hate that you were in danger, Ash."

"Celia said something that I've tried to forget." Ashley exhaled. "I told her I was pregnant. That I'd been with Jean-Claude Pierre. And Celia's eyes became so wide, you know? Like this information terrified her."

"Did she say why?" Landon pulled her closer, so their bodies were touching. As if he could protect her from the past. "Did Celia know him?"

"She didn't. Her friend did. A friend she'd had all her life growing up." Ashley felt sick. "Her friend had dated

Jean-Claude the year before and gotten pregnant, too. When . . . when she didn't have an abortion, Celia's friend went missing." Ashley shivered again. "They found her body in the Seine a few days later."

Ashley heard Celia's warning again, as clearly as she'd heard it then. "Celia told me I had to move. 'Leave this place,' she told me. 'Jean-Claude is a famous artist, but he is a very, very bad man. You'll be dead in days . . . and it'll never be traced back to him. That's his way.'"

"What?" Landon started to move, like he might find a police officer and get this figured out here and now. But then he relaxed and kept his hold on Ashley. No one was going to hurt her while she was in Landon's arms. That was for sure. "Ash . . . you should've told me. We could've hired someone, checked into it and made sure the danger was past."

"Yes." She nodded. "I should have. I just . . . I didn't want to think about it." She thought for a moment. "I did look him up once, to see if anyone had ever filed criminal charges against him."

"And?" Landon's heart was beating harder. Ashley could feel it.

"Actually, someone had. And a host of cases were finally solved. After his death, Jean-Claude was linked to the murder of at least three girls."

Landon didn't state the obvious. That Ashley could've been the fourth. He was trembling now. "Baby . . . I'm so sorry." He kissed her forehead and then her lips. "You're safe now. That's in the past."

Ashley had thought that if she finally told Landon, her fear over the matter would fade. In a single moment, even. And she wouldn't have to feel sick about that part of her time in Paris ever again. But that wasn't how she felt. If anything, the fear and terror of those last months in Paris were alive once more.

As if the two men were still following her.

"I'm sorry. For not telling you." She shook her head. "I didn't tell anyone. Like maybe if I just never talked about it, I could believe it never happened." A sad laugh came from her. "And now I ruined our anniversary."

"Hey." He ran his hand over her hair and took her face in his hands. "You did not ruin our anniversary. Hardly." He kissed her, longer this time. "You made it better."

"Better?" Ashley felt her heart growing lighter. "How in the world did telling you that terrible scary story make it better?" She stepped back and this time her laugh was more carefree. "I can't wait to hear this."

"Well . . . see . . . " He nuzzled his face up alongside hers and kissed her neck. "Now, we have nothing secret between us. It's like a moment." He kissed the other side of her neck and then her lips. "Here on the Pont des Arts . . . the Love Lock Bridge. A new memory."

Everything bad and frightening about the story she'd told him left her entirely. She grinned at him. "I like that."

"Me, too." He took her hand and led her out onto the center of the bridge. "And to commemorate such an occasion, and since putting locks on this bridge is still allowed . . ." He stopped and felt in his other pocket. Then he pulled out a slim silver lock and a key. "I brought this."

"Landon!" She couldn't believe it. "What else do you have in there?"

He raised his brow. "That, my love"—he lowered his voice—"I will show you later."

She laughed out loud. "You're so funny. Please . . . always make me laugh."

"I will." He chuckled. "That's my job." He handed her the lock. "Read it."

The silver lock was so small Ashley struggled to read the words engraved on the front. Landon turned on his phone's flashlight and there it was, the message in the prettiest font. Delicate and beautiful and deep, like everything about this trip.

Tears filled Ashley's eyes and she hugged Landon for a long time. Then the two of them attached the small lock to the Pont des Arts. They used the key to set it forever in place, and Ashley threw the tiny key into the Seine. There was nothing else to say as they walked back to the hotel.

The message on the lock had said it all.

7-13-21

FORGIVING PARIS

17

Landon could feel the change in Ashley even before she fell asleep in his arms that night. Every dark and dangerous detail she'd been carrying since her first time here was gone now. As if she'd passed it from her own heart to his.

The information she'd shared concerned him. No doubt the Pierre guy had intended to harm her. Landon thought back to his own life during that time, when she would've been going through that, when two men would've been following her.

Possibly planning to kill her.

He ran his fingers over her bare arm and stared at the ceiling. College was busy that semester, and he had spent more time with Hope. His buddy Jalen had talked him into being a volunteer firefighter and God was whispering to him that maybe this was how he would spend his life. Fighting fires. Rescuing people.

One night the truth of that had come over him, as if he were getting a message straight from the Lord Himself, the ultimate Rescuer. Yes, for sure, he would spend his life helping people. Pulling them out of burning buildings and helping them however he could. Even if it cost him his life.

But that night in his dorm room, Landon's revelation was accompanied by the saddest thought. The one person he could not help, the one who wouldn't take his phone calls and might never come home again, was the girl he still loved. No matter how much time he spent with Hope Freeman.

Then he had an idea. Actually, there was something he could do. He climbed out of his upper bunk, careful not to wake his roommate. Landon slipped into the common area and near the beaten-up old sofa, he fell to his knees.

There, for almost an hour, he begged God to protect Ashley Baxter.

He had no idea what she was going through or why she had so completely severed ties with him and with her family. But Landon knew the One who had the answers. The One who could see Ashley even that very moment, and who could do the thing Landon could not.

The God who could protect her.

Landon could see himself, there on his knees, tears in his eyes, calling out to God on behalf of Ashley. A chill ran down his arms and legs. Was that one of the days the men in black had been following her? It was possible. Either way, God had answered his prayers from that night and many nights after it.

Not only had He watched over Ashley, He had saved her life. He had brought her back home and now . . .

Landon held her close . . . now she was here in his arms. Only God could've done that.

But what about the men? Landon stared at his beautiful wife. If they'd been ordered to kill her, had they passed that job on to someone in the States after Ashley left? His heart beat faster than before and he realized he'd been holding his breath.

Gradually he exhaled. Surely not. More than two decades had passed since Ashley had been here, and Jean-Claude had been dead for much of that. Everything was fine. The story had shaken him, for sure, but Ashley was not in danger now. Obviously.

Still, that night, despite every wonderful thing about their anniversary, and even with Ashley in his arms, Landon dreamed that he was wrong. That other bad men were being paid by some evil employee of Jean-Claude's estate, someone still checking off a master hit list, maybe. And now with Ashley back in Paris, indeed, someone was after her once again.

In the dream, Landon was walking with Ashley down cobblestone streets and narrow dark paths at night. He would hear footsteps behind them and turn around, but no one would be there. Then they were at a restaurant, only the place was cavernous, and cobwebs hung from the ceiling. Landon had to use the restroom, but the pathway there was barely passable and the ceiling kept getting lower.

When he finally returned to their table, Ashley was gone.

He raced from one side of the building to the other, crying out for her, screaming her name . . . but he still couldn't find her. *The police,* he thought to himself. They could help him! But his phone wasn't where it was supposed to be, and even when he ran outside there wasn't another person anywhere.

"Help me! Someone help!" He shouted into the empty street. "Ashley!"

That's when he woke up, out of breath, his heart racing. The sheets clung to the sweat on his bare stomach. What had happened? Landon reached for his wife as he opened his eyes and she was there. Ashley was fine, asleep beside him. It had all been a nightmare.

Nothing more.

But even after they got morning lattes at Terres de Café and headed to the Louvre, Landon struggled to shake the feeling. Ashley could've been killed. He worked to stay in the moment, smiling at his wife and trying to share her excitement about the museum morning ahead.

"You could spend a week at the Louvre and never see it all." She practically danced beside him. Her pretty face somehow looked a decade younger, as if everything that had weighed her down, every bad memory and terrifying secret was finally and fully gone.

They were walking up to the main entrance and Ashley stopped. "Can you believe it?" She looked at Landon. "We're really here!"

"We are." The bad dream was leaving him. They didn't have much longer in Paris. Just the show tomorrow and one day after that. He wouldn't waste another minute being concerned over nothing. "You know something, Ash?" He felt himself relax a little more.

"What?" She turned to him.

"I've always wanted to take you to the Louvre." He put his hands on her shoulders. "You, my artist girl, my love." He smiled. "I think I was in high school the first time I thought about it. How one day I wanted to bring you here."

"Really?" Ashley looked smitten, the way she had on their wedding day.

"Yes." Landon remembered something else. "I did a paper on the Louvre my junior year in high school." He chuckled as the details grew clearer. "I was obsessed, Ashley. Chasing you . . . hardest thing I did in all my life."

She winced. "Yeah . . . sorry about that." Her eyes lit up again. "I guess I forgot about that English paper. Do you remember any of it?"

"Let's see." He narrowed his eyes. "The Louvre was originally a fortress built sometime around the year 1200. Then three or four hundred years later it was redesigned to be a grand royal palace. The goal was that the Louvre be breathtaking, one of a kind. With every change of monarchy, the Louvre was made bigger, more ornate until there wasn't another building on earth like it."

Ashley looked back at the front of the museum. "Mission accomplished."

When they stepped inside, they read a plaque on the wall. "Looks like it became a museum in 1801."

"Mmm." Ashley looked intently at the description. "Today it's the largest museum in the world. Thirty-five thousand art pieces on display." She shook her head. "I can't even imagine that."

"Well." He took her hand. "We have to at least try. What time are we meeting Alice and her mother?"

"Four o'clock." Ashley walked with him through the museum entrance. "So much to see, so little time to see it!"

Over the next five hours, they first visited Leonardo da Vinci's famous *Mona Lisa*. Ashley stared at the eyes in the painting. "What did she know?" She linked arms with Landon. "Do you ever wonder that? What was behind that expression of hers?"

"No, my love." Landon hid his laugh, in keeping with the quiet of the museum. "I must say I never wondered. But now . . . I always will."

In the same room was the *Les Noces de Cana* by Paolo Veronese—a realistic painting of the biblical wedding at Cana. The place where Jesus performed his first miracle. Landon studied the piece. "I've never really looked at this painting. Like in textbooks back in college."

"I have." Ashley pointed to the lower right side of the piece. "Look at that cat, all smiling and happy. And the friendly dogs and little birds." She folded her arms. "Reminders that all are welcome around Jesus."

He shifted his attention to her. "You know what I love most about today?"

She smiled at him. "The coffee?"

"No." He smiled. "Seeing the Louvre through your eyes. That's what I'll remember most."

Next they visited *La Dentellière* by Johannes Vermeer in the Richelieu wing.

"The Lacemaker." Ashley didn't need to read the sign beneath the work. "Renoir thought this was one of the most beautiful pieces in the world."

Landon could see why. The painting was of a woman in the seventeenth century, dressed in yellow fabric with white lace. She was sitting at a sewing desk using bobbins to stitch a lacy pillow. Landon took a step closer. "The detailing is incredible. Like she's sitting here working in front of us."

"Yes." Ashley stayed at his side. The Louvre was filled with tourists, of course, but here there were only a few people. Ashley let herself get lost in the art piece. "I always thought we would be friends, the woman in this painting and me."

Only Ashley would say something like that. Landon's heart swelled. "Friends? You and her?"

"Look at her face. She's so intent on making sure her creation is just right. But there are no lines on her forehead or near her eyes." Ashley looked at him. "She's not worried or fretting. She just loves what she does. And she wants her work to show it."

Amazing, Landon thought. "If that's the case, then yes. The two of you would've been best friends."

"Right?" Ashley turned to the painting again. "She could work on her lace in one room. I'd paint in the other."

She grinned. "Then we'd take a walk around Square des Batignolles and talk about the beauty we'd created that day."

In the Sully wing they joined a crowd of people looking at the popular *Venus de Milo*, the nude statue of a woman missing her arms. Landon put his hands on his hips and stared at the work. "I never really got it about this one. I mean . . . technically, it's broken."

"The art world would disagree." Ashley smiled, her eyes never leaving the sculpture. "They called her Aphrodite, the Greek ideal of beauty. Sculpted in 100 B.C., found on Greece's island of Milos and presented to King Louis the Eighteenth in 1821."

"Ash."

"Yes." She turned to him.

"If we ever move to Paris, you could work here." He touched her cheek. "All that information in your pretty head."

"We had to study famous art in junior college, the different time periods and classics. I knew even more back then." She looked at the statue again. "I remember a lot of what I learned . . . because it mattered to me."

Of course it did. He looked at the piece once more. "She may have been the ideal." He put his arm around her. "But old Venus has nothing on you. Just saying."

"At least I have arms." She tried not to laugh, tried to stay serious.

"A whole lot more than that." He kissed the side of her head. "Let's go to the bedroom."

Ashley spun around. "Landon!"

"Not that bedroom." He covered his smile. "The bedroom of Charles the Ninth!"

The Chambre de Parade du Roi was where King Charles IX greeted the court every morning. "Strange place to hold a meeting." Landon cocked his head and studied the room. "But I've never seen anything so ornate in all my life."

The walls dripped with massive gold embellishments, fine detail, and accoutrements. Red velvet curtains hung from the towering ceilings. "That chandelier must have hundreds of candle lights." She touched her new necklace. "Light. The theme continues."

From the bedroom, they wandered through many parts of the royal palace including Napoleon III's apartment, the Grand Salon, and his dining rooms. Landon wasn't an art critic by any means, and he didn't make it to many museums. But even to him, every inch of the royal quarters was breathtaking.

Almost as much so as Ashley's expression as she took it all in. "I never made it inside the Louvre when I lived here. I couldn't afford it." She took his hand as they left the museum later that afternoon. "Touring the Louvre . . . this was on my bucket list, Landon."

"And taking you here . . . that was on mine." He worked his fingers between hers, thankful for her. For their life together.

And for their two bucket list items that—after today—could finally be checked off.

. . .

LANDON HAD LOOKED forward to this meal.

Alice had told him she'd made reservations at the exact address of the boulangerie where she and Ashley had worked. In the twenty-three years since then, someone had obviously renovated the place. Now it was a vibey café with bright windows and shiplap wooden walls. They met at a corner table and introductions were made. Marie Michel was a carbon copy of her daughter, older but pleasant and pretty, with kind brown eyes.

They ordered pastries, croissants, and chicken salad—the house specialty according to the waitress. Jessie and Gabriel wouldn't join them today, and Landon was grateful for the time alone with Marie and Alice. He had a feeling that after today, Ashley would have yet another reason to know the truth.

Paris hadn't been all bad.

Alice clearly wanted her mother to tell her side of the story, what it was like having a daughter addicted to heroin and how she had felt when Alice came home.

Landon kept his eyes on Ashley. She had found her laugh in the last few days. Gone were the worry lines on her forehead and the concern in her eyes. It should've been the same for Landon. Typically, if Ashley was happy, he was happy.

But he caught himself checking the door, staring out the windows and looking for strange men who might be following them. *Ridiculous*, he told himself. Two decades later? The people in the Pierre camp would've forgotten about Ashley by now. *It's the dream,* he told himself. *That's what this is about.*

He took a deep breath and settled in next to Ashley. Enough of that. Marie was about to tell her story.

Landon didn't want to miss a word.

18

Marie Michel rarely revisited the heartbreak of Alice's lost years. Most days it seemed like that time had never happened. Like Alice had gone from being the charming middle school girl to the lovely young woman she was today.

Without any break in between.

But it did happen, and now she would share that time again with their new friends—Ashley and Landon Blake. Marie steadied herself.

"I told my mère how I wouldn't be alive today if it wasn't for you, Ashley." Alice looked into Marie's eyes. "I thought together we could tell the rest of the story."

"Oui." Marie had no words to adequately thank Ashley for the impact she'd made on Alice. But maybe telling the story would help. "I remember that afternoon, the day Alice came home. She . . . she knocked on the door and just waited. Skin and bones, dressed in rags. But her belly . . . I could see she was with child."

"My heart was pounding out of my chest." Alice's smile faded. "Every time I thought about coming home I told myself ma mère would turn me away. That she hated me for what I'd done to her."

Marie gave Alice a gentle squeeze. "That was never true, of course." She faced her daughter. "I took Alice in my arms before I said a single word. And we stood there." She removed her arm from Alice and faced her. "We just stood there on the front step, both of us crying."

Across the table, Ashley nodded. "It was that way for my family, too. When I came home from Paris."

There was a break in the conversation as their food arrived. When the waitress was gone again, Ashley looked at Marie. "What was that like, having her gone for so many years? Not knowing if she was okay?"

"It was hell." Marie shrugged slightly. "I apologize for the word. But it is the only one that fits that time in my life."

Hurt flashed in Alice's eyes. "I'll always be sorry for that, Mère."

"I know, baby girl." Marie gave her daughter a sad smile. Then she turned to Ashley again. "I had to change the locks." In some ways, those days felt like yesterday. "The police said that way she'd have no money to buy drugs."

Alice folded her arms. "Of course it didn't work that way. I found the drugs. On the street, there's always a way to find them."

"Exactly. As you know . . . my girl was living under an overpass. She overdosed and nearly died." Marie's heart stuck in her throat for a minute. "When she woke up in the hospital, she learned she was pregnant. I didn't know about any of that."

"I wasn't on drugs, but my family must've felt that way about me, too." Ashley's voice was tender.

Marie smiled at the American. "Most nights when I couldn't sleep, I would slip across my bedroom floor and find our photo album, the one I kept in my dresser drawer." She paused. "Pictures of my daughter through the good years. Before she found heroin. There are many tears on that book."

Marie explained that after Alice returned, there was no looking back. "I loved her then, I loved her still. All I wanted was to help her."

Across from Marie, Ashley nodded. "My mom and dad felt the same way."

"It's a parent's job. To love our children, no matter what. When Alice returned, she wanted help." This wasn't a time to cry, but the story would never be easy. "God answered my prayers."

The rest of the tale came out in broken bits and pieces as Marie remembered the details. She had helped Alice find her way back to school, and not long after, Marie had met a wonderful man and the two married. "Money was less tight. Alice had the best schools. She became a teacher and she met Paul Arquette."

"My husband." Alice smiled. "The love of my life."

Marie explained that Paul had loved Gabriel from the moment he met the boy. "Paul is the only father Gabriel has ever known."

Ashley looked at her husband and the two shared a brief embrace. "Landon is my Paul."

"I thought so." Marie smiled. "Ashley, I began praying for Alice before her overdose, before she found out she was pregnant. Long before she came home." Marie hesitated. "But you . . . you were the answer to my prayers. I wanted to look into your eyes and thank you. From this mother's heart, thank you for giving me my girl back."

Tears shone in both Ashley's eyes and Landon's. "Your story is very important to us." Landon cleared his throat. "Thank you . . . for sharing it."

"And now look . . ." Marie laughed and it eased the heaviness at the table. "God has brought you two friends back together. And our Gabriel is dating your niece. We need only look to see the miracles of our God."

They ate their dinner, and Ashley invited Marie and Alice to her show. They both agreed to go. "We wouldn't miss it!" Alice reached across the table and took brief hold of Ashley's hand. "You're having an art show in Paris, Ashley. Look at us! All because of God."

Indeed. Marie sat back and watched her daughter laugh and talk with her American friend. *Thank You, Father, for this.* She kept her prayer silent as she blinked back tears. What if she hadn't fallen to her knees that long-ago night in her chilly bedroom? And suddenly Marie wished for just one thing. That she could tell her own mother how things had worked out, how they were still working out.

All because Marie had finally been willing to pray.

• • •

THE MORNING OF her gallery show, Ashley woke up just before sunrise. Landon was still asleep, so she slipped out of the bedroom and moved to the desk on the other side of the door. It sat near the window, and from there Ashley could watch Paris come to life.

Somewhere out there, people are making plans to attend my show tonight, she thought. *How is that even possible, God?*

Her heart felt deep and full, like she could stare out the window and cry a million tears over the faithfulness of the Lord and the love of Landon and her family. If only her dad and Cole could be here today. The two of them would make her feel like her own mother was actually here.

Which she was.

Mom . . . you'll always be with me. And tonight . . . you'll have a window. I believe that.

Tears trickled onto Ashley's cheeks and she blinked them back. No matter how many years it had been, she felt close to her mother this morning. Hearing Marie's story had done that for her. Listening to Alice's mother say many of the things her own mother would've said if she were still alive.

The heartache of the silent months, the longing for a daughter lost, the photo albums with proof of happier times. All of it had been Ashley's mom's life, as well. If Ashley could have it to do over again . . . If only she had another shot at that year, she never would've let so much time go by without calling home.

Of course the messages from her mother had gotten

through to Ashley. She simply hadn't wanted to call back. Selfish and young, caught in a web of immorality and wretched decisions. The last thing she wanted was to hear her parents' voices on the other end of the line.

Especially her mother's.

Ashley wiped at her tears. Light was piercing the darkness over Paris. A smile tugged at her lips. Wasn't that the truth, though. She felt for her new necklace again. The sunrise was nothing to the way heaven's light had shattered the darkness of her days in Paris.

She closed her eyes for a moment and let the memories come again. Not about Jean-Claude, but about her time at the boulangerie. The days when the men were following her. When she wondered if she'd live to see the morning.

Of course, she remembered giving Alice the Bible and showing her the pregnancy book. She had purchased the guide because she had no idea what to do. What to eat or how to care for the child growing within her. And by then she was too ashamed to call home.

Ms. Martin had turned into a completely different person when she heard about Ashley's baby. And she definitely knew—before Ashley even had the chance to tell her.

"Marguerite informed me of your pregnancy." Gone were the warmth and camaraderie. The woman rolled her eyes. "You will pack your things and be gone in the morning, Ashley." Her look screamed disappointment. "I had such hopes for you."

Ashley looked at the city lights again. With nowhere to turn, she had hauled her suitcases to the hostel twelve blocks away, not far from the bakery. She was running out of money and had no friends, no phone to call home even if she could muster the courage to do so.

And it was in that desperate place, across the street from the hostel, that she saw the old bookstore. "I need help, God," she had whispered. "If You love me, show me."

She walked into the bookstore with eleven francs in her pocket. Just eleven francs. Somehow she found the used pregnancy book. *Six francs.* And then, on the next aisle tucked between dusty cookbooks, was a Bible. In English. Seven francs, the orange sticker read.

Too much. Ashley's heart sank. She was about to pay for the pregnancy book when a shop clerk walked up. "You want that Bible, mademoiselle?" The man was probably in his seventies, but he had a sparkle in his eyes. Like he loved being surrounded by old books.

"I do." She felt so ashamed. A pregnant American with nowhere to turn. "I . . . I can't afford it. Maybe another time."

The man reached for the Bible. "Here." He handed it to her. "Today is buy one, get one free." He grinned. "For you, mademoiselle."

When Ashley walked out of the store, she knew two things. First, God had heard her feeble prayer outside the bookstore. And second, she wasn't alone.

The sun was breaking across the Seine, and Ashley leaned back in her chair. Her eyes were dry now, and it no longer felt like she was looking out over today's city. But the one that had been so hard on her years ago.

Whether she was alone or not, every hour was hard back then. Finding clothes clean enough to wear to work . . . getting food within her meager budget. Trying to sleep in a bed surrounded by strangers.

But when Ashley met Alice something happened. For the first time since her plane had touched ground in the City of Light, Ashley had a reason to think of someone else. Rather than waking up hating herself and wondering how she was going to raise a child on her own, Ashley began climbing out of bed thinking about Alice.

The girl had been even worse off than Ashley.

Since they were both pregnant, she began taking her new book with her to the restaurant. Together they talked about how big their babies might be at that point and what was going to happen in each of the trimesters of their pregnancies.

But then Ashley had realized something. Alice needed more than knowledge about her baby if she was going to survive. Heroin called to the girl day and night. So even though she was still angry at God about the accident, and though she was the farthest thing from a Christian, Ashley knew there was only one Source strong enough to help Alice with that sort of addiction.

The Bible.

Ashley leaned forward and rested her elbows on the windowsill. *God, I could never have known what was at stake. That Alice was about to take her life.* Her eyes stung again at the magnitude of it all. *You used me to save her life. When I was my ugliest, my absolute worst.*

Ashley, precious daughter, I never stopped loving you.

The voice was as clear as the view across Paris. *God . . . You're here. I can feel You. Thank You, Lord . . . for redeeming my time here. I . . . I didn't deserve You then and I don't deserve You now.*

She could remember when it all changed, when she knew that she couldn't live another day without Jesus.

The men had been following her, Ashley was sure. They wanted to harm her. Finally Ashley knew she had to call home. Never mind how long it had been or the wicked things she had done since she last spoke with her parents. She had needed to hear her mother's voice more than she needed her next breath.

At a bank, she exchanged several francs for coins, and she practically ran down three streets to the nearest pay phone. Inside the booth, with shaking fingers, she had dialed home.

Her mom answered on the first ring. "Hello? Ashley . . . is this you?"

The sound of her mother's voice was as vivid now as it had been then, and again tears spilled onto Ashley's cheeks. *You never stopped believing in me, Mom. No matter what I had done . . . no matter how I hurt you.* If only her mom could have been here yesterday to share together the goodness of God's rescue of Ashley and Alice.

The memory continued. "Yes . . . it's me." Ashley hadn't known how to explain the awful decisions she'd made, so she didn't try. Instead she said the only thing that mattered. "Please . . . I want to come home."

Arrangements for a flight came together quickly. Her parents paid for the ticket and had it waiting for her at the airport the next day.

The only hard part had been leaving Alice. Ashley went back to the boulangerie to put in her notice and tell the owner thank you. But Alice wasn't working. "Good things are happening to that girl." Her boss shook his head. "I have to think that's because of you, Ashley."

Of course, Ashley had doubted that. There had been no final conversation with her friend, no way to know what had happened to her. Not until a few days ago. And to think . . . the son saved back then was now dating Jessie.

Streaks of dusty pink worked their way across the sky and a sense of wonder came over Ashley. Her mom must've been praying for her back then. Her dad and Landon, too. Because Ashley never should've made it home.

She remembered the flight back to Indiana, her suitcases in the belly of the plane. Her paintings safe and intact. There, thirty thousand feet off the ocean surface, Ashley realized exactly what she had done. The gravity of it. The guilt.

Jean-Claude was married. She had no right touring Paris with him and kissing him. Sharing a bed with him. All of it was disgusting, and finally, there on that airplane, she could see the truth clearly.

The tears she cried in the air between Paris and New York, her first stop, were enough to make her flight attendant concerned. "Miss, do you need help?"

Ashley only shook her head every time the woman asked. *There is only One who can help me now*, she had thought. And for the entire seven hours on that flight, she had called out to Him. *Forgive me, God . . . I'm so sorry. Please help me.*

Finally, when the plane was an hour from landing, a peace came over Ashley and she heard a voice, the same one she'd just heard here in her hotel room.

I sent my Son to die . . . so that you would be forgiven, daughter. The past is gone . . . along with every bad decision. You are free.

The words still soothed the edges of her soul and gave her a reason to draw breath. She was free. Then and now and always. God forgave her. What she'd done in Paris was forgotten.

Forever.

No, Ashley hadn't gone home with a perfect faith or a willingness to step back into her old church circle. She still felt like an outcast, even after her parents had greeted her at the airport with love and understanding. Even when they saw that she was pregnant. But her siblings had struggled to understand. Ashley's story had been difficult for all of them.

Especially Landon.

It had taken years before she stopped fighting against God and the person He was calling her to be. But one thing was certain. From the moment she laid her sins down on that transatlantic flight, she was free.

And she was forgiven.

Ashley drew a deep breath. In the far distance she could see the Eiffel Tower. Funny. She never took the trip to the top. Another promise Jean-Claude hadn't kept. But that was behind her now. She smiled again. Before they left Paris, she and Landon would visit the iconic landmark, and the famous Eiffel Tower Carousel, just in front of it. She had thought herself too old to ride the white horses of the merry-go-round when she was here last time.

That wasn't true now. She would never be too old to see life through the eyes of a child.

She stared over the city. Jean-Claude was the utter counterfeit of love. He was a liar, like the devil. A fake and a fraud, intent on destroying a young American girl. And she had been his willing partner.

But Landon . . . Landon was the real deal. Full of love and faith and compassion.

Yes, she would miss her mom and dad and Cole tonight. But when the doors to Light of the Seine opened for her very first Parisian show, Landon would be standing beside her. And that was so much more than enough.

Thank You, God. Thank You for forgiving me. Thank You for giving me this life. And thank You for Landon Blake. Him most of all. She stood and stretched. This was about to be one of the greatest days in all her life.

Ashley had never been more sure.

19

The timing had to be perfect. Cole already knew that.

So when his car made a sputtering noise three hours out of Bloomington, he felt a wave of concern. *No, please, God. Keep the engine working.*

As if on command, the engine kicked into gear once more. Smooth and without a sound. *Thank You.* Cole smiled. This trip wasn't going to work out without help from the Lord. That much was sure.

Cole checked the time. He had been on the road for most of the day. The plan was tight. Another meeting had been added by the leadership team at Liberty yesterday. So he couldn't leave campus till this morning. "I'll be on the road early. Don't worry," he had told his grandpa John last night after he was back in his dorm. "Everything will be fine."

Cole rolled down the window. It was just past three in the afternoon. The plan was to arrive in Bloomington by six that night, leave the house at 7:30, and be at the airport by nine. They were booked first to New York, and then an overnight flight to Paris, one that left just before midnight.

So, every minute was critical.

The engine still sounded good, purring right along. Good thing, because coming up was the last exit with an open gas station for thirty miles. Cole turned up the car speaker. He was listening to Matthew West's *All In* album and a song came on, one that he loved.

"The Beautiful Things We Miss" it was called. He settled back in his seat and let the song play across the surface of his heart. The first verse talked about a couple—maybe in their forties like his parents. Only in the song, the man doesn't notice his wife. Doesn't care about her like he should.

Thank You, God, that my parents aren't like that, he thought. *They love each other so much.*

The chorus was what really spoke to him. Cole turned it up again and sang along. The message was beautiful, about not missing the things that mattered, the things right in front of him. "Open up my eyes, Lord," he sang at the top of his lungs. "Keep me in the moment just like this. Before the beautiful things we love . . . become the beautiful things we miss."

It should've been an anthem for college students like him. Just yesterday he had been home, heading off to high school each morning and sharing dinners with his parents and siblings. Every single night. But now . . . now he was almost finished with college and his girlfriend was talking about marriage. "We don't get this back!" he sang.

His voice wasn't the best. But he loved to sing, especially on I-64 west on the long car ride home. No danger he'd fall asleep singing songs like this one. Traffic was light as he passed the exit. He couldn't break down now. Not if he was going to make the flight.

Cole settled back into his seat. The day had been hot, nearly ninety degrees when he stopped for food in Charleston, West Virginia. But it was cooler now, and the breeze that filled the car smelled summer sweet. He turned the radio down and listened.

Good. The smooth sound of his engine was almost better than the song. At least this afternoon. He switched playlists. Ben Rector this time and another favorite song. "More Like Love." The whole world needed this song. A song that called for more love. More kindness. And the prayer . . . to actually look a little more like love.

Cole was about to sing the second line in the chorus when the engine jolted and jerked so hard it nearly stopped the car. *No . . . not now. Please . . . God, I need You.*

But whatever had happened, the engine was finished. Cole barely had time to get the car to the shoulder before it died altogether. His heart pounded as traffic whizzed past. Cole tightened his grip on the wheel. What could it be? He tried starting it again and again. Nothing.

He studied the gauges. Everything looked fine. He even had plenty of gas. Almost as much as back when . . .

"The gas gauge!" That was it! Why hadn't he figured it out sooner? When he stopped for food, he'd only given a quick look at how much gas he had. But after hours of driving, he should've needed a refill.

Instead, he hadn't even topped off his tank.

Now as he looked at the gauge he could easily see the problem. It read the same as it had on campus that morning. He let his head fall back against the seat. What was he going to do now? He was miles past the last exit and the afternoon sunlight was waning fast. He grabbed his cell phone and used his GPS to figure out where he was exactly. Then he called the gas station at the last exit.

"Please . . . someone answer."

Finally, a man picked up on the other end. "Harvey. Texaco." The guy sounded tired. "How can I help you?"

Cole explained the situation. "It wouldn't be so bad, but I have a flight to catch."

"Sorry? Can you say it again?" The man had a drawl that was almost impossible to understand. "You're breaking up."

The call dropped. Cole forced himself to take slow breaths. Getting worked up wouldn't help anything. He was about to call Harvey at the Texaco again when a tow truck pulled up behind him. *Yes.* Cole's shoulders dropped as an ocean of relief came over him. He must've gotten enough details to the man, after all. Despite the bad connection.

A tall blond man walked up to the car and stopped at Cole's window. "Out of gas, is that right, son?"

"Yes." Cole couldn't look away from the man's eyes. Like they weren't of this world. "Um . . . did Harvey send you?"

"Harvey?" The man smiled. "No. Your father called. Said you were out of gas and needed help."

"My father?" Cole couldn't make sense of the story, but it didn't matter. "I'm . . . I'm trying to catch a flight out of Indiana in a few hours. My gas gauge broke and I'm completely empty."

"Then I'm your guy." The man gave a slight salute. "I've got five gallons in the back of my truck. That should get you to the next station."

"Definitely. Thank you." Cole was in shock. Who had called the man and how did he have just enough gas to get his car to the next station? He was about to climb out to help the guy when the man looked back at him and shook his head.

"Stay in your seat. I've got this." He glanced at the traffic. "Most dangerous place on the interstate is the shoulder."

The man was right. Following his orders, Cole stayed seat belted in his car and watched the guy fill his tank with the contents of three containers.

When the stranger was finished, he walked back to Cole's window. "Your father knows about your flight, Cole. You'll make it just fine." He patted Cole's hand, which was still on the steering wheel. "Keep your eyes open. There's more going on around you than you'll ever know."

"Yes, sir." Cole caught a glimpse of the man's name tag. The one stitched into his tow truck shirt. A simple name, just three letters.

JAG. And his company was Blue Sky Towing.

Cole shook the man's hand and again he had the

strangest feeling. Like this guy wasn't any ordinary person. Cole chuckled. "Anyway . . . thank you. I'm not sure how it all worked out, but you were exactly who I needed to see. Again, thanks."

"You asked for help." The man grinned at Cole and made the strange salute sign again. "So here I am. At your service, Cole. Have fun in Paris."

"Yeah. I will. Thanks . . . Jag." Cole watched him climb back into the tow truck and pull out into traffic. But even before he could do the same thing, Cole's mind began to race. When had he told the man his name? And he was sure he hadn't told him about Paris.

Just that he needed to catch a flight.

Also how in the world could his dad have contacted the man? His father was in France. He never would've known the trouble Cole was in or even that he was headed to his mother's show. Let alone that he was out of gas somewhere on the interstate, hours from home.

His heartbeat wouldn't slow down as he merged back into traffic. Jag hadn't asked for any sort of payment. He'd have to look up Blue Sky Towing later, when they were on the way to the airport. He'd call tomorrow and find out what he owed. Maybe he could pay a little extra as a tip for Jag. Or maybe jump on a call with the guy and ask him a few questions. Like how the whole thing had played out and where he had actually heard about Cole's roadside trouble.

He found another Matthew West song and sang along. Not until he pulled into his grandpa John's driveway did he remember Jag and Blue Sky Towing and the strangest help he'd ever gotten.

When they were both in the car headed to the airport, Cole looked at his grandfather. "I almost didn't make it."

"Wow. That would've been bad." His papa looked at him. "What happened?"

Cole told him the whole story, right up to the part where Jag told him his father had reached out.

"Your father?" Grandpa John kept his eyes on the road. "Cole. That's impossible. Your dad doesn't even know you're coming."

"I thought about that after he left." Cole felt chills on his arms. "He said some other strange things." One at a time, Cole remembered them. "He told me to stay in my seat, said that the shoulder was the most dangerous place for people on the interstate."

"True." His papa nodded. "What else?"

Cole stared out the windshield. "He said my father knew about my flight. Then he told me I'd make it there just fine. And he said something else. He told me to keep my eyes open. Because there was more going on around me than I'd ever know."

Grandpa John was quiet for a long time. "Your dad didn't call that man, Cole."

"I know." It took Cole a few minutes, but eventually he turned to his papa. "Do you think . . . maybe the man was . . . ?"

For a while his grandfather didn't say anything, either. Then he shot a quick look at Cole. "Who else?"

"So you think he was—"

"An angel?" His papa raised his brow. "I guess there's just one way to know for sure. Contact Blue Sky Towing." He laughed, but it was more the sound of sheer amazement. "I'll say one thing for sure. Someone wants you to make that flight to Paris."

"Definitely." Cole grabbed his phone and did a search for the tow truck companies in the area of the interstate where he'd broken down. There was A-1 Towing and Impound Towing and half a dozen others. But one was very plainly missing. The one Jag worked for.

Blue Sky Towing.

20

Albert had figured it out.

Each of his original plans had flaws.

He had thought that in the hour before Ashley Baxter's show he might walk past the catering van at the back of the gallery and slide a bag with the poisoned cheesecake inside with the other pastries and drinks. The bag would be marked with the artist's name. But the caterer might know that cheesecake wasn't on the list of items being delivered to the gallery. He couldn't afford a missed opportunity.

Not this time.

Another option also fell flat—planting an incendiary device in the American artist's car, so that when she left the show, she wouldn't make it back to her hotel. But that sort of hit worked best if the victim had a longer drive, ideally through the countryside. It was too risky in the city, too many ways of being caught.

Now, though, he had the perfect plan.

Thallium, of course. The tasteless, odorless poison wouldn't kill Ashley tonight. But a week from now, when she was back in the States, she would fall sick. Food poisoning, it would seem. Her demise would follow soon after and no one would suspect foul play.

They never did.

Albert was in his Jean-Claude room again, pacing the floor, going over the details for tonight. In his hand was a vial of thallium with the finest possible needle at one end. Albert would mix in with the people awaiting her arrival at the red carpet and in the happy chaos, he would appear to be jostled by the crowd straight into Ashley Baxter.

He would apologize, but the damage would be done.

She wouldn't feel a thing.

• • •

SINCE HER SHOW wasn't until that evening, Ashley had plans with Landon for the day, more of his surprises in honor of their anniversary. After breakfast at the café across the street, they took a ride to eastern Paris and Parc des Buttes-Chaumont in the nineteenth district.

Landon brought a bag of hot sweet beignets. The smell took Ashley back to that first day, hours after she'd gotten off the plane when she was twenty. This time she was getting to do more than smell them. She and Landon shared them in the car, and they were delicious.

Everything about this time in Paris was better. Even the food.

When they got out of the car, Jessie and Gabe were waiting at a picnic table twenty yards away. Ashley spotted them and waved. Then she turned to Landon. "What's this?"

Landon grinned at her. "Gabriel turns out to be a very smart young man."

"Oh, really?" Ashley had no idea where this was going. "How so?"

"Well . . ." Landon stood a little straighter. "Gabriel wants to talk to me about Jessie. About how to do things right. You know." He chuckled. "Seriously. He's asking me."

"That's so nice." Ashley was touched by the young man's request, proud that Landon was the sort of man young guys wanted to be like. "So . . . you and Gabe are going to talk?"

"Yes." He pointed to the distant lake. "And you and Jessie are going to walk around the water. Pretty views, hilly paths, and enough scenery to keep you busy at your easel for a year. What could be better?"

Ashley hadn't seen this coming, but she could hardly wait for her walk with Jessie. She hadn't had a long talk with her niece in forever. Not since she graduated from high school.

When they reached the table, Gabe shook Landon's hand. "Thanks for doing this."

"My pleasure." Landon looked back at Ashley. "Seize the moment. That's what my wife always says."

Landon sat down at the picnic table, opposite Gabriel, and Jessie stood and walked with Ashley toward the path. Her niece grinned. "You ready for a walk?"

"You bet." Ashley put her arm around Jessie and gave her a quick hug. "This park is beautiful."

"Gabe's brought me here a few times already. It's our favorite."

Once, a lifetime ago, Ashley had come here with Jean-Claude. But she was a different person back then and the park was different, too. Everything about the beautiful lakeside area was fresh and new. Ashley set the pace, slow enough so they could focus on talking. "So . . . tell me about Gabe."

Nothing could've stopped Jessie's smile. "He's amazing. Smart and funny. He loves reading the Bible with me and he treats me like royalty."

"Which you are." Ashley raised her brow. "Don't forget it."

She laughed. "That's what Gabriel says." They walked for a while without talking. Jessie broke the silence first. "The problem for us is sort of obvious."

"You live an ocean away." Ashley felt a subtle sadness. She thought about her sister Kari. "Your mom would be crushed if you moved to Paris forever."

"I know." Jessie lifted her face to the blue overhead. "I like it here. She'd understand if it was really what I wanted."

"True." Ashley and Kari agreed that it was time to let their children were mostly grown now. Time to let them take wing. "Your mom would be okay."

Jessie drew a deep breath as they kept walking. "The thing is, I don't want to live in France. I'm only here for the summer session and already . . . I miss home. I do."

"Hmm." Ashley could see where this was going. "And Gabriel?"

They passed the first part of the lake. From here the path wound up a hill and along the rim of the lake. The view took their breath for a moment. "Sometimes I just want to sit down and draw everything I can see." Jessie looked at her. "You know?"

"I do. Exactly." Ashley stopped for a moment and took in the sight. She pulled out her cell phone and took several pictures, including one of Jessie. "Material for another day." They started walking again. "You were saying . . . about Gabe?"

Jessie gazed at the lake. "I think he loves me. But"—she turned to Ashley—"I can't imagine taking him away from his mother. Alice . . . you heard her story. Gabriel is everything to her."

Tears stung Ashley's eyes. There would be pain in this story however it played out. A goodbye at an airport in a few months, or a mother saying farewell to the only child she'd ever had. Ashley nodded. "I see."

"Right." A pair of squirrels ran across the path in front of Jessie, and she stopped short. "I feel like we're in a painting come to life."

"Exactly." Ashley laughed. "Even the critters are colorful."

After a while, Jessie found her spot in the conversation again. "Sometimes I want to tell Gabriel things are over between us. His mother needs him more than I do. Or at least it seems that way."

"Awww, yes, Jessie. Growing up is hard. The letting go and holding on." Ashley thought about Cole in his junior year at Liberty. In a few years he could be married with a full-time job. God and life could take him thousands of miles from Bloomington. She waited to find her voice. "Your mother told me something a long time ago. Maybe it'll make sense to you . . . with all that's in your heart."

"Okay." Jessie was so sweet, so pure. Nothing like Ashley at her age.

But that didn't mean Ashley couldn't help the girl through the conflicts in her young heart. "She told me time could often solve today's troubles. If you just let enough of it pass by."

They slowed their pace. Jessie seemed to let the words work their way into her heart. "Time." She nodded. "Of course, my mom said that. She's such a writer." The heaviness in Jessie's expression lifted. "So maybe don't worry about it today. Right?"

"Yes." Ashley took her time. "God's waiting for you in your tomorrows, Jessie. Just like He is for all of us." Ashley breathed in the scent of gardenias that lined this part of the path. "If you and Gabriel fall in love, then God brought him to you. And God will show you a way to make it work. Even for Gabe's sweet mother, Alice."

"Yes." Jessie was quiet for the next twenty steps or so. "You knew my birth father, right, Aunt Ashley?"

This was the last thing Ashley expected her niece to say. She took a quick breath. "Yes . . . yes, I knew him."

"Was he . . . was he a bad guy? Like did you think he was wrong for my mom?"

This was fragile ground. Conversations like this were better between Jessie and her mother. But Ashley could lend a little insight, at least. "Tim Jacobs. No, sweetheart. He wasn't a bad man. He just . . . made a bad decision."

"Having an affair with one of his students." Jessie clearly knew the story.

A whisper of familiar shame swept over Ashley. Tim was certainly not the hero in the Baxter family story. But then what he'd done . . . Ashley had done also. The reality hit her for the first time. "People . . . they do things they shouldn't. I think if your dad would've lived, he would've spent a lifetime regretting that affair."

Jessie nodded. A breeze played in the trees overhead and a few leaves drifted along the path ahead of them. "So . . . did you think he was wrong for my mom? You didn't say."

The answer was quick and obvious to anyone who had known Kari all her life. But this was Jessie's birth father they were talking about, and Ashley chose her words with care. "Your mother was in love with Ryan Taylor from the day she met him. It was at a picnic at Ryan's house a year after we moved to Indiana from Michigan."

"She says she looked down and her heart was gone." Jessie grinned. "The way I feel about Gabriel."

"You know what happened. The misunderstanding between her and Ryan and how your dad came along at just the right time." Ashley stopped walking and turned to Jessie. "Your mother loved Tim Jacobs. I can tell you that, Jessie. It was different, but it was deep and real. She married him because she believed she'd have forever with him."

Jessie was quiet, so Ashley touched the girl's shoulder. "Things worked out like they were supposed to, Jessie. God gave us you because of Tim Jacobs."

Ashley's answer seemed to hit just the right chord for Jessie. She lifted her head some and nodded. "True. I hadn't thought about that." She started walking again, her step a little lighter. "Besides, Ryan is the only dad I've ever known. And he's the best, Ashley. He's such a good daddy."

They finished the loop and ended back at the picnic table where Landon and Gabriel were still talking. The conversation looked light now, like whatever serious matters Gabe had wanted to discuss, they were behind them now.

Jessie and Gabriel bid Ashley and Landon goodbye and Jessie called out as they walked their separate directions. "We'll be the first ones there tonight! Can't wait."

Ashley felt a wave of exhilaration. In seven hours she'd be at the gallery welcoming guests to her very own Parisian show. It was still hard to believe.

This time the driver took them to a spot between the twelfth and thirteenth arrondissements. The boundary between the two districts was the Seine and here there was another scenic ancient foot bridge. It arched over the river and at the center was a bench with the sweetest view.

"Sometimes, the Seine is this bigger-than-life river." Landon took her hand and together they walked to the bench. There were no other people on the bridge. This was a residential area, not somewhere tourists frequented.

"You're right." Ashley nestled in next to him as they sat down. "It can seem that way."

"That's why I brought you here." He turned to her. "You're like the Seine, Ashley. Famous with your artwork one minute and meandering across the landscape of my heart the next."

"Oooh." She tapped his foot with hers. "Who's the artist now?"

He laughed, but he didn't look away. "I'm serious. You're the most beautiful, complex woman I've ever known. I still can't believe God gave you to me."

"Mmm. I feel the same. About you." Ashley looked out at the water. "Landon? Does this have something to do with little boats?"

A chuckle came from his lips. "Smart girl."

"I wondered." At this spot, several barges moved along the waterway. Every few seconds another one passed beneath them and continued west into the city. Like Landon said, the pace would pick up miles from here. But for now . . . in this place the water seemed to take its time.

"Here's what I want to say." He sat a little straighter and stared into her eyes. "You do understand that the only reason we're here is because of Paris. Twenty-three years ago."

Ashley narrowed her eyes. "What?"

"Think about it. Who knows what would've happened if Paris had gone differently? If you hadn't gotten connected with that evil artist and . . . if you hadn't come home pregnant with the very great gift of Cole."

"Okay . . ." Ashley still wasn't sure where this was going.

"I was mad at you, Ash. You didn't want to talk to me, so I didn't want to talk to you. I remember how I felt." He kept his tone light, but the admission was a tough one. "I might never have . . . "

"Ouch." Ashley nodded. "I get it. You might have kept your distance even after I got home."

"But . . . when I saw you again for the first time, once you came home from France, you had Cole. Which gave us a reason to talk." He smiled even as tears filled his eyes. "I loved that little boy from the first time I saw him. He was so you, Ashley. His eyes, his heart. His joy for life."

"He's all that, isn't he?" Ashley ran her thumb over Landon's hand. "Even now . . . all grown up. My precious Cole."

"Yes. And then . . . "

The details were adding up. "Then you were nearly killed in that house fire. You saved the life of that child."

"And you came to see me in the hospital." Landon didn't look away, didn't blink. "Where you first spoke the words you'd never said till then."

"I told you I loved you." She paused, seeing it all again. She leaned up and kissed him. "I meant it, Landon."

"I know." He kissed her and then he put his arm

around her shoulders. A tourist boat moved from beneath the bridge and sailed on down the river. "You see, Ash? All the boats?"

"If I hadn't told you I loved you at the hospital . . . we never would've started dating."

"Right." He kept his eyes on the river. "And I wouldn't have ached for you when I moved to New York after 9/11. I thought about you every day, all day at Ground Zero. You didn't think the two of us could make it, Ash. Remember?" He turned to her again. "But I knew. I knew you still loved me. That you always would."

"Which was why . . ." The pieces were still coming together. Landon's best friend from college, Jalen, had been one of the firefighters killed when the Twin Towers collapsed. Because of Jalen, Landon was a firefighter by then. He worked at Ground Zero until they found Jalen's body. Ashley sighed. "The love you felt for me and Cole . . . that was why you came back to me after they found Jalen's body in the rubble."

"I saw you painting in the front yard of our house . . . your parents' house, back then." His voice was soft, the memories clearly vivid for him, too. "I walked up behind you. Remember?"

"Of course." She looked deep into his eyes. "I was painting the Baxter house, thinking of you."

"As soon as you were in my arms, I knew." He searched her face. "I was sure I was never going to leave you. Not you . . . not Cole. Not ever again." The love in his eyes was so great it was like a physical force. "Even when you thought you were sick . . . when you wanted me to leave and find someone else."

"You didn't . . ."

"Which was why . . . eighteen years ago . . . we stood before our family and friends and said, 'I do.' "

"Mmm." Ashley's head was spinning. "All because of what happened in Paris."

Landon stood and helped her to her feet. He took her in his arms and kissed her, this time long enough that she almost forgot where they were. When he drew back his eyes were bright. "All the little boats, Ashley."

"When God calmed my storm."

"Yes."

For a long while they stood there, holding on to each other and watching the boats on the Seine. Soon they would have to get back to the hotel room and get ready for tonight. For the big event. But for now it was enough to be here in the middle of nowhere Paris, standing on an old forgotten footbridge and remembering. Every time God had been faithful in the twists and turns of their story. That . . . and something Ashley would never forget.

More little boats than she could count.

21

They had the same driver that night for the ride to Light of the Seine, and everything felt like a dream. Not just that they were heading to her show, but the realization that she would hold on to forever.

Landon . . . Cole . . . their marriage . . .their family. All of it was because of the brokenness of Paris.

From the seat beside her, Landon let his eyes move up and down the length of her. "You're gorgeous, Ashley Baxter Blake." He grinned. "There's a fifth-grade boy somewhere inside me who still can't believe his dream of marrying you came true."

She eased her fingers between his. "And there's a fifth-grade girl inside me who still remembers you taking my hand at the zoo that day, when we were lost."

"Because you just had to draw that giraffe." He shook his head. "Had to get the neck just right."

"Good memory." She laughed. "We thought the zoo-keeper was after us, remember?"

"I just kept hoping he'd never find us."

"Me, too." She smoothed her navy blue sequined dress. It came up around her neck and cut away to expose her bare arms. The hem came to just below her knees and the color matched the spiky heels she'd bought for the occasion. "I hope I'm not overdressed."

"Not at all." Landon wore a black suit and white shirt and tie. "You're perfect, Ashley. Absolutely perfect."

They pulled up at the gallery and Ashley uttered a quiet gasp. "Landon . . . look."

There on the sidewalk, starting at the nearest intersection, was a long stretch of red carpet. Velvet stanchions separated the walkway from the rest of the sidewalk. Landon only grinned. "I told Emilie it was okay."

"A red carpet . . . for me?"

"Yes, my love. This is your night. The world is waiting for you." He helped her out of the car, and they stepped onto the stretch of red.

That's when Ashley noticed the photographers. Gathered on the other side of the divider, they started snapping photos as soon as Ashley and Landon began the walk toward the gallery.

"Ashley Baxter . . . Ashley?" A man lowered his camera. "How does it feel to be the most famous American artist in Paris?"

How does it feel? Ashley stopped and turned to the man. *Was this really happening?* "It . . . it's wonderful." She looked at Landon. "I've loved Paris since I was a young girl."

With her husband's arm around her, they continued the red carpet walk past three storefronts, the entire time smiling for photos and pausing so Ashley could answer questions from reporters. This had to be a dream. How did so many people know about her work? When they reached the front door, Ashley saw one more thing that took her breath.

A line of people in the opposite direction, all clearly waiting to enter the gallery. Fifty people at least. "Ashley," someone called out. "Over here!"

She waved and smiled at the people and at the same time she could see Jean-Claude Pierre again, making his way into the Montmartre Gallery past a crowd like this one. Could it really be that Marguerite and Jean-Claude were wrong? That her work not only was good enough for public display . . . it was loved by the very people who knew art best?

The people of Paris?

"This is all for you, Ash," Landon whispered near her ear. "Come on . . . Emilie is waiting for us."

"Yes." She waved once more to the patrons in line, and then to the paparazzi. And in a moment straight from a movie, she breezed into the gallery. With the fanfare outside the building, Ashley expected more of the same inside.

And definitely the place looked all done up, same with Emilie. There were tables with sparkling cider and pastries, and all of Ashley's twenty paintings graced the walls and display areas.

But Emilie didn't look right. She was standing with Edward, her husband, at the back of the gallery. There was another man with them. A man vaguely familiar.

Ashley felt her excitement fall. What was this? And who was the man?

When Emilie spotted them, she motioned them close.

"Something's wrong." Ashley was suddenly afraid. "That man . . . I've seen him before, Landon. I . . . I don't like this."

Landon stepped in front of her. "Emilie . . ." His voice was stern. "Please tell us what's going on."

"I'm sorry." The gallery owner sounded distressed. "It's . . . it's okay. I promise, you can join us."

After a few seconds, Landon brought Ashley back to his side and led her to the others. "Please . . . can someone explain this?" He put his arm around Ashley's shoulders, and he looked at the stranger. "Does my wife know you?"

"He's with our foreign intelligence agency." Edward spoke up. "He's police. There's nothing to fear. I'm sorry you were startled."

As amazing as the entrance to the gallery was, this was taking a hard turn in the other direction. Ashley blinked a few times. Why in the world were the police here? "You . . ." She stared at the officer. "You look familiar."

"Yes. I'm sure I do." The man took a badge from his pocket and showed Ashley and Landon. "I wasn't always with the secret police like I am now."

Edward nodded. "His badge is legitimate."

"Please . . . explain." Landon still sounded upset. Or maybe he was just being protective. Whatever it was, Ashley liked it.

"My name is Guy Hollande." He paused and looked

straight at Ashley. "First, madame . . . you were in serious danger this week. But not any longer."

"What . . . how?" Ashley's knees grew weak.

Landon tightened his hold on her. "Danger?"

"Oui." The man paused. "Twenty-three years ago, my colleague and I were hired by Jean-Claude Pierre . . . to kill you."

If it wasn't for Landon's arm around her, Ashley might've fainted. She'd been right all this time. The danger she'd been in had been real, after all. "I knew it . . . I saw you. You and another man. A . . . number of times."

Monsieur Hollande nodded. "When we failed, Jean-Claude attempted to kill us."

Emilie and Edward looked horrified. Same with Landon. "So . . . what happened?" Landon still had a tight hold on Ashley.

"I was shot and left for dead." Monsieur Hollande crossed his arms. "And my crime partner escaped to London. The secret police found me and helped me heal. In exchange for my cooperation. They asked me to work for them." He drew a deep breath. "I told them everything."

He went on to explain that he had secretly worked with Paris authorities to bring down Jean-Claude Pierre. "But the man died of natural causes before they could bring a strong case against him."

Ashley could barely believe this.

"How does this involve my wife tonight?" Landon didn't sound as upset. But the question was a good one.

"Oui." Monsieur Hollande nodded. "The other day I

saw the poster advertising your show, and I became concerned." He paused, as if there were no easy way to say what was next. "My former partner—Albert Arnaud—is back in Paris. Madame, he is a very dangerous criminal. We believe he's behind a number of murders . . . but he never leaves a trail."

Ashley and Landon were both quiet now, waiting.

"Albert was dangerously obsessed with Jean-Claude Pierre. We suspected he still might be." He looked at Ashley. "Killing you was the one job Albert Arnaud failed at. And sure enough, he's been trailing you again these past few days."

Landon tensed up again. "I knew something was wrong."

"Yes." Monsieur Hollande stood a little taller. "When Albert showed up in the crowd waiting to enter the gallery tonight, we made our arrest. He definitely planned to harm you, madame. We've since searched his flat and found evidence to link him to three recent murders. He'll spend the rest of his life in prison."

Ashley was stunned.

"I thought you should both know." The man looked at Ashley and then Landon. "Truly . . . there is no danger now."

Landon sighed. "I . . . don't know what to say." He took a step toward Guy Hollande and shook his hand. "Thank you. For looking out for my wife."

Monsieur Hollande nodded at the group. "I'll be on my way."

"Wait." Ashley had a question for the man, the one who had once tried to harm her. She stayed at Landon's side. "Twenty-three years ago you were right behind me. Several times . . . I saw you. Both of you."

"We were." The man looked like he regretted his past.

"So why?" She shook her head. "Why didn't you kill me? You had your chance."

"We would have. That was our job." Monsieur Hollande paused, as if he thought Ashley should know the answer. "It was your bodyguards. There was no way either of us were going to get past them."

Chills ran down Ashley's arms and legs. She stared at Monsieur Hollande and blinked. "Sir . . . what bodyguards?"

Now it was the officer's turn to look puzzled. "There were ten of them at least. They seemed to come from everywhere. As soon as we got close, they would surround you. On every side." He hesitated. "And they were armed. We could see their guns."

Ashley was shaking. She wasn't sure whether to laugh or cry. "Do you . . . believe in God, Monsieur Hollande?"

"Funny you should ask." He shifted from one foot to the other, like he was slightly uncomfortable. "I've been considering that, honestly."

"Good." Ashley looked at Landon and then back at the officer. "Because those weren't guards you saw around me." She paused. "I had no guards. Not at all."

"So . . . who were the men?"

Ashley smiled. No one was going to hurt her. Not now

and not twenty-three years ago. "Simple." She raised one hand toward heaven. "They were angels."

• • •

EVEN AFTER MONSIEUR Hollande was gone, Landon didn't leave her side, not for a minute. Not until Ashley turned to him and touched his face. The doors would be open in ten minutes, and she didn't want him worried about her all night.

"I'm okay, Landon." She actually felt giddy. "God was with me. When I was at my absolute lowest. I feel so happy, so thankful. Can you picture it? Angel armies surrounding me when the enemy of my soul wanted me dead?"

Landon eased back a little. "Are you saying I can do a little shopping?"

"Yes." She laughed. "But you didn't have to come all the way to Paris to shop for one of my paintings, crazy love."

"Hold on." He pulled her close, swaying with her, flirting with her again. "Did you ask me which paintings you should take? No! You asked your sister. And how would Kari know which one of your pieces I couldn't part with?"

She tried to answer but all she could do was shake her head. "Really?"

"Actually. Yes." He took a few steps back. "So . . . if you're sure you're okay . . . I have a certain painting to secure." He nodded to the growing crowd outside. "Before those people buy my favorite one."

"Go . . . you crack me up, Landon." She was still laughing, still loving everything about how he made her feel. She watched him join Edward across the gallery where her row of paintings began.

At the same time, Emilie approached her. "You ready?" The woman looked as relieved as Ashley and Landon. This was supposed to be a happy night and now it would be.

"I am." Ashley took the woman's hands and smiled at her. "Thank you, Emilie. For believing in me. For asking me to do a show here."

"It wasn't just me. Look at that line." Emilie turned toward the gallery window. "There are a lot more than me who believe in you." She hesitated, then she held out a sealed envelope. On the front it said simply: *From Mia.*

"What's this?" Was there no end to the surprises tonight?

Emilie gave a slight shrug. "A woman came by the gallery a few days ago. She said she wouldn't be here for your show. But she wanted you to have this." Emilie handed the envelope to Ashley. "Maybe read it later."

"I will." *Strange*, Ashley thought. "Can you please hold it for me?"

Emilie agreed and then she hesitated. "Ashley . . . the very best artists create from a broken place." She studied Ashley for a quick moment. "I don't know your whole story, but whatever yours is, I know this much." She smiled. "That place is beautiful now."

"Yes." Ashley blinked back happy tears. "It is, Emilie. By the grace of God it is."

Emilie checked the time. "One minute." She hurried to the desk and put the letter in a drawer. Then she raised both hands. Almost like a conductor ready to lead the greatest symphony. "Edward," she called out, "would you please open the doors?"

"Yes, my dear." And with that Edward Love opened the gallery and a stream of people poured inside.

The first to enter were Jessie and Gabriel, Alice and her mother, Marie. They came to Ashley and gushed about her pretty dress and the art that surrounded them all. "You are a very beautiful artist, Ashley." Marie patted her cheek. "And your work is stunning, also."

Alice looked so happy for Ashley. She clapped her hands. "Paul wanted to come, but he had to work late. He'll meet up with us later." She hesitated. "You're really here, my friend. Look at you!"

Ashley hugged her. "God is so good. That's all I can say."

"Yes, He is." Tears glistened in Alice's eyes. "Go on . . . we don't want to keep you."

They shared a long look, one that spoke of their broken yesterdays and their beautifully redeemed todays. Finally, Ashley nodded. "We will talk more later."

One after another, people came up to Ashley, congratulating her on the collection and asking her about various pieces. For the most part, Landon was at her side. But sometimes he helped answer questions. Already Ashley could see that one had a red dot beside it, which meant the piece had been sold. *Landon*. She smiled. She knew why he had purchased it.

Ashley was grateful. She shouldn't have brought it.

As the first half hour of the show played out, all the fear and shame of the past was finally and fully gone. Ashley did wonder about the letter from Mia. Whoever she was. Whatever the woman wanted to tell Ashley, she had a feeling it was important. And when her show was over and tomorrow had come, Ashley knew exactly where she was going to read it.

But that could wait.

For now she wanted to soak in every moment, welcoming her guests and watching one after another of her paintings find new homes.

Here, of all places, in Paris, France.

22

The roller coaster of emotions that night still had Landon on edge, even if he was back to laughing with Ashley. This was her night, and she was whole and healed and safe. She had come so far in her days here. But it was still hard to believe someone had been following them, intent on killing her.

Landon wished he could've had a shot at Jean-Claude. And this Albert guy.

But that was behind them. No one was going to think about hurting Ashley now. Not ever again.

Once the patrons joined them in the gallery, he put the crazy scene with the officer out of his mind. Ashley was safe . . . God had protected her. Landon held on to that truth. This was Ashley's shining moment, and he was only thankful to have a front-row seat.

He talked with the guests, but mostly he watched his wife. Beautiful and elegant, talented and poised, mingling with one patron after another. Then there was her artwork. Her paintings truly were more beautiful than anything they'd seen at the Louvre yesterday. At least through his eyes.

Landon visited with Alice and Marie and Jessie and Gabriel while the show continued. Gabe had admitted yesterday that he was in love with Jessie. Yes, it was soon and yes, they lived in different countries. But he loved her.

And he had no idea what to do about it.

Later Ashley told him about what Jessie had said. As it turned out, they'd given the young couple the same advice. Let God lead. Take it one day at a time. Even an ocean away, no goodbye was forever. Not for people who believed in the promises of Jesus.

Landon took a deep breath and glanced toward Ashley again. It was so easy to see her the way she looked a thousand different times in their lives. But right now, he remembered her on their long-ago prom night. The first time he kissed her.

He could hardly believe that when the show was over, he got to go back to the hotel with her, that they could kiss anytime they felt like it. He started to walk toward her, but as he did, he felt his phone vibrate. Instantly he was on alert again.

Who would be calling him in Paris? No one here had his number. He pulled his phone from his pocket and saw his father-in-law's name on the home screen. *John Baxter?* Why was he calling now? Then it hit him. The man must've figured out the time difference and he was calling to congratulate Ashley. So kind of him.

"Hello?"

"Landon! How are you?"

"Great." The connection was surprisingly clear. "Good

to hear from you, John. Her show is still going on. She has another hour left. Let me get her for you."

"Wait!" John laughed on the other end. "How about you step outside, instead."

Maybe his father-in-law had hired a local flower delivery. "Okay." Landon stepped out into the cool July night. He wasn't five feet from the building when he stopped short.

John Baxter and Cole were standing there at the curb, both of them dressed in dark suits, dress shirts and ties. Landon could've cried, but he was too happy to see them. "Are you kidding me? You actually pulled this off? How did you . . . when did you decide to do this?"

"We talked about it, remember?" John was still laughing, his eyes damp.

"But you never told me you actually . . . John, this is amazing."

"I couldn't miss it."

"Me, either." Cole threw his arms around Landon's neck. "Hi, Dad. You look sharp."

"You, too." Landon couldn't begin to imagine what their being here would mean to Ashley. "I still can't believe this."

"Wait till you hear! I almost didn't make it." Cole looked back at his grandpa and grinned. "It's a long story. Let's just say only God could've gotten us here." He gave Landon a hearty pat on his shoulder. "Okay, already. Take us to her. I need to see Mom in her element."

Even after everything that had happened today, this

moment, seeing her father and son at her show, was going to leave Ashley speechless. After this, Paris would be an entirely different place for her. A place of true romance and laughter, accomplishment and blessing. And something else.

The very sweetest redemption.

• • •

ASHLEY WAS MID-CONVERSATION with an older woman who spoke little English, and Emilie was standing nearby translating when out of the corner of her eye, Ashley noticed a group of people enter the gallery. An hour into the show, most patrons were here and deciding which painting to purchase.

She looked that way and gasped. "How . . . Dad! Cole!" Ashley looked at the older patron. "I'm sorry, pardon me."

Emilie was grinning, like maybe she had known about this. Ashley would find out later. All that mattered now was that they had come. They had flown across the ocean to surprise her on her big night.

Her heart was so full she wondered if she could take it all in. She moved past other gallery visitors, and in as much time as it took her heart to beat again, Ashley had her arms around both of them.

Landon stood next to her dad and Cole. "Look who I found outside."

"You came!" Ashley hugged Cole for a long while, rocking him, breathing him in. Cole, who wouldn't be alive if her first trip to Paris had turned out differently. "I love you, son. I can't believe you're here."

"It was Papa's idea." He stepped back and put his hand on Ashley's father's shoulder. "He asked if I wanted to surprise you." Cole kissed her cheek. "I wouldn't have missed it. Being in Paris with you, Mom." He looked around the gallery. "Seeing all of this." His smile lit up the room. "Congratulations."

How was this really happening? The child she had nearly lost, the one who changed her life, was here in Paris and they were celebrating her greatest artistic achievement? The miracle of it was almost more than she could take in.

"Yes, honey, congratulations." It was her dad's turn. He took her in his arms and held her close, his hand on the back of her head. "I always saw this. Your mom did, too. She would've loved to be here."

Ashley couldn't stop her tears. The happiest and saddest tears she'd ever known, all mixed together. "I feel her with me, Dad. I do." She pressed the side of her face against her father's. "Thank you . . . you'll never . . . you'll never know how much this means to me."

He stepped back a few inches and smiled at her, that look of love and pride and approval that could only come from a father. "I was there when you made your first drawing, Ashley. I took you to your first art gallery." He put his hand on her cheek. "I do know. That's why I had to come."

"Yes." Ashley had no idea how she was going to pull

herself together for the other patrons. She glanced back at the gallery floor. Emilie and Edward were handling things. She turned to her father again. "Can you believe it?" She looked over her shoulder once more. "All of this?"

"Of course, honey." He pulled her into another quick hug. "I always believed it."

Cole and Landon were still standing there, and now Ashley took their hands, the four of them forming the happiest little group. Her family was living proof that God had forgiven her, that He had given her this week in Paris so she could never look back at this city ever again without smiling.

Without longing for every minute they'd spent here.

Especially now . . . now that her dad and Cole had come.

One of the patrons handed Ashley a tissue and she laughed through her tears. "Merci madame."

The woman smiled. "Nothing better than happy tears."

"True." Ashley laughed again, and when they were alone once more she looked at Cole and her dad. "Are you here tomorrow, too?"

"We go home with you and Landon. On the same flight." Her father smiled at her husband. "We'd love to tag along and see some sights."

It was the greatest gift, the two of them being here. "Yes!" Ashley squeezed Landon's hand and smiled at her dad and then Cole. "We'll have the very best time."

"Uh . . . hey, Mom." Cole nodded to a few guests wanting to talk to her. "They're waiting for you. Go on. We want to watch you do your thing."

"Right." Ashley nodded. She dried her face and dabbed at her eyes, then she motioned to the patrons that she would be with them in a moment. She leaned in close to Cole. "First . . . I want you to meet someone."

She led the group across the gallery to the place where Alice and her mother, and Jessie and Gabriel were looking at Ashley's painting of Lake Monroe. As Ashley walked up they turned to her.

"I'm buying this one." Alice looked back at the painting. "I imagine you at this lake, Ashley. Finding your way back when you returned home."

"Yes, that was the place." For a moment, Ashley stared at the piece. Then Cole moved up beside her. "This is Cole. My firstborn." She turned to her son. "Cole, this is Alice. She was my only friend when I was here the first time." The rest of the story could come later.

Cole shook Alice's hand and smiled. "Nice to meet you."

Alice looked almost as surprised as Ashley. "You mean . . ." She glanced at Cole. "He is the baby . . . the one . . ."

More tears, and this time Ashley's laugh was pure joy. "Yes. This is him."

Alice covered her eyes with one hand for a moment, and when she lowered it, there were tears on her face, too. "Well, then, Cole . . . this is Gabriel." She uttered a single sound, more laugh than cry. "You two have more in common than you'll ever begin to understand."

The two young men shook hands. Cole chuckled. "Sounds like we have some talking to do."

"Definitely." Gabriel nodded. "We'll connect on WhatsApp before you go."

Ashley introduced her father to the others, and she slipped her arm around his waist. "He never stopped believing in me." She dabbed at her face once more. "And now he's here."

Alice and Marie took turns shaking his hand, then Landon raised his camera. "Tears and all . . . we need a picture."

They all talked at once, agreeing that the moment had to be remembered. Ashley and Cole and her father . . . Alice and Marie . . . Jessie and Gabriel. Ashley had a feeling she would frame this one.

Only then did Cole seem to notice his cousin Jessie. "Hey . . . I forgot you were here!"

The two hugged and Jessie looked back at Gabe. "It's been quite the summer."

"Looks like it." Cole smiled. "Let's get coffee tomorrow. All of us."

Plans were made and then they sent Ashley back to her adoring fans. It was time. Ashley didn't care that most of her makeup was cried off. Her father and son had come. Who needed mascara? She made her way to the patrons waiting for her.

"Hello! I'm sorry about that . . . How can I help you?"

A man stepped forward. "Family is so prevalent in your paintings. Can you tell us about that?"

"Well . . ." Ashley felt the sting of tears once more. A single laugh came from her and she looked back at Landon and Cole, her father and Jessie and her friend, Alice. Then she turned to the man again. "Family is God's greatest gift. And . . . there's a lot more to that. But let's just say I wouldn't be here without them."

There were other questions and other visitors who made their way to her. Another hour passed and one by one, each of Ashley's twenty paintings was sold. The last guests to leave were Alice, Marie, Jessie, and Gabriel. They all said their goodbyes, Alice last.

"Your m'man . . ." Alice looked at Cole, who was standing nearby. "She saved my life, Cole. Ask her to tell you about that, one day."

Cole seemed surprised. He nodded and smiled at his mother. "I can't wait to hear."

Alice hugged Ashley. A hug that came from the desperate teenager she had been all those years ago. Clinging to Ashley like a drowning person clung to a life preserver. "I will never . . . never stop thanking God for bringing you back to me." She cupped Ashley's head with one hand and stared into her eyes. "You will always be my miracle."

Their eyes filled with tears, but neither of them cried. Their newfound friendship was too happy for that. "We'll see each other again." Ashley smiled. "Come visit us in the States."

"We will." Alice looked back at Paul. He had shown up thirty minutes ago, and now he nodded.

"If Alice says we're coming for a visit, then we most certainly will." He chuckled. "God has given you women this friendship. This is just the beginning."

Alice and Ashley hugged once more. And Alice worked to find her voice. "I didn't get to say goodbye last time." She hesitated. "Goodbye, Ashley. Thank you." She looked across the room at Gabriel, her son, and then back at Ashley. "Thank you for everything."

When the group was gone, Emilie and Edward closed the doors and raised their hands again. "You did it!" Emilie smiled so big at Ashley. "Such a raving success, Ashley. You'll have to come back. Whenever you can bring us another batch of paintings."

"Yes." Ashley hadn't even considered the possibility. That this wouldn't be just the most unbelievable Paris gallery show, but that it would be the first of several. Many, even. She was standing between Landon and Cole, and she put her arms around both of them. "I think we could make another trip back." She looked at her husband and then at their son. "What do you think?"

"Next time we bring the whole family." Her dad looked beyond happy at the idea. "All the kids and grand-kids and Elaine."

"Yes." Ashley could picture it. "That would be one for the ages."

"Now." Landon turned to Emilie and Edward. "If you could help me find a bag for that painting. I'll ship it from the hotel tomorrow. So Ashley and I can have one night with it on display in our room."

They all laughed, and Emilie motioned to them. "Follow me."

Landon and Cole walked with Emilie and Edward to the desk. As they did, Ashley's father stepped closer. They were alone now, near a velvet bench at the middle of the gallery. "Can we sit?" Her dad touched her elbow. "I brought you something."

Classical music played through the room, soft and subtle. Ashley hadn't noticed it until now. She sat next to her father and turned so she could see him. "You didn't have to do that."

"Yes, I did." His smile was tinged with sadness now. "You'll see." He pulled a wrapped gift from his suit coat. "I've been hiding it here all night. Waiting for this moment."

Ashley's heartbeat quickened as she took the small silver-wrapped gift and opened the paper. Whatever it was, the gift mattered dearly to her father. She could see that much. Beneath the wrapping was a slim black box, and inside the box was . . .

A used cell phone.

"Isn't this yours?" Ashley held up the phone. "This is your case, right?"

"Right." Her dad took the phone from her. "I'm not real tech savvy. You know that."

"Yes." Her laugh was quiet now. What was this? "So . . . you're giving me your cell phone?"

"No, sweetheart." He scrolled through the phone's home screen and into his handful of apps. "Luke helped me with this."

Luke. Ashley's heart melted a little more. The brother who had been so mean to her when she came home from Paris twenty-three years ago and who now was one of her best friends. Of course he had helped with whatever this was, whatever their dad had wanted to do for Ashley.

"Here." He handed the phone back to her. "On the day I decided to come see your art show, I looked back at the box of letters your mother had written. And tucked between the cardboard pieces at the bottom of the box was a cassette tape."

Ashley felt her heart beat harder again. "And we'd missed it all this time?"

"Yes." Her father looked bewildered. "I have no idea how. Or why I didn't find it before." He paused. "Anyway, all those letters? Your mother read them. She recorded herself. So every word she ever put on paper for you, Ashley . . . for your siblings . . . when she got sick she must've decided to read them. Every letter. Every single letter is on that cassette tape."

Her mother's voice? Ashley reached for her dad's hand. This was more than she could imagine. "So . . . Luke helped you make a sound file? With Mom's words?"

"Yes. That's it. A sound file." He allowed a soft laugh and he pointed to a link marked *Your mother's words—for your Paris art show.* "You'll want to listen to the whole thing later. When you have an hour. But Luke helped me make a shorter recording, some of my favorite things your mother said about you as an artist, Ashley." He blinked back tears. "I wanted you to have it tonight."

Ashley held her father's phone, her fingers trembling. "Can . . . I listen to it now?"

"Yes." He nodded. "Please." He swiped at a tear on his cheek. "On this day . . . this momentous day . . . you should know your mom used to say you painted with more than reds and blues." Her dad put his hand on her shoulder. "She believed you painted with times gone by. With the memories of family and the certainty of faith. I had to be here to tell you that." He looked at the phone again. "And to bring you this."

A part of her was thrilled to hear the compilation of things her mother had said about her being an artist. But she was almost afraid to push the play button. Afraid she wouldn't be able to breathe from the weight of missing her mom. Especially on a night like this.

Finally, she couldn't wait another moment. They were still alone, so while it was quiet enough to hear the recording, Ashley started the clip and held the phone a little closer.

"Hello precious Ashley, I must say I love this project. Reading my letters to each of you kids and recording myself. Because some far-off day I have to believe that hearing this will make you smile."

Ashley hung her head and let her tears come again. *Mom . . . you're here, after all.* She squeezed her eyes shut and focused on her mother's words.

"Anyway, about your artwork . . . Ashley, you are the most talented artist." The recording was edited so seamlessly, Ashley felt like she was listening to a single letter. A message from her mom to her alone, for such a night as this.

"There's something so special about a blank canvas. I know you—of all people—agree, precious daughter. Oh, the things you create on a blank canvas. You see things that aren't, Ashley, and you bring them to life as if they had been there all along. I love that about you."

Ashley took her father's hand as she kept listening.

"I know I tell you all the time, Ash, but you are such a talented artist. You really are. Today I was missing the moments when you were in fifth grade. Remember that Peter Pan play you and your friends put on when you were in Mr. Garrett's class? You were Wendy and you had your own ideas about how things should go at the end. Neverland forever! That was your way of playing the part, and so you did. It was a moment I will remember always, sweet girl." Her mother's soft laugh was full of light and hope. Nothing to indicate how sick she was. "Your love for your life, your determination to never grow old! Such good times, Ashley."

She paused the recording and laughed. "Remember that? I was so rebellious."

"You were creative." Her dad patted her knee. "Your mom and I always loved that about you."

"Thanks, Dad." Ashley held his eyes for a moment before starting the message once more.

"So, since I was missing those days, I went down to the basement where you keep your paintings. Every one of them. And I was simply breathless, precious daughter. You have been given such a great gift from God." Sincerity rang in her mom's voice. "Precious Ashley, I can picture you being old and gray one day and finding these letters and knowing—to the core of your being—that your father and I believed in you. Truly, honey, one day people will line up to buy your artwork. And all the world will see home and family and faith through your beautiful eyes."

Again Ashley stopped the recording. It was like her mother was sitting here beside her. She worked to collect herself.

"See? Why I had to bring it to you?" Her dad put his arm around her shoulders and gave her a long hug. "Your mother always knew you would be here one day." He took his time. "Listen to the rest."

"Ashley, my dear, look at what your simple drawings have become! I believe that one day, Ash . . . one day you will have a gallery show in Paris, France. Yes, all the way across the ocean in Paris. Where art is so important, and people expect the very best. And there you will be, among the greats."

"What?" Once more, Ashley paused her mother's voice. "How could she have . . ." Ashley felt the sense of wonder grow, proof that God was here. Giving her this very great gift. Her mother's voice, her words of encouragement. Her love.

The recording began again. "But between you and me, you're already that good. Even if your gallery is only here in the basement for now." There was a slight pause on the message. "Ashley, we haven't heard from you in a while. You're still in France, and I know you're figuring things out, and that's okay. Your father and I are praying for you every day. God is with you, we know that.

"But even though you are struggling, I am convinced of this. You're supposed to be in Paris right now. I'm not sure why, Ashley, but I can feel it every time I pray. God is using you there. Maybe because you really are going to showcase your paintings in France.

"Or maybe He's doing something else with your time away. Whatever it is, I am at peace. Because God is working in your life, sweet girl. I know He is.

"I love you always, Mom."

Ashley stared at the phone and then she held it to her chest, to her heart. "I miss her so much." She put her arms around her father and held him tight. "Thank you, Dad. I'll listen to this a million times."

"I know you will." Her dad kissed her cheek. "I couldn't think of a greater gift."

She took a few seconds to send the sound file to herself. So she could share it later with Landon and Cole, and keep it forever. Her mother's words, and more than that her mother's belief that one day she would be here, having a show in Paris. Her certainty that God would make good out of whatever had gone wrong the first time she was here.

Which He had done so clearly.

And the best part, the part that would stay with Ashley always. The chance—here at a gallery in Paris—to hear her mother say, "I love you."

One more time.

23

Rain fell across Paris the next morning, so Ashley and Landon slept in. Once they were out of bed, Ashley took a little longer washing her face. Her head still hurt a little from the tears and laughter of yesterday.

But the groggy feeling was no match for the joy in her heart.

She met Landon in the living room, where he was staring at the painting he'd insisted on bringing back to their suite. Ashley shook her head. "I still can't believe any of it . . . that it happened. That you were here and my dad and Cole. Alice and Gabriel and Marie. Jessie." Disbelief filled her voice, the way it always would when she remembered this past week in Paris. "It's like a dream, Landon."

He held out his arms and she came to him. "That's exactly how I was just feeling about this painting." Together they turned and looked at the piece.

As with all her work, the people were only seen from the back. A couple of young teenage kids on a large rock, overlooking a pretty stream. Dreaming about life and the days to come. "The two of us. We always found our way to that spot." He brought his face close to hers. "Remember?"

"Like it was yesterday." She angled her head. "I love that we still live there. That we can still go out there and watch the stream. We can even sit on that same old rock."

"It's not the Seine, but . . ." Landon always knew how to lighten a moment. He kissed her cheek. "Speaking of which . . . it's our last day. We should get going."

He was right. Despite the pouring rain and gray skies, they would take the trip Ashley had been looking forward to all week. Her dad and Cole were having breakfast with Jessie and Gabriel, and later they would all meet up at the Eiffel Tower and for a tour of the Notre Dame Cathedral.

Somehow the weather only made the day feel more unforgettable. Paris in the rain.

They got ready and packed quickly, and Ashley grabbed her red umbrella. The one she'd had all these years since her first trip here.

Before they left, they took the painting to the concierge and arranged for it to be shipped. Landon gave her a light elbow in the ribs as they waited at the desk. "That'll teach you to sell one of your paintings without showing me first." He grinned. "Especially this one. I have my favorites, you know."

"They're all your favorites. You're biased." She laughed, and the feeling was wonderful. Never had she imagined being so happy at the end of this week. So free.

Once the painting was safely packaged and on its way, they took an Uber to the seventh arrondissement, and the Champ de Mars that led to the Eiffel Tower. When they were out of the car and at the beginning of the long stretch of green space, they stood under Ashley's umbrella and Landon faced the iron structure. "I did my homework on this one."

"Oh, you did." She laughed. "I can't wait to hear."

"Little-known facts. The tower wasn't originally supposed to be a work of art. Did you know that?"

Ashley did, but she kept the fact to herself. "Okay."

"Right . . . so it was built by a guy named . . . wait for it . . ."

Ashley loved this, loved being married to him. Standing here in the rain in Paris with her best friend. She finished his sentence. "Monsieur Eiffel."

"Very good." He looked to the top of the well-known structure. "It's over a thousand feet tall, tallest building in the world for a while." He held up his hand. "Wait for it. You can't possibly know this. The tower was built out of puddling iron." He shrugged. "Not sure what that is, but I'm surprised it's held up all these years." He cast a glance at the pouring rain. "Especially in this weather."

"Puddling iron. Hmm." Ashley took his hand, and they started their walk toward the tower. "Interesting."

"Yes. And it was originally made for the World's Fair of 1889." Landon had a few more noteworthy details. How a person could walk up to the first and second floors, but only an elevator could take them to the top of the tower.

Ashley's dad and Cole planned to meet them there in half an hour. So, Ashley and Landon began their ascent. The ride up was as breathtaking as Ashley had imagined.

The glass elevator rose through the rain to the top, while the structure became more and more narrow.

She held tight to Landon's arm. "Glad I'm not afraid of heights."

They got out at the first level of the summit, the part that was indoors. But even on a rainy day like this, Ashley had no intention of staying there.

"Come on. I can't wait." She hurried with him to the stairs and in less than a minute they were at the very top. Mist from the rain swirled around the open space, but Ashley didn't care. She felt around in her bag for her red umbrella.

But it was gone.

"No . . . I must've left it near the entrance. When we first started walking up." Ashley hesitated. "They'll have it for me. Someone will have turned it in."

"I'm sure." Landon nodded.

Besides, Ashley didn't care if they got a little wet. They were really here! She took a deep breath. The air was fresh, the smell of summer rain.

At the top of the Eiffel Tower.

Ashley had to remember to breathe. "Can you imagine this?" She was barely moving now, taking slow steps to the railing at the edge of the summit floor. "To be up so high? To see all this? How it must have felt back in 1889?"

"Or . . ." He wasn't looking at the expansive view of Paris. He was looking at her. "How it feels right now. I think this might be even better."

She turned to him and they came together in a long

hug. "Thank you, Landon. For insisting I take this trip. For being with me every moment of the way." She kissed him, slowly with the passion of a lifetime. Then she pulled away a few inches. "I'll remember this forever. You . . . the show . . . our time here. This." She looked out again. "It's all I'll think about now . . . when I think about Paris."

They walked around the summit to the other side, where there were fewer tourists. The spray from the wet sky wasn't as strong here because of the direction of the wind. Together they leaned against the center wall, as far from the rain as possible. Ashley pulled a letter from her jeans pocket. "I brought this."

Landon hadn't seen it before. He looked at the writing on the front. "Who's Mia?"

"I don't know." Ashley slid her finger beneath the envelope flap, careful to keep it dry. "Emilie gave this to me. Before the show last night." When it was open, Ashley lifted the contents from inside. There was a letter and also . . . a photograph.

A blond woman maybe in her forties . . . and a younger one, the woman's daughter maybe. That must've been it, because the pair looked so much alike. The girl was maybe in her late teens or early twenties.

"Do you know them?" Landon peered over her shoulder at the picture.

"I don't think so." There was something slightly familiar about the woman's face. And the girl . . . she almost looked like Cole. But Ashley was sure she didn't know either woman. "Here." She handed the photo to Landon.

A strong breeze made its way across the open summit. Ashley held tight to the paper. "I'll read the letter."

She opened the single page and started at the top. "'Dear Ashley, . . . you don't know me. My name is Mia Barrons. I'm enclosing a photo of myself with my daughter, Estelle. We live in Normandy, where my husband and I are dairy farmers.'"

"Dairy farmers. Hmm." Landon glanced at Ashley. "Maybe they're inviting you to come milk the cows."

"Stop." She swatted at him. Ashley still didn't know where this was going. She kept reading. "'We have a big family and a beautiful life. But all of that . . . all of it is because of you. Because of your courage. Let me explain.'" Ashley lowered the letter and looked at Landon. "What in the world?"

"Let her explain. Keep reading."

"Okay, okay." She lifted the page and found her place. "'Twenty-three years ago, you were not the only one traipsing around Paris with a married man. With Jean-Claude Pierre. I, too, was one of his many paramours. I escaped the man's evil empire by moving to Normandy.'"

For a minute, Ashley and Landon said nothing. The pieces were beginning to add up. Did that mean . . . was the girl . . . "Dear God . . ."

Landon wasn't laughing now. He moved closer to her. "Read the rest."

"'Yes, my time with that horrible man left me pregnant. Just like you.'"

"Ashley . . ."

She took the photo from Landon again. "The girl . . . she's Cole's half-sister. I can't believe this." Her hands were shaking now. The rain was falling harder, and Ashley raised her voice to be heard. She found her place in the letter. "'Anyway, I was in the waiting room in the clinic about to have an abortion when they called your name. I knew who you were. I worked in the shop across the street from the Montmartre Gallery, and I would sometimes see you with Jean-Claude.'"

Suddenly the memory came back. "I saw Mia with him, too. A few times. I knew he was having an affair with her . . . same as me."

"I'm sorry." Landon rubbed her back. "I love you, Ashley."

Those were the only words she needed to hear. Her time with Jean-Claude had been so tawdry, so shameful and dirty. Ashley took a shaky breath and finished the letter. "'As fate would have it, there we were . . . you and me . . . at the same abortion clinic. Both of us pregnant . . . by the same man.'" Ashley exhaled. This was so much. Not in a million years would she have imagined this coming. "'You didn't see me, but when they called your name to take you back, you didn't go.'"

Ashley's voice cracked under the weight of this. She forced herself to keep reading. "'You didn't do it. Instead . . . you ran from that clinic. You ran and never looked back.'" Ashley paused. *God, help me get through this.*

She found her place once more. "'Five minutes later, I

ran out of that clinic, too.'" Ashley lowered the letter and lifted her face to heaven. "Thank You, Jesus. Thank You." She had seen someone else in the waiting room that day, she remembered that now.

"Ashley . . . this is incredible." Landon pressed his face to hers. The wind was picking up, making the moment feel intimate. Like the Eiffel Tower was theirs alone.

She steadied herself and read the last few lines. "'So you see, because of your courage I have my daughter. My Estelle.'" Ashley pressed her fingers to her lips. *God . . . You are so good.* "'And I . . . I believe our children would be half siblings. I'm including my phone number and email address. If you ever want to be in touch. If not, that's okay. We had to leave before your show, but I wanted to thank you. I've always wanted to do this. Sincerely, Mia Barrons.'"

"Cole has a half-sister he's never met." Landon sounded dazed. "A girl who wouldn't be alive if . . ."

"Just like Cole." Ashley put the letter and photograph back in the envelope and returned it to her pocket.

"Like Gabriel, too." Landon turned to her. He put his hands on either side of her face and searched her eyes. "That Scripture we read together . . . before the trip." He shook his head. "God gave that to us, Ash. So we'd be looking. Can you see that?"

Ashley nodded. This was more than little boats. "Lives were saved . . ."

"Because of your time in Paris." Landon kissed her then, just long enough to remind her how much he cared.

No telling whether Cole would want to meet Estelle. But what had happened was hardly fate, as the woman had written. Ashley would share that with Mia at some point, she was sure.

The connection here was arranged by God Himself.

Ashley turned to face the city. The outlines of the buildings were foggy and dreamy and as she looked out over the landscape the view was no longer of Paris. Not for Ashley. It was of her own life. Shiny and sparkling, old and new. A verse came to mind from Romans, chapter 8. Something she had read that morning before her shower.

And we know that in all things God works for the good of those who love Him, who have been called according to His purpose.

His purpose. Yes, that's what this was all about. The entire trip and every miraculous moment she and Landon had shared together. Moments like this one.

"Mom!" It was Cole's voice and Ashley turned at the same time as Landon to see their son and Ashley's father hurrying toward them.

Cole was carrying her red umbrella. "This has your name in it . . . I thought it was yours, so I picked it up."

She took it from her son. "It is mine. You know me . . ."

"Always forgetting things." Cole laughed as he looked around. "It's gorgeous up here. Even in the pouring rain."

Her father started to tell a story about someone they met at breakfast and Landon chimed in with his Eiffel Tower facts. Ashley wasn't really listening. She stared out over the city and smiled.

This week God had given her purpose here in Paris. Marguerite and Jean-Claude were wrong. Her paintings were cherished and loved, and they'd sold out at her first French gallery show. She had a new friendship with Alice Arquette and now she was about to connect with Mia and Estelle.

A long time ago, God had forgiven Ashley. She had felt His grace first on the way back to Indiana, on that long ago flight. He didn't hold against her all she'd done wrong here . . . the terrible choices she had made. So this week she had come to forgive Paris, to move on from the past and let this city be something new. New faces and places. Fresh memories with Landon.

She laughed as the wind spritzed rain across her face. Now it was time to move on with her life. Because here, in this moment, she had finally done something she had felt God wanting her to do more than two decades ago. Something she would take back home with her tomorrow. It was another very great gift, and the truth of it would stay with her always.

Ashley Baxter Blake had forgiven herself.

ACKNOWLEDGMENTS

This book took me to Paris, if only in my mind.

But to make it work, I had to do my research. I had to feel the grass beneath my feet at the parks and smell the catacombs. The bridges and waterways, the monuments and famous art pieces all became so real I could see them. And so I hope you found yourself visiting the different arrondissements of Paris along with the characters. You may not be able to take a trip to Paris just yet, but this book took us both there through the pages of the story.

Now I am honored to thank many people who helped make *Forgiving Paris* possible. I simply cannot leave the Eiffel Tower Summit without giving thanks where it is so deeply deserved.

First, thank you to my amazing Simon & Schuster editor, Trish Todd, and my publishing team, including the keenly talented Libby McGuire, Suzanne Donahue, Lisa Sciambra, Isabel DaSilva, Paula Amendolara, Karlyn Hixson and Dana Trocker, along with so many others! It's an honor to work with you!

Also thank you to Rose Garden Creative, my design team—Kyle and Kelsey Kupecky—whose unmatched tal-

275

ent in the industry is recognized from Los Angeles to New York. Very simply you are the best in the business! My website, social media, video trailers and newsletter—along with so many other aspects of my virtual conferences, signature events and television pieces—are cutting edge and breathtaking all because of you two. Thank you for working your own dreams around mine. I love you and I thank God for you every single day.

A huge thanks to my sisters, Tricia and Susan, along with my mom, Anne. You give your whole hearts in helping me love my readers. Tricia, as my executive assistant for fifteen years, and Susan, as the president of my Facebook Official Online Book Club and Team KK. And, Mom, thank you for being Queen of the Readers. Anyone who has ever sent me an email and received a response from "Karen's mom" is blessed indeed. The three of you are making a tremendous impact in changing this world for the better. I love you and I thank God for you always!

Thanks also to my son Austin, for coming onto my staff as my event director. I couldn't have finished this book down the stretch without all the work you took on. I treasure working with you, Aus.

Thanks to EJ for praying for me every day while I was writing this book, and to Tyler for doing more than his share of the work on our other projects while I camped out on the banks of the river Seine.

Also, thank you to my office assistant, Aurora Galvin. You create space for me to write! My storytelling wouldn't be possible without you.

I'm grateful to my Team KK members, who step in at the final stage in writing a book. The galley pages come to me, and I send them to you, my most dedicated reader friends and family. My nieces Shannon Fairley, Melissa Viernes and Kristen Springer. Also Hope Burke, Donna Keene, Renette Steele, Zac Weikal and Sheila Holman. You are my volunteer test team! It always amazes me, the typos you catch at the final hour. Thank you for loving my work, and thanks for your availability to read my novels first and fast.

Also, my books only happen with the help of my family, especially my amazing husband, Donald. Honey, thank you for your spiritual wisdom and leadership in our home, and thanks for talking through books like this one from outline to editing. The countless ways you help me when I'm on deadline make all the difference. I love you!

And a special thanks to a man who has believed in my career for two decades, my amazing agent, Rick Christian. From the beginning, Rick, you've told me to dream big, set my sights high. Movies, TV series, worldwide reach. All of it for God and through Him. You imagined this, believed it and prayed for it alongside me and my family. You saw it happening and you still do! While I write, you work behind the scenes on film projects and my future books, the Baxter family TV series and details regarding every word I've ever written. You are brilliant and driven, compassionate and dedicated. I used to dream of having you as my agent. Now Tyler and I are the only authors who do. God is amazing. Thank you, Rick, and thank you for praying for me and my family. That most of all.

Finally, my greatest thanks to God Almighty, who is First and Last and all things in between. I write for You, through You and because of You. Thank you with my whole being.

Dear Reader Friend,

Many years ago, the idea of *Forgiving Paris* came to me. I couldn't move my heart past the days when Ashley made her worst decisions in Paris, back when she was just twenty years old. In many ways I had told that story, of course. I had covered the details in broad strokes in the Redemption series, and I hit on it again in *The Baxters: A Prequel*—in stores next year.

But I had never dealt with Ashley's shame. The way she still hadn't forgiven herself. In Ashley's mind the only good thing to come from Paris was her son Cole. And while that was wonderful, it didn't change the fact that she had made awful choices, done terrible things.

And haven't we all? The Bible says we are all sinners. We all fall short of the glory of God, and the only perfect person to walk the earth was Jesus. I believe that. So I figured why not take a deeper look at the shame and regret Ashley carried . . . and ultimately the grace and freedom that comes from forgiveness.

Convinced that the story needed to be told, I shared the idea with my editor, Trish Todd. Her delight at the concept and title was all the proof I needed. It was time to go back to France. Time to tell Ashley's story. And of course, *Forgiving Paris* was the perfect title.

I must say, I wept writing the last two chapters. The idea of Ashley back in Paris was one thing. But Cole showing up at his mother's art show? John Baxter bringing a recording of Elizabeth's words to Ashley? I still have a headache from all my crying. But . . . they were good tears, tears of hope and healing for bad decisions in my own life. I love Ashley Baxter like a sister, and to see her experience such redemption in this story was good for my soul. I believe it will be good for your soul, too.

As you close the cover on this book, do me a favor. Please think about who you can share it with. A friend who never overcame something in her past. A sister who can't seem to forgive herself for something she did. Someone looking for hope in the midst of a world gone mad. Or just that person who loves to read.

A book dies if it's left on the shelf. So please share it.

As with many of my other books, this novel gave you the chance to spend a little time with our favorite family—the Baxters. And now very soon you will be able to have the chance to watch the first season of *The Baxters* on TV. Something I only dreamed about back when God gave me these very special characters. The series is expected to become one of the most beloved of all time. I know you'll be watching.

You won't find the Baxters in my upcoming book— *Just Once*. It's a stand-alone love story about Irvel and Hank, who first appeared in the Baxter book *Remember*. But this one is set against the backdrop of World War II. It is a love story that will take your breath and have you reading it again and again. I can't wait to tell you more!

Visit my website, KarenKingsbury.com, to find out more about *The Baxters* on TV and about my other books.

At my website, you can sign up for my free weekly news-letter. These emails come straight to you and offer stories, devotions, and news you will not find anywhere else. Sign up today! You can also stay encouraged by following me on social media.

Remember, the Baxter family isn't just my family. It's yours. And with them at the middle of our lives, we are all connected. Until next time . . . I'm praying for you.

Thanks for being part of the family. Love you all!

THE BAXTER FAMILY: YESTERDAY AND TODAY

For some of you, this is your first time with the Baxter family. Please know that you don't have to read any other Baxter books to read this one. Like my other recent titles, *Forgiving Paris* stands alone! But if you read this and want to start at the beginning, the starting place is my book *Redemption*.

That's where the adventure of the Baxters begins.

Whether you've known the Baxters for years or are just meeting them now, here's a quick summary of the family, their kids and their ages. Also, because these characters are fictional, I've taken some liberty with their ages. Let's just assume these are their current ages.

Now, let me introduce you to—or remind you of—the Baxter family:

• • •

THE BAXTERS BEGAN in Bloomington, Indiana, and most of the family still lives there today.

THE BAXTER HOUSE is on ten acres outside of

town, with a winding creek that runs through the backyard. It has a wraparound porch, a pretty view and memories of a lifetime of love and laughter and faith. John and Elizabeth Baxter moved in when their children were young. They raised their family here. Today it is owned by one of their daughters—Ashley—and her husband, Landon Blake. It is still the place where the extended Baxter family gathers for special celebrations.

• • •

DR. JOHN BAXTER: John is the patriarch of the Baxter family. Formerly an emergency-room doctor and professor of medicine at Indiana University, he's now retired. John's first wife, Elizabeth, died long ago from a recurrence of cancer. Years later, John married Elaine, Elizabeth's longtime friend, and the two live in Bloomington.

• • •

DAYNE MATTHEWS: Dayne is the oldest son of John and Elizabeth. Dayne was born out of wedlock and given up for adoption at birth. His adoptive parents died in a small plane crash when he was 18. Years later, Dayne became a very famous and popular movie star. At age 30, he hired an attorney to find his birth parents—John and Elizabeth Baxter. He had a moment with Elizabeth in the hospital before she died, and years later he connected with the rest of his biological family. Dayne is married to Katy. The couple has three children: Sophie, 11; Egan, 9; and Blaise, 7. They are very much part of the Baxter fam-

ily, and they split their time between Los Angeles and
Bloomington.

• • •

DR. BROOKE BAXTER WEST: Brooke is a pediatrician
in Bloomington, married to Peter West, also a doctor. The
couple has two daughters: Maddie, 23, and Hayley, 20.
The family experienced a tragedy when Hayley suffered a
near-drowning at age 3. She recovered miraculously, but
still has disabilities caused by the incident.

• • •

KARI BAXTER TAYLOR: Kari is a designer, married to
Ryan Taylor, football coach at Clear Creek High School.
The couple has three children: Jessie, 22; RJ, 14; and
Annie, 11. Kari had a crush on Ryan when the two were
in middle school. They dated through college, and then
broke up over a misunderstanding. Kari married a man she
met in college, Tim Jacobs, but some years into their marriage he had an affair. The infidelity resulted in his murder
at the hands of a stalker. The tragedy devastated Kari, who
was pregnant at the time with their first child, Jessie. Ryan
came back into her life around the same time, and years
later he and Kari married. They live in Bloomington.

• • •

ASHLEY BAXTER BLAKE: Ashley is formerly the most
troubled of the Baxter family, married to Landon Blake,
who works for the Bloomington Fire Department. The

couple has four children: Cole, 22; Amy, 15; Devin, 13; and Janessa, 9. As a young single mom, Ashley was jaded against God and her family until she reconnected with her firefighter friend Landon, who had secretly always loved her. Eventually Ashley and Landon married, and Landon adopted Cole. Together, the couple had two children— Devin and Janessa. Between those children, they lost a baby girl, Sarah Marie, at birth to anencephaly. Amy, Ashley's niece, came to live with them a few years ago after Amy's parents, Erin Baxter Hogan and Sam Hogan, and Amy's three sisters, were killed in a horrific car accident. Amy was the only survivor. Ashley and Landon and their family live in Bloomington, in the old Baxter house, where Ashley and her siblings were raised. Ashley typically creates her paintings on the front porch, and in addition to Light of the Seine, she sells her work in local boutiques.

• • •

LUKE BAXTER: Luke is a lawyer, married to Reagan Baxter, a blogger. The couple has three children: Tommy, 19; Malin, 13; and Johnny, 9. Luke met Reagan in college. They experienced a major separation early on, after getting pregnant with Tommy while they were dating. Eventually Luke and Reagan married, though they could not have more children. Malin and Johnny are both adopted. They live in Indianapolis, about forty minutes from Bloomington.

FORGIVING PARIS

KAREN KINGSBURY

1. In your opinion, what is the theme of *Forgiving Paris*?

2. How is *Forgiving Paris* an allegory to your life?

3. The devil has several common names according to Scripture. Tempter. Liar. Accuser. Killer. How do you see all four of these play a role in Ashley's life the first time she went to Paris?

4. How do you see these playing a role during Ashley's current trip to Paris?

5. Ashley survived professionals telling her that her paintings were trash. What can words like that do to a person? What did they do to Ashley?

6. How did shame manifest itself in Ashley's story?

7. Is there a place you're afraid to revisit because of the memories associated with it? Tell about that.

8. Everyone has regrets. Ashley's weighed on her for twenty-three years. If you are comfortable, share a regret of yours. Tell how you were able to overcome it.

9. What role does God's grace play in overcoming a bad decision?

10. For Ashley, there was a difference between believing she was forgiven by God, and then forgiving herself. Have you experienced this? Share your story.

11. How did you ultimately forgive yourself for something in your past? Why is forgiving yourself healthy, once you've been forgiven by God and others?

12. In *Forgiving Paris*, Ashley remembers her flight back to Indiana when she was just twenty. On that flight she repented of the things she'd done. What does repentance mean to you?

13. How is repentance linked to healing, when it comes to something in our past? Look up Bible verses that deal with repentance and forgiveness. Share one that landed on your heart.

14. Landon was a steady help for Ashley from the beginning, through her first time in Paris, to current day. What traits do you admire in Landon? How are you most like him?

15. John Baxter is the sort of father we all would want to have. Was your father as supportive as Dr. Baxter? Talk about that.

16. John gets the idea to surprise Ashley at her art show. Talk about a time when you surprised someone you love . . . or someone you love surprised you.

17. Cole was most definitely the personification of God's grace after Ashley's first trip to Paris. What good has come from a bad decision or a terrible storm in your life?

18. Landon and Ashley read about Jesus calming the storm in the Bible and Landon noticed the bit about the little boats. Think of a difficult time in your life. What other people or situations were affected positively by what you went through. What are your little boats?

19. The necklace Landon gives Ashley is a burst of sunlight. In what ways did you see light used in *Forgiving Paris*?

20. Is it important to revisit painful places and make new, happier memories? Why or why not? Tell about a time when this happened for you.

YOU WERE SEEN
MOVEMENT

His name was Henry, and I will remember him as long as I live. Henry was our waiter at a fancy restaurant when I was on tour for one of my books. Toward the end of the meal something unusual happened. I started to cry. Slow tears, just trickling down my cheeks. My husband was with me and he looked concerned. "Karen, what's wrong?"

"Our waiter," I said. "He needs to know God loves him. But there's no time. We have to get to our event, and he has six other tables to serve."

Henry was an incredibly attentive server. He smiled and got our order right and he worked hard to do it. Everywhere he went on the restaurant floor, he practically sprinted to get his job done. But when he was just off the floor, when he thought no one was looking, Henry's smile faded. He looked discouraged and hopeless. Beaten up.

That very day I began dreaming about the "You Were Seen" movement. Many of you are aware of this organization, but I'll summarize it. Very simply, you get a pack of You Were Seen cards and you hand them out. Where acceptable, tip—generously. From my office in the past few months more than 250,000 You Were Seen cards have gone out. We partner with the Billy Graham Evangelistic Association's plan for salvation and other help links.

And so it is really happening! People like you are truly seeing those in their path each day. You are finding purpose by living your life on mission and not overlooking the delivery person and cashier, the banker and business contact, the server and barista, the police officer and teacher, the doctor and nurse. You are letting strangers see God's love in action. Why?

Because Christians should love better than anyone. We should be more generous. Kinder. More affirming. More patient. The Bible tells us to love God and love others. And to tell others the good news of the gospel— that we have a Father who is for us, not against us. He loves us so much that He made a way for us to get to heaven.

Hand out a pack of You Were Seen cards in the coming weeks and watch how every card given makes you feel a little better. Go to www.YouWereSeen.com to get your cards and start showing gratitude and generosity to everyone you meet.

Always when you leave a You Were Seen card, you will let a stranger know that their hard work was seen in that moment. They were noticed! What better way to spread love? The You Were Seen card will then direct people to the website—www.YouWereSeen.com. At the website, people will be encouraged and reminded that God sees them every day. Always. He knows what they are going through. Every day should be marked by a miraculous encounter.

www.YouWereSeen.com

ONE CHANCE
FOUNDATION

The Kingsbury family is passionate about seeing orphans all over the world brought home to their forever families. As a result, Karen created a charitable group called the One Chance Foundation.

This foundation was inspired by the memory of her father, Ted C. Kingsbury. Ted always said, "Life is not a dress rehearsal. We have one chance to love, one chance to truly live!"

Karen often tells her reader friends, "You have one chance to write the story of your life!"™ Now, with Karen's One Chance Foundation, readers can join her in the belief that all of us have one chance to make a difference in the lives of orphans.

In the Bible, James 1:27 says people with pure and faultless religion look after orphans. The One Chance Foundation was created with that truth in mind.

The dedications below were the result of a donation to the One Chance Foundation. If you are interested in giving to Karen's One Chance Foundation and having your dedication printed in one of Karen's upcoming novels, visit www.KarenKingsbury.com. Below are dedications from some of Karen's reader friends who have contributed to the One Chance Foundation:

- Mary, I wish I was here forever, to hold you tight at night.
  To be there in your heart, and to be your guiding light.
  15 years together, how wonderful it's been!
  If I had the chance, I would do it all again! Love, Mark Erickson

- Happy 70th Birthday Nana-Brenda Goodwin! We love you & we are thankful for you! Love, Your family

- To my most amazing reader friends: You are the best and most loyal readers an author could ask for. May God bless you and yours always! Love, KK

- Bralen, you're a blessing. Love you, Momma

- Dear Diane, As you follow GOD, He will lead you to wonderful places! Love, Gary Bowman

- Hi Mom-Juanita, You are loved this side of heaven and the other. Thanks for life! John, Helena, Sus & Teri

- To our friends in celebration of the love and support we've shared in our life's journey. Dave & Jan Kukkola-Miller

- Faith, Hope & Love to MOM! Love, Lisa Johnson

- Patty: You are a reflection of God's love. Jen O.

- Memory of A. Martin & Helen Maylard. Keep Trucking -Amanda Kalinovich

- For my mom, Paulette, who has long loved all Karen's stories and loves others well. Love you! Laura

- For you Andrew. You will understand. Love you honey

- To the entire group from the Believe writing intensive, write well! Philippians 2:13 -Tiki

- To my mom, Vi Stockdale! Love, Davey

- For Bill Stone - Happy 90th birthday, Dad! We honor & thank you for your brave service to our country & appreciate all you sacrificed for our family. You are forever loved! Sheila & Kurt

- Mama, you're with Jesus now. I love you! -Sammie

- To Megan, for our shared love of Karen's books. Love, grandma

- Dedicated to my parents: Ron & Jane Dotson; angels on earth loving and caring for children!! Love, Pam Gatz

- To Jesus my Lord, who took my place on the cross! -Linda Zimmerman

- Shayna - The momma loves you!!! Hope it inspires!!

- Happy 40th Marie. Love Beck

- Dear Lindz, Paris isn't Forever. Remember God's Love & Redemption. You're in my heart always. Love, AH

- In loving memory of my grandmother, Daisy Day!
  Love, Barbara Day

- Thank you and God bless -Sedi Graham

- Merry Christmas, Madilyn! May you always have a
  forgiving spirit! Love, Mama Year 2021

- Michele A, you inspire me! -Hilary Esposito

- Kristina/Shane, Kayla, Lucas. John/Bri, Brad,
  Brooke. Brian and Dave. Make every day count.
  Love, Mom

- Blessings to my bestie BWTF! Love you! ~AB Cho

- For Aubrey, Love you more! -Dana Tedder

- To the book lovers in my life, Carolyn and Jen. Love
  from, Michelle Berry

- In honor of family. Love Donna L. Davis

- To KLK & CAF, Love LAK

- To my amazing mother, Mary. You are a gift from God
  and I am forever grateful for you! -Michelle

- To Delia and Mary, Thanks for inspiring me! Love,
  Renette

- For Princess Morgan Adams! Love, Pamela Sheldon

- Blessed by the adoption of Erica, Emily and Laiya.
  -Dave & Marva Lubben

- Dedicated to A. Martin & Helen Maylard 2012 & 2021
  Love, Amanda Kalinovich

- Dad, I am forever grateful for your love, guidance, wisdom & continual support that you give to me. You are 1 of the most precious gifts God has given me. -Andrea Chaney

- Happy 50th Stacy P! Your friend, Leah L.

- To Mom (Suzy): You faithfully pointed me to Jesus and loved others well! All my love always, Whitney

- To Jan Hager: Family connects us from the beginning; but our connection thru God has meant an even stronger bond. God is Good! Love, Cousin Jan Kukkola-Miller

- Darla TibenRivera give God the glory in everything!

- My Erica VH. I love you & I know you'll love this. -Laura

- To my mom Jan, who chases sunsets and loves well!

- To Karen & family for being such bright lights. CRUSADE was THE highlight of Kylie & Caroline's trip. - Love, The Evans Family

- To my 2 beautiful daughters Nicole & Kristen love you! -Mom

- I love my family to the moon and back! -Vicky

- Carolyn Rogers-We love you so much! You are the best! Love, Jenny

- Dedicated to Tyler & Hannah for adopting a Brother & Sister Thank you, JoAnne

- To Sheryl Buttrick! Love, Erin Marcello

- In memory of my parents! Love, Perlina

- To my mom, Edna Raes, who taught us to love reading! Love Linda

- Love you, Emma Roo! Love Mom

- Amy, A true friend over 30 years -Love Pam E.

- My hero is Jean Chaney! Love Deborah

- To my wife (Sandi Teague) . . . my true love. Thank you for loving me through the good and bad. David Currie

- Erin Kiu, to God who is doing more than we could ask or imagine through the power in us! (Eph 3:20)

TO SOMEONE SPECIAL

In *Forgiving Paris*, Alice Arquette prayed for twenty-three years that she might have the chance to thank Ashley Baxter Blake. You see, Ashley had changed Alice's life for the better. Her entire story was different because of Ashley.

Now it's your turn. I asked who in your life made an impact? Who made a difference? In less than twenty-four hours, you provided me with the 1,258 names listed below. We didn't have room for more than this. Also a special nod of appreciation to my publisher for letting these names be included.

Because sometimes it's worth everything to take a moment and say thank you to that person who made all the difference. If your name is listed below, then you are such a person. You are loved and appreciated, and you made a difference in the life of one of my readers. I hope you feel honored!

Aaron Famosi	Abby Shields
Aaron Snellings	Abigail Patterson
Aaron Thomas Brainard	Abigail Smith
Abbie Palmer	Abigail Wheaton

Abraham Landman

Abraham Thompson

Adam "Shnookums"
    Pritchett

Addi Joy Masten

Addie Crawford
    Barkman

Addison Rapp

Adebukola David

Adeline & Briella

Adiya

Aggrey Kanu Oji

Aidan Donan Guilfoyle

Alan T. Billett

Alberto (Woensie)
    Hendricks

Aldonia Francois

Alechenu Ogbole

Alex Cassmeyer

Alexis Nikolle

Alexis Renee Edge

Alfred

Alfred William Nydegger

Alice Nesselrolt

Alice Baker

Alice Howell

Alice McMurray

Alicea Fournier

Alison Koutzas

Allen Baker

Allen Shepherd

Allie Mae Moody

Allison

Allyson Hays

Alma Swanson

Alyssa Joy Wiles

Alyssa Marie Oliverio

Amanda Cunningham

Amanda M. Greene

Amanda Sanzari

Amanda Watts

Amber Majors

Amber Mazuera

Amber Smith

Amelia H. Valenzuela

Amy E. Adams

Amy McMahon

Amy Park

Amy Porter

Amy Stark

Andressa Petarli

Andries Burger

Angela Lowery

Angela Rey

Angelina Lynne

Angeline Solgat

Angie McGowan

Angie Moore

Anita Lange
Anita Hamilton
Anita Strickland
Anita Tosser
Ann Eubanks
Ann Musser
Ann Pounds
Ann Thrift
Ann Voigt
Anna E. Neuwirth
Anna L. Carson
Annabelle Lee Browning
AnnaMarie Desimone
   Crisalli
Anne Vanden Hoek Jones
Annie
Annie Keaton
Annie Nikole Metcalf
Anthony Dale Driver
Antony
Antony Robinson
Anuolwapo Olutimilehin
April Freeman Hines
April Hopkins
Arleen Dodson
Arlene May Ball
Armana Irvine
Arno
Ashley Gordon

Ashley Jones
Ashley Langford
Aubrey Ray Freeman
Aunt Shirley Moorhouse
Barb Higgins
Barb Schroeder
Barbara Adams
Barbara Carlos
Barbara Drye
Barbara Leidig
Barbara Rossillo
Barbara Tester
Barbara Wilson
Barry A. Root
Becca McGillis
Becky
Becky Eacott
Becky Sundberg
Becky Wooten
Belinda Church
Ben Conyers
Benjamin Holmquist
Berna Jo Mellenthin
Bernice Gadd
Berri & Ashleigh Locklear
Berry Greenwood
Bertha Wittrock
Bertie Gebbert
Beth Hutcheson

Beth Koscak

Beth Pace Johnson

Beth Wordsworth
   McCarty

Bethany

Betty Driggers

Betty Jolly

Betty Queen

Betty Walker

Beulah Davis

Beverly Bonnie Stieglitz

Beverly Hoffmaster

Beverly Huddleston

Beverly Reams

Bill Kline

Bill Parham

Billie Montgomery

Biye Amakoromo

Blanche Martin

Blondie Eaves

Bobby Kevin Sherron

Brandon Parsons

Branson Ayscue

Breanna Driezen

Breanna Tanner

Brenda Adams

Brenda Foster

Brenda Gresham

Brenda Horton

Brenda Joyce Hopkins

Brenda Shockey

Brenda Spencer

Brenda Sue Murray

Brent & Jennifer Salmons

Brian Harrison

Brian Parker

Brianna Chambers
   Stanley

Bridget Callis

Bridget Moore

Bridgette Newsome

Brieanna Nicole Cannon

Brittany Adams

Brooke Drumeller

Brooke Duffy

Brooke T. Higgins

Brooklyn McCurley

Burt Atkinson

Caitlin Baker

Cal Klopp

Callie Smith

Calvin Waugh

Cameron Hicks

Candi Duran

Carla Lamond

Carla MacLachlan

Carla Ryan

Carla Swihart

Carol

Carol Baldwin

Carol Lee Fritzler

Carol Renner

Carol Sue Matthews

Carole Vess

Caroline

Caroline Andrews

Caroline Couts

Carolyn Bing

Carolyn Sue Richmond

Carroel Blair

Carter Lee Gray

Casandra Cyster

Cassandra Poe

Cassie Hunter

Catherine Ann Posey

Catherine S. Barry

Cathy Hand

Cathy Huhnerkoch

Cathy Lynn Sigler

Cathy St. John

Chanell

Chantelle Groenewald

Charlene Harris

Charlene McDonald

Charles D'Armetta

Charles Goodson

Charles W. McCammon

Charlyn Spicer

Chelsea Sandham

Cherilynne Marsalis

Cherry Moore

Cheryl Boesch

Cheryl Dubois

Cheryl Huffman

Cheryl Millsap

Cheryl Moles

Cheyenne Cole

Cheyenne Moore
    (McMiles)

Chloe Baas

Chris & Judy Crowe

Chris Criel

Christi Cummings

Christian Gilstrap

Christie Bales

Christie Greenia

Christine Ahline

Christine Crittenden

Christine Smith

Christine Thorp

Christopher Connell
    Thompson

Christopher N.
    Huneycutt

Christy Blanchard

Chuck Fannucci

Chuck McFarland
Cindy A. Bunch
Cindy Elliott
Cindy Harvey
Clayton & Barbara
    McCurdy
Cole Williams
Colleen
Colleen Dunlap
Comfort Adetutu
    Adeniji
Connie Bader
Connie Becker
Connie Lee Roberts
Connie Parker
Connie Renfro
Connie Schaeffer
Connor Tanner
Constance Ann West
    Irvine
Constance Lynn Nelson
Cornelia Buchanan
Corrine Huyser
Courtney Poda
Courtney Williams
Crystal Brumfield
Crystal Burns
Crystal Lynn Merrick
Crystal Tayman

Cynthia Duncan
Dale Glomski
Dan Thompson
Dana Kim Warren
Danette Badger
Daniela Vatamanu
Danielle Siltala
Danny Wood
Darcey Juzwiak
Darlene Paaaina
Darrell Estus
Darrell G. Hill
Darrin Gibson
Darwin E. Meacham
David Baldridge
David Ellis
David H Martin Sr.
David Hall
David Kerkvliet
David L. Pratt
Dawna-Marie Elizabeth
    Gauthier
Dayna Ingle
Deanne Huitema
    Zuehlke
Debbie Bernhardt
Debbie Burgess
Debbie Dass Kallap
Debbie Fortenberry

Debbie Grooms
  Browning
Debbie Lane
Debbie McCoy
Debbie Matherly
Debbie McLaughlin
Debbie Metcalfe
Debbie Peeters
Debbie Teal
Debbie VanderWyst
Debi Marks
Deborah Hill
Debra Gail Lane
Debra Heatherly
Debra Jones
Dee Hawkins
Deidra Faith Lambert
Delight McClure
Della White
Delma Williamson
  Griffin
Delores Wright
Denise Philander
Dennis & Bertha Lovell
Dennis Flowers
Dennis White
Dennise Botha
Denver Barker
Deonna Shake

Derri Ohm
Derrick J. Horne
Destin Legieza
Dexter Ramirez
Diana Banks
Diana Creque
Diana Kirby
Diana McKowen
Diane Dvorak
Diane Rassi
Diane Stamper-Liette
Diane Welcher
Dianne Stokes
Dick Rickert
Diedre (DD) Zelin
Dixie Ellen Meachum
Doc & Mary Lou Eckart
Dolly M. Heath
Dolores Will
Don Nichols
Don Norman Wood
Donald Banks
Donald Blankenship
Donald Lemieux
Donald Lowe
Donald Schulze
Donna Barnett
Donna Bentley
Donna Berry

Donna Fahy

Donna Faye Reasner

Donna Friesen

Donna Keathley

Donna Lee

Donna Lemmon

Donna Marie Tyree

Donna Marie Witt

Donna McVey

Donna Arlene Merrick

Donna Powers

Donna Rae Evans

Donna Zirkle

Donnette Schidecker

Donnie S. Harkcom Jr.

Doris Jean Cobbler

Doris Olson Bright

Dorothy Arlene Lippiatt
    Hutmacher

Dorothy Marcott

Dorothy Meyers

Dorothy Mollen

Dorothy Robinson Belton

Dottie Geigley

Doyle Ginn

Dr. Carol Erb

Dr. Jan Bentley

Dr. Kevin Rouse

Drew Staggs

Edna Mae Derocher

Elaine J. Bobeldyk

Elias & Doris Hartman

Elijah James Oatley
    Poteet

Elisa Branan

Elizabeth Fallow

Elizabeth Frey

Elizabeth Grace

Elizabeth M. Hoelle

Elizabeth Marie Nees

Elizabeth Messer

Elizabeth Pharazyn

Elizabeth Ward Harris

Elizabeth Wilson

Ella Dalton

Ella Jane Varner

Ellen Brittain

Eloise McCarley

Elsa Flores

Emma Jean Burke

Emma Kathryn

Emogene King

Eric Donnal

Erica George

Erica Wilbanks

Erin Ogle

Ethel Mae Madewell

Eugene Solgat

Eunice Willis

Eva Sherrell

Eva Skelton

Evelone Chapman

Evelyn Funk

Evelyn Howard

Evelyn Nichols

Faye Bentley

Felicia Pease

Fern Hoff

Fiorella Siu

Florence Boyd

Florence Cuff

Florence Elsie Wright

Florence Haney

Frances Bianculli Risavich

Frances Prouse

Frances Risavich

Frances Smith Spearman

Fred Habiger

Funmilayo

Gaby Siu

Gail England

Gail M. Wack

Gary Braley

Gayle Maples

Gene Dailey

Geneva Waggoner

Genevieve Bowers

George & Mary Gilmore

Georgietta Johnson

Gerhard Steffen

Geri Buchenot

Gina Wessel

Gladys Jenkinson

Gladys Purkey

Glenda Fleming

Glenn Coffelt

Glenn Dawson

Gloria Arrowood

Gloria Davis

Grace Coleman Deal

Grace L. Echols

Grace Lorraine Anna
    Zibrun Lowe

Grace Vaters

Gracie Ruthie Gasparri

Grady McLean

Grandma Apsey

Grandpa Calvin Waugh

Greg Hubbard

Gregory Rebernick

Gretchen Schoenberg

Gwyn Mauk

Hailey Marie Forgues

Hannah Elizabeth Sipes

Hannah Isbell

Hannah J. McDonald

Hannah Rich

Hansen-Ayoola
  Olugbenga I

Happy Hinton

Harlan Moore

Harold Clark

Harry Schaub

Haydee-Elyse

Hayley Holmes

Heather Abbott

Heather Brooks

Heather Frey

Heather Hale

Heather Houle

Heather Lynn Sellers

Heather Mohr

Heather Sapp

Heidi Anderson

Helen

Helen Beck

Helen Gilde

Helen Hart Havens
  Becker

Helen Holder

Helen Shinn

Helena Combs

Henry Gershman

Herb Nelson

Heritage Januario

Hester Hall

Hilda Anthony

Hilda Robertson

Holly R. Sullivan

Howard Goins

Hubert Redburn

Hugo Martinez

Ian Hendry

Ifeoluwajoba Adeagbo

Inez Patterson

Ione

Iqbal Mamdani

Irene Helen Mitchell

Irene M. Lee

Irene Squires

Iris Cash

Irma Espinoza

Irma Roets

Isabella Juliann Lombardi

Jack T. Nelson

Jackie Lambert

Jackie Rich

Jackie Weaver Shaffer

Jackolyn Tara (Nelson)
  Hyman

Jacob & Bailey Renteria

Jacqueline Tibbs

Jacquelyn Patterson

Jacquie Covill

Jade Brumfield

Jaime Winters

James

James Britt

James Erick Muriithi

James Griffis

James Hallett

James Wolhoy

Jamie Amanda Walton

Jan Horner

Jan Jubin

Jan Ridley

Jane Starr

Janet Jarvie Smith

Janet Leman

Janet Roby Benton

Janet Singleton

Janice Louise Phelps

Janie Key

Janie Lynch

Janie Rolfe

Janis Faulkes

Janis Gooden Davies

Janise Cantoy

Jann McAfee

Jared

Jared Gardner

Jared Hatfield

Jared Nelson

Jason Horton

Jason Michael Eastman

Jason Patrick Stewart

Jaxon Daniel Sparks

Jay Thomas Noble

Jaycee Pruitt

Jayne Dulas

JB Norman Jr.

Jean

Jean Blair White

Jean Hasenauer

Jean House

Jean Melvin

Jeanette Foster

Jeanette Larsen

Jeanne Boyle

Jeannie Tabscott

Jeff Owens

Jenna Rae Sarr

Jenna Rose Larsen

Jenni Nungester

Jennifer & Kayla

Jennifer Burleson

Jennifer Edwards

Jennifer Jayne

Jennifer Rediker

Jennifer Zarnke

Jenny Collins

Jenny Eberhardt

Jenny Kruger
Jenny Murray
Jeremy Curl & Kevin
  Hartgrave
Jerry Downs
Jerry Solgat
JerryLizzyGab Akinsola
Jess Bosma
Jessica & Devan
Jessica Hardin
Jessica Kell
Jessica Valle
Jill Stiffler
Jill Walsh
Jim Zinn
Jnese West
Jo Woodard
Joan Bell
Joan Chipman
Joann Riggs
JoAnn Pieczulewski
Jodi VanOrder
Joe & Paula Oliverio
Joe Richards
Joe Wilson
Johan Snyman
John Dee
John E. Brown
John Gilliam

John H. Miller
John Paige
Johnny Mack Brown
Jordan Stivers
Jose Luis Barron
Jose Santiago
Josef Taylor
Josh Bickler
Joshua McHale
Joy Branning
Joy Sandner
Joyce Brown
Joyce Clevenger
Joyce Duke
Joyce Hope Shepherd
  Umstead
Joyce Martin
Joyce Owen Moody
Joyce P. Keeler
Joyce Peoples
Joyce Ramsey
Joyce Reece
Joyce Krom Smith
Juanita de Jong
Juanita Ketterbaugh
Juanita Kirby
Judy Blecha
Judy Holtrop
Judy Phillips

Judy Reinhart

Judy Shab

Judy Yandell

Julia Barrios

Julia Gundorin

Julie Bolen Jordan

Julie Copp

Julie Culpepper

Julie Gamache

Julie Hendrix

Julie Phelps

Julie Plocher

Juliet Bulias Obat

June Bausum Powers

June Evans

Justin Brubaker

Kaitlyn Carlton

Kaitlyn Sien

Kaleigh Brandon

Karen Cordell

Karen Hufman

Karen Lafargue

Karen Lynn Miller Howe

Karen Oosthuizen

Karen Ramos

Karen Wimberly

Karey Nicole Rolland

Kate Moody White

Kate Stanley

Katherine D. Jackson

Kathi Ellen Dee

Kathleen P. Smith

Kathryn Barber

Kathy Hall Williams

Kathy Manchego-Martin

Kathy Reifers

Kathy Shirah

Kathy Wimer

Katie Johnson

Katie Miller

Katy Hollingsworth

Kay "Mooma" Jennings

Kay Ewing Henderson

Kay Whitaker

KayLyn Miller

Keisha M. Williams

Keith Driscoll

Kelly Ashley

Kelly Boer

Kelly Pickel

Kelsey Gillman

Ken Krupke

Ken Sparkes

Kennedi Williams

Kenny Fritzler

Kera Gonzalez

Keri Novak

Kevin Len Tanner

Kevin Phelps

Kevin Smith

Kevin Stika

Keyla Carnahan

Kim Bradford

Kim Falke

Kim Harper

Kim Hurst

Kim Robinson

Kimberly Adams

Knox & Genie Bennett

Koen Taekema

Kris A. Newman

Kristi James

Kristi Kirchgestner

Kristina Marie Albright

Kristy Tate

Kyle Summers

Lacy (Bella) C. Nelson

Lakshmi Morgan

Larry Buchholz

Larry Kelley

Larry Reeves

Larry Renfroe

Laura Cueva

Laura Doege

Laura Kalfas

Lauren Hutchinson

Laurie Kiger

Laurie McGowan

Laurie Zoyiopoulos

Laurie-Ann Platt

Lee Smith

Leigh Ann Ward

Leo & Emily Kight

Leonard Weston

Lesley Robertson

Leslie Peters

Liam Gracin Alexander
　Poteet

Lidia Marinca

Lidiya Minchuk

Linda Bloch

Linda Bollinger

Linda Couts

Linda Dore

Linda Fullerton

Linda Gilchrist

Linda Inskeep

Linda Kay Cook

Linda Lawley

Linda Lindsey

Linda Lou Jackson

Linda Mae Hillis Salvage

Linda Ohlinger

Linda Orewiler

Linda Partridge

Linda Rae Spangler

Linda Sue Laymon

Linda Sutherland

Lindi van Wyk

Lindsey Wilson

Lirfa Benjamin Dashe

Lisa Anderson

Lisa Ann Miller

Lisa Askew

Lisa Harper

Lisa Millison

Lisa Mullins

Lisa Pinkston

Lisa Scott-Dzwonczyk

Lisa Stark

Lisa Wright

Liz Rooney

Lloyd Critch

Loie Jaggard

Lonny Butler

Loraine Boyd

Lorene Walker

Lori Benthin

Lori Hansen

Lori Morrison

Louise Catton

Louise MacDonald

Louise Timpa

Lucie Costa

Lucille P Heath

Luke Asher Wade

Lupy

Luuk Kramer

Lydia Burger

Lyla Marquis

Lynda Annette

Lynda Oesterreich

Lyndal Bonds Stott

Lynn Morgan

Lynne Russell

Lytisha Shuler

M. Taylor

Mackenzie Nichols

Maddox Robert Rusnak

Madelyne Leopard

Madilyn Donovan

Malachi Bowman

Malisha Burson

Mandy Gartlan

Marbie Edwards

Marcia Nelson

Marcile Hale

Margaret Hanna

Margaret Kensinger

Margaret Mary
    Hershberger

Margaret Ruth Glenn

Margaret Simmons

Margaret Simpson

Margie Sasnett

Margie Sherry

Maria Angelou

Maria Cecilia Ogoc

Maria Escalera

Maria Gundorin

Maria Oscarsson

Marian Mulvaney

Mariann "Ammie" Kubas

Marie Callahan

Marie Fuller

Marie Saldivar

Marietjie Snyman

Marilyn Hindsley Haynie

Marina Colonna

Marisa Croushorn

Mark (Edward) S. Smith

Mark Brasure

Mark Kilmer

Mark Madera

Marla Dufur

Marla Perigo

Marleen Drenth

Marlene Bernard

Marlene Friesen

Marlene Stout

Marlene M. Yowell

Marlys Schoedel

Marsha Stanley Rhoads

Martha Ntho

Martha Evelyn Rousseau
Henderson

Martha Jackson

Martha Jo Brown

Martha Snyder

Martins Nkem Philip

Mary Agbomma Agbu

Mary Alice Baker

Mary Ann Martin

Mary Beth Weikal

Mary Carlson

Mary Elizabeth Cannon

Mary Grace Giaimo

Mary Jane Demster

Mary Lane

Mary Love

Mary Murphy

Mary Sumner

Mary Verline Tatum
Sellers

Mary Yancey

Marzee King Tew

Mathilde Labelle

Matisse

Matthew Segura

Maude Meacham

Mavie Baker Lewis

Mavis Garrett

Maxine
Maxine Keoughan
Maydeen Ponts
McKenzie Dawn White
Meda Hawthorne
Megan Regit
Mel Richardson
Melanie Lillie
Melinda Copeland
Melissa & Zachary
    Funk
Melissa Freese
Melissa Patterson
Melissa Ross
Melissa Webb Zurek
Melonie Brown
Merissa Garman
Merry Jo Hopkins
Micah Christopher
    Raymond Hilliard
Micah Alexander
    Abernathie
Michael
Michael B. Baker
Michael Montalbano
Michael Wayne Leidig
Micheal Hopkins
Michele Brinkerhoff
Michelle Armbruster

Michelle Britton
Michelle Bryant
Michelle Carroll
Michelle Givler
Michelle M. Descent-
    Brown
Michelle Parry
Mike Brennan
Mike Peterson
Mildred ("Maggie")
    Hammock
Mildred Schallert
Mishi Grubb
Misty & Allen Sayers
Mollie Preston
Mom & Dad
Morgan Zoeller
Mossie Oosthuizen
Moyinoluwa Ajayi
Mrs. Dorcas Olorunju
Mrs. Donna Berry
Mrs. Geneva L. Grim
Mrs. Grewal
My Dad
My Girls
My Mom Anita
My Mother Betty
Nan Daniels
Nanci Tolliver

Nancy Anderson
Honeycutt
Nancy Dupont
Nancy Hutchison
Nancy Lopez Jacobsen
Nancy McGarry
Nanny
Naomi Emory
Nathan Keener
Nathan Lee Donart
Nathaniel Brown
Navada Marzka
Nee Holdsworth
Neely LeBlanc
Nelma Pauline Hutchins
Nevaeh
Nicole Vandress
Nikki Carpenter
Nina D'Agostino
Nola Lewis
Nora
Norma
Norma Blackgrave
Norma Jeffcoat
Norma Montgomery
Norma Pettitt
Norma Phillips
Nova Tikvah Brown

Odesanya Beatrice
Foluke
Olivia Verdusco
Olivia, Megan, Mallory &
Gabbee
Olufunmilayo Giwa
Orene Head
Owanna Dement
Paige Preissner
Paige Wimbish
Paloma Urbano
Pam Melton
Pam Shapiro
Pamela Davis
Pamela Moore
Pamela Schrieber
Pamela Symonds
Paris Walker
Parker Blaine Means
Pastor Brenda Nevitt
Pastor Bruce Ingle
Pastor Inemesit Oluseye
Pat Armstrong
Pat Broten
Pat Etheridge
Pat Fletcher
Pat Ford
Pate Bauldree
Patricia Brewer

Patricia and Jack
     Flaningan
Patricia Forcier
Patricia Germer
Patricia Glaspie
Patricia Jean Koubek
Patricia Moody
Patricia Rigby
Patricia Salrah
Patricia Schaub
Patricia Sumner Herndon
Patricia Torres
Patricia Wrench
Patrick
Patti Lacey
Patty Shepherd Cavender
Patty Szalay
Paul Ledbetter
Paul Morrison
Paul Willoughhby
Paula Mans
Paula Stetson
Paula Zuniga
Penny Washington
Phil & Lee Vos
Phil Tribby
Phyllis Love
Phyllis Sterler
Polly Louise Taylor

Priscilla Greene NP
Racha Semaan
Rachel Christman
Rachel Cline
Rachel Lynn Huff
Rachel Meeker
Rachel Toler
Rainbow Zoyiopoulos
Ralph L. Magill
Rebecca Ann Wilhite
Rebecca Lin Chema
Rebecca Robinson
Rebecca Wiley
Rebekah Burgess
Rebekah Jo Mitchell
Regan Laine Brooks
Regina Fankboner
Remington Meadows
Rena Lehman
Rene Normand
Renee Newton
Reta
Rev. Allan Monson
Rev. James Merrick
Rex Framon M. Salas
Rhoda
Rhonda Bonisch
Rhonda Eastham
Rhonda Madge

Rhonda Mashburn

Rhonda Plotts

Richard & Pauline
  Boytim

Richard Burns

Richard L. Kerr

Richard Van Egtern

Rick & Cathy Wall

Rick Hartley

Rick McGowan

Ricky Liederbach

Rika Harper

Rita Gillman

RJ Gallaher

Robert Bailey

Robert Carlson

Robert J. Schell

Robert Louis Bruns Sr.

Robert Mau Sr.

Robert P. Mason

Robert Snyder

Robert T. Sanders

Robin Elaine Blake

Robin Goolesby Farley

Robin White Darmon

Roger Fegan

Ronald Paul

Ronnie Terry

Rosalie Barton

Rosalie Ryan

Rose Boyd

Roseline Afebuame

Rosina A. Hodges

Rosmarie Hibbs

Roswell Hill

Rudy Speckamp

Rulan Smith

Russ Mills

Rutamu Uwera Fabiola

Ruth Cole Wegscheid

Ruth Harlow

Ruth Weinsteiger

Ryan Lynn Shane

Sally Acord

Samantha Hardin

Samantha Huff

Samuel A. Owonibi

Samuel Haynes IV

Sandie Bassett

Sandra McGary

Sandra Murphy

Sandra Nelson

Sandra Noble

Sandra Zimmerman

Sandy Aracena

Sandy Breckel

Sandy Brotherton Lyles

Sandy Parks

Sara Bateson
Sara Jane Joned
Sara Lynch
Sarah Anderson
Sarah Andreoni
Sarah Beth Carton
Sarah Goetzinger
Sarah Ortiz
Sarah Valdez
Scarlett Tandy
Scott & Kim Cowling
Scott Klinger
Sedi Graham
Selena Heard
Selma Kloog
Seugnet Snyman
Shania Castillo
Shanna Deleon
Shannon Clayton
Shannon Goodrich
Shari Godley
Sharlene DeBlaay
Sharon Schüttenberg
Sharon Baugher
Sharon Frey
Sharon Glenn
Sharon M. Hahn
Sharon Manz
Sharon Roth

Sharon Schwalm
  Dempsey
Sharon Woods
Sheila Boyd
Sheila Osborne
Shelda
Shelia Pylant
Sheree Hied
Sherri Walker-Bowman
Sherry Davidson
Sherry Stedman
Sheryl Gossett
Sheryl L. Kaufman
  Moore
Sheryl Nabozny
Shirley Brashears
Shirley Farrell
Shirley Gregory
Shirley Minton
Shirley Scalia
Sidney Robert Pace
Sonja Jean Williams
  (Harbin)
Sonya Richardsons
Sophia Gemignani
Stacey Buher
Stacey Hance
Stacey Hargon
Stacy Fox Myers

Stanley Cooper

Stanley Kehr

Stella Brumfield

Stella Harris

Stephanie Boothroyd

Stephanie Cooper

Stephanie Davis

Stephanie Holloway

Stephanie Tawney

Stephanie Wilson

Stephanie Witt Crum

Stephen Epps

Steve Willis

Steven Brent Southall

Steven G. Smith

Steven Strauch

Sue Anderson

Sue Dorris

Sue Gasper

Sue Isbell

Sue Straley

Sue Wagoner

Susan Benjamin

Susan Burton

Susan Dennis

Susan Griffin

Susan Muhlenhaupt

Susan Oliver

Susan Shaw-Simon

Susan Sims

Susan Stricklin

Susan Thevenard

Sutherlan Cope

Suzanne Bryant

Suzanne Neff

Sydney Marie Casto
Cooke

Sylvia A. Burchett

Szilágyi Sára

Tamara Banning

Tammy Martin

Tammy Mitchell

Tammy Tobin

Tana McDonald

Tanya Holmquist

Tapanga Ward

Tara Meke

Teresa Aguirre
Ornelas

Teresa Chong

Teresa Johnson

Teresa Manfredo

Teresa Morgan

Teresa Napier

Teresa Parkhurst

Teresa Pool

Teresa Sours

Terri P.

Terri Smith

Terry Brown

Terry Gray

Terry Miller

Terry Van Syoc

Tessy Chinwendu Igwe

Thanpuia & Manuni

Theresa Robertson

Theresa Sidloski

Theresa Smithson

Thomas A. Foreman

Tiffany Sapp

Timothy Kleimgartner

Timothy Wheeler

Titi

Todd Lee Yates

Tommie Wilkes

Tony Helveston

Tonya Helveston

Tori Ann Root

Traci Yingling

Tracy Brooks

Travis Lemaire

Treyton Stanton

Tricia Beaver

Trudy Bisbing

Trudy Thornton
Whittaker

Trudy Wade

Tshepiso Joystified
Molakeng

Tyler Baldridge

Tyler Moon

Ullysses Sheridon Ogle

Valerie Sherrer

Vanessa Garcia

Vasha Ragbir

Vennie Elizabeth Thomas
Johnson

Vera Riffel

Vershendia Hoffer

Vesta Burgess

Vicki Ingram

Vicki Marra

Vicki Maupin

Vickie Flowers

Vickie Kirchner

Vickie Laucello

Vickie Sparks

Victoria Hernandez

Vida K. Barnes

Violet Huddleston

Violette Linda

Virginia

Virginia Foshage

Virginia Kaiser

Virginia Self

Vivian Martorana Payton

Vivian Yap
Wanda Coetzee
Wanda Joy Lane
Wanda Motes
Warren Talbot
Wesley Adam
    McCormick
Wesley R. Garlock
Wesley Sykes
Whitney Reynolds
Will Tidwell

Willa Dean Williams
William
William Hand
William James
William Mulhern Sr.
William Volkmer
Wilma McKinney
Wyatt James Levi
    Gibson
Zane Yates Curtis
Zona Hayes-Morrow